For Christine.

With thanks for editing advice from Robin Derrick and Martin.

If you enjoyed this book, please review it on Amazon.

1

It was a new life Donald Leckie wanted after his friend Grant's death. Alone so often, as dark took the street, he'd empty a bottle and the past went. Next day it was back. Today was a first day; maybe the beginning of something good. Beginnings always seem good till the past intervenes. Been so many beginnings: the big school in his new blue uniform, boys everywhere running, shouting, kicking balls. Boys are never still. Max and his guitar. Your turn and it was a magical sound. You never recovered. Then girls and the parties; the shyness going, the lips the fingers the smells. God. Then her. That day at Cramond, you in your blue suit, she in that white puffy dress. It was raining. Raindrops on her nose that you kissed dry. That night when her waters broke at the table. Megan's first cry that you heard as you tottered along the corridor…

In Portobello, gulls wheel, gutters gurgle. Wipers of the Saab judder to a halt. First day as an Investigator. Late. Park on a single yellow outside a pub. Up the stairs. Rancid fat and toilet spray. Someone's trying.

Findon greets him. They sit in his office. A quick eulogy for Grant, an ex-employee. Fine guy. Fucking shame what happened, yeah? Findon brushes his hand over his pink skull. Stares at Leckie with watery blue eyes. He has stubby yellowed fingers: a life lived. Leckie wonders what next. Findon gets up moves to the window. He's about five eight, but you wouldn't want to argue with him. He addresses the glass. 'Background!' he barks. As if it was an order. Findon's jacket concertinaed with sitting. Cloth strained at the shoulders. Leckie shifts uneasily. Findon's story. He'd been in Baghdad with a security operation. Jumped ship when one of his mates parted with his brains. Shot dead in front of him by a rooftop sniper.

'Ever seen a man shot dead, Donald? One minute laughing, the next down, his brains coming out of his nose. No?' Leckie doesn't answer. The question didn't want an answer. This guy's seen things you don't see in Gorgie on a Saturday night. 'Good money in Security,' Findon barks, resuming his seat. 'Fills the pockets but empties the fucking bowels. A few real baddies out there too. On both sides. Hard bastards that don't care who they take down.' He leans forward and fills Leckie in on the routine work of the Office. Surveillance, fraud stuff, missing persons. Other activities would be handled by a guy called Will. IT geek. 'Keep your distance though, breath like a rotting corpse.' Leckie laughs.

He pours Leckie an orange juice. A clouded plastic tumbler you'd avoid pissing in. 'If you're driving, the days of the snifter are over Donald,' Findon says, as if he knows something. Leckie laughs. Leckie sips. Chemical stink of dying plastic. A test? Should have said something. Findon rambles on about protocols and fees.

Day rates, night rates, two-man jobs and what to avoid, says Zoe would give him a Canon T3i. He shows Leckie to his office.

It's a cubicle posing as a room. A small Afghan rug. A box with aspirations. A desk and swivel chair; a faux-leather armchair for clients, a pad, an Apple, an answerphone and a four-drawer filing cabinet. Well, this is him. Cubicle man now. Leckie thought he'd get Grant's office, but the IT man had moved in there. Needed space for his gear, Findon said.

Better than The Station, anyway, Leckie thinks. Employed again. A clock-watcher on slack days but maybe a bit of excitement. 'Don't expect this to be like the Force,' Findon had said, smiling, 'You won't have a shiny warrant card to frighten the buggers. We've made ours up to look similar, so the punters just glance and accept. Funny how none of the punters ever says, "Hold that still a moment." Ha!'

Zoe, the receptionist knocks and comes in and Findon says something to her before excusing himself. Zoe says she's sorry about Grant and Leckie smiles as if he's lost a brother. He sits and reads through the Protocol section where the name Grant has been scored out. The phone rings in the corridor. Zoe knocks and brings in his first customer, a Mrs Gilhooley. The door slams. Springs gone. Gilhooley laughs. Jesus that was quick. He'd hoped for an hour or two to get used to this, but here she was, first customer for shaving. Leckie brushes his lap. Crumbs, or a day-dreaming dick? He stands up slowly.

'Come in please. Mrs Gilhooley? I'm Donald Leckie.' Good strong, confident voice of one who's done this often. 'Have a seat.' Leckie's heart rises. She's about five-five with long blonde hair and a smile that could melt brick. Mid-forties, he guesses. A few lines
by the eyes. She's lived. Drink and fags leave calling cards. She's wearing jeans and an expensive looking blue leather jacket. A cream silk scarf.

'Hello.' The voice deeper than he'd expected. A hint of Kirsty Wark. 'I'm Paula. Paula Gilhooley. Shall I write it down for you? 'A smile. Leckie smiles back, hoping she won't notice his recently removed pre-molar. Seven hundred quid for a crown and root deal. Robbery. He could afford to lose the damn thing.

'I think I can manage that,' says Leckie. 'Used to deal with a Gilhooley when I ran a gallery.

'Ah.'

'No relation, I suppose? A Norman Gilhooley, lived out Musselburgh way.'

'No relation.' Settled in the armchair, she crosses her legs. He moves his chair from behind the desk and faces her.

'Well. Down to business Mrs Gilhooley...'

'Oh, call me Paula.' She smiles again and opens her handbag. Glitzy with a logo and a gold chain strap. Must have cost a few bob, he thinks. 'Excuse me,' she says, 'Managed to get another blinking cold.' She delicately brushes her nose with a little lace handkerchief. Pops it back in the bag.

'My husband's having an affair and I'm damned if I'm having it. Well, that sounded a bit Irish.' Leckie laughs. She feels a need to fill the silence. 'That's it.' she said. Leckie bites his tongue to avoid thoughts becoming words. Someone screwing someone they shouldn't tickles him. Always has. 'I'm sorry to hear that...er… Paula. And you're looking for proof?'

She settles herself in the chair and leans forward. She really is a stunner. He crosses his arms and tilts his head.

'I've suspected he was having an affair for ages, but I had no proof. Two days ago, I saw a mail on his computer. It was obviously
from a woman. It said, "Miss you." No-one I know, would write that to him. His father's dead and his mother who he hates, is in a
home, and not exactly into e-mailing. We don't have kids. Oh, and
in case you're thinking what a nosey bitch I am; I never look at his computer. He's been so cold lately that I knew something was wrong. A word from the wise Mr Leckie— if

you're a man and having an affair don't start using aftershave. Not when you've gone without for twenty years.
Bit of a clue.'

Leckie laughed. 'I'll try to remember that.' Nice feed. They could make a pair.

'Have you any idea who the woman could be, that is, if there really is a woman. You can never be sure of these things. Some men...'

'Some men just can't keep it in their trousers, Mr Leckie. This isn't the first time, but by God it's going to be the last.' She takes a deep breath, stares at a spot on the ceiling above Leckie's head. 'It's my money Mr Leckie. Every bloody penny that we have is my money. My father owned the McRae Bakeries. When he died, I sold out. Didn't fancy keeping an eye on folk who think four o'clock in the morning is time for lunch. Shortly after, I met Duncan and we got married.

He was the golf pro at a club where I took lessons. Bastard's got strong arms. The rest is history. After we married, I told him to give up his job and we'd go travelling. Well, we did, but Venice and Paris and Bangkok lose their charm after a while. Now he spends his time playing golf, or so he says, and playing the trumpet in a jazz band. Gordon, I want...'

'Donald.'

'Sorry. Donald, I want proof of what he's doing so that I can divorce him. We discussed a pre-nup, but in the throes of love, it was never done. How stupid can you be, eh?'

'I see. How often is he out on his own?'

'Maybe a couple of nights a week and some afternoons.'

'Have you tried following him yourself to see where he goes or is that not possible?'

'Oh, I've followed him, Donald. I have my own car. Each time he's visited his mother. Which is weird enough. Not much to go on there then, unless he's into screwing eighty-year-old biddies.'

'OK. Any idea at all of who he might be seeing? Any clues you've come across? Anything in the car you've noticed for instance; ticket stubs, parking receipts that might give a clue to where he's been. His phone?'

'No. I haven't looked in his car. Perhaps I should have. Haven't managed to look at his phone.'

'Do you have a picture of him? I need to know who I'm watching.' She passes a photograph to Leckie. A square-jawed good-looking man in his thirties with close cropped fair hair and a mouth brimming with teeth. They both looked happy in a palm-tree heaven. How times change.

Leckie chats for a further twenty minutes and with Gilhooley's address and registration number he reckons a bit of reccy would solve the problem. Every Tuesday evening, he practises with his band. The following Tuesday Leckie would tail him and watch.

Leckie suddenly remembers that the protocol is to offer clients a cup of something. Luckily, she declines. Christ knows what the tea would be like. Her face had changed now, the soft smile morphing into something more serious.

'So, are we agreed on a course of action?' asks Leckie, and he gets to his feet not really knowing why, only that his legs have grown twitchy.

She looks up. Her breathing has quickened. 'I'm angry Mr Leckie. I'm being made a fool of, and I don't like it. You know what I want? Pictures. Pictures of him and her. I want to throw them in his face and tell him to fuck off.'

Leckie brushes his hand over his lower face. He needs a shave. He rises, offers his hand, and she shakes it.

A scribbled number for him. As she moves to the door, he notices the subtle swell of two buttocks at war beneath the jeans. He leads her out and sees her down the stairs, the buttocks boxing with each step.

Zoe is putting on her coat. Findon has gone. He says he'll lock up and sits at his desk to make a few notes. He still has Megan's photo in his rucksack. He puts it on the cabinet. Home from home. It's a couple of years old but one of his favourites. A day they spent down at Gullane when she was seventeen. Hair blowing over her cheeks and that grin. OK, this is it. A cupboard, and a dodgy job. Day one of a new life

2

Annabell Lithgow's face was turned to the wall away from her new-born child asleep by her bed. Her body ached, her face in the mirror the nurse had offered, still ruddy as if a force ten gale had battered it for hours. Those ills she could accept, for this was her second child and she knew the price of giving birth: what hit her now however was the distaste she felt for this creature she had brought into the world. As she'd held him for the first time, her first thought was how little she felt. How numb to maternal feelings she was.

With Robin she remembered the surge of joy, the sense of a perfect gift that had been bestowed on her. And the joy of his tiny cries. This one had been quiet, oddly quiet, as if to confound her expectations. She could see the blonde hair, the pale blue eyes and the pert nose of the Lithgows, but his face seemed somehow too perfect, too immaculate to suffer the development that the years would bring. In truth, she felt nothing for him, but she knew it wasn't unusual for new mothers to feel this way, and troubling as it was, she hoped in time she would grow to love her youngest son.

As the months rolled by and the baby grew, stronger and more
adventurous than Robin had been, it was clear that the toddler could not be left unattended for a moment. Those piercing eyes with their determined look took him tumbling down the upper landing stairs
while nurse had turned her back. A lump the size of an egg appeared in moments and a little later the nurse disappeared down the drive wheeling her buggy.

It was a difficult time for the family as financial problems piled up. Digby was often absent from home in the Glasgow office while Annabell ran the house and the garden. Her studio, with its easel and tables vivid with tubes of paint, was visited rarely. She coped, but she was not happy.

As the children grew, however, school fees cut a swathe through the household budget. There had never been a doubt that the boys would be sent to boarding schools: it was what folk like the Lithgows did, so there would be no saving in that direction. It was also a relief that the constant bickering between the children could be silenced for a time. Robin, quiet Robin, seemed constantly harassed by his younger brother whose advancing years had equipped him with ever more devious provocations. Books were scribbled on, a pet rabbit which Robin doted on was released, it was discovered, by Blair, and mangled by a dog on the front lawn. At meals, the usual sibling bickering would often result in Robin running upstairs in tears. He was taller than Blair, but there was no violence in him, and Digby's advice that he stand up to his younger brother failed to influence things.

So in time, Robin went to school in Edinburgh, and later, Blair together with his guitar, went to an institution in the Borders. An admission interview in the latter school involving Digby and Blair with a tall thin Headmaster, had ended with the Head remarking on the six-year-old's self-confidence and what an asset he was sure he'd be to the school. At home, Digby tilted his glass and winked at Annabell. 'You wait, he'll be a credit to us before you know it.'

As Annabell watched each of her boys leave - Robin clinging and tearful, Blair later, with scarcely a backward glance, she felt the same mixture of relief and emptiness. With Blair gone, the house was quiet. The weather was turning cold and for once, in a lifetime it seemed, she had time for herself. Digby had grown closer to Blair before his departure, and the child's irrepressible spirit seemed to have calmed. He had changed, it seemed to Annabell and she wondered how he would fare at school.

'He'll be fine,' Digby assured her. 'He's a clever wee bugger.'

'He still needs to learn to respect others more. He needs to realise he's not the most important person in the universe. Maybe that's our fault. That cherubic little face that grins and gets away with murder. You know when he was born, I didn't have any strong feelings for him.'

'Yes, I know. But you've been a good mother to him. To both. They're both different. Life will sort them out. You wait and see. Any more roasties?'

3

As the last turret disappeared behind the gaunt birches, Blair Lithgow summoned up a new wave of anger towards the world. It was a coat he wore that brought warmth in the chill winds of decency that surrounded him. He was slumped in the rear of the Toyota, his right ankle resting on his left knee. His toe nudged the rear of his father's seat, and he kept it going, nudge, nudge, nudge, a Chinese Torture in its subtle insistence. He expected an angry face in the rear mirror or perhaps a brush off from his father's large hand, but nothing came. Sometimes anger transcends irritation, Blair mused, but the thought of his old man's anger comforted him. Anger was a currency he was familiar with. It was kindness that discomfited him.

The countryside flashed by the driver's suppressed rage tilting the speeding vehicle this way and that along the twisting country
lanes. Of course, it's not every day you pick up your errant son who's been booted out of another public school. Blair imagined his father in Edinburgh at some club fielding questions about his younger son. 'Oh we took him away from that place. It wasn't what
was needed at his stage...' Nothing like the bourgeoisie for invention, when their cosy little world seems less cosy.

A year before, through an avenue of arching leaves, the same sleek black Toyota 4 by 4 driven by his mother had delivered Blair to the imposing front entrance of Birchbrae School. He was seventeen years old, the youngest of an older brother and a sister, tall and well-built, with a new large-size green blazer on his back. They didn't normally take new boys into the sixth form, but a sob story made up by Digby had done it.

At first, he'd settled to the routine, being well acquainted since the age of six with the ways of the British Public School, making friends with two boys who shared his taste in music and books and whose inclinations tended to the subversive in a regime based on conformity. While Simon Crichton and Tom Birnie had been there since the age of twelve and had managed to curb their inclinations through fear of expulsion and family disgrace, it was Blair's influence which ignited the bonfire of their malevolent talents. In class he shone, his intelligence sharp and his tongue eloquent, but after Prep it was as if a new Blair emerged like some nocturnal animal fired by bloodlust. He stalked the dorms provoking, taunting, seemingly eager to detect any sign of weakness in the younger boys whose only defence was obedience or avoidance, the latter stratagem requiring a cunning few of them could muster.

For most, Blair's words were law: he spoke with a kind of authority that made his peers listen. He was clever, he read books, they didn't understand and it was clear he had a self-confidence that the others lacked. On trips to the woods the three would attempt to shoot birds with the air pistol Blair had smuggled into his room, and on one occasion, rebuked by the PE master, Blair stuffed a hedgehog he'd shot in the wall-bars in the gym. It was a school full of boys and such activities, if not condoned, were accepted as the natural poor choices that the maturing male makes. Boys meant fees after all, and it would be counter-productive to over-react to every little indiscretion. The Head knew most of what went on, but not all, Housemasters agreeing that some misdemeanours should be treated in-House as it were.

On a drizzling Wednesday afternoon, a week before his expulsion and as Autumn was well established, Blair and his two friends found themselves back markers on a four-mile cross-country course which bordered fields and a forest to end up a twisting leaf-strewn path to The Tap, a hill overlooking the school. The multi-coloured shorts of the others darted on ahead and out of sight. The Games Master, a man called Hastie, would jog along in the middle of the leading group leaving the tail enders the prospect of a jeering finish and the possible loss of House Points. Blair hated sport of any kind, a developed reflex to his father's sporting achievements.

Taking a short cut through the dying bracken in the forest the three could cut the course by a third. The trio fought their way through the rusting fronds and lounged behind a large beech just off the path till the rest of the group trundled past and along the edge of a field with much moaning and cursing. They were about to join the tailenders when a young third-former called Tim Pringle (known as Yum-Yum-- his surname that egregious nibble favoured in the dorm) noticed them and stopped.

'Go on Yum-Yum 'shouted Blair, 'You'll be left behind.' But Tim merely stood and shook his head.

'You've been cheating,' he shouted, 'You've cut the course. I saw you.'
Blair and the others broke from hiding and took hold of Tim who by now had begun to realise the folly of calling out the trio.

'What'll we do with the little toad, lads?' said Tom, flicking his floppy ginger hair from his eyes. 'Shall we kill the little fucker?'

'Stop it! I won't tell. Don't care anyway.' He pulled away from Tom and began running after the others as if he really did believe his life was in danger. Blair shoved Tom angrily. 'Why'd you let him go, you idiot. We could've had some fun.'

Simon said they'd better get a crack on, or old Hastie would be wondering where they were, so they jogged their way after the others, arriving some four minutes after the last man.

'Where the devil were you lot?' said Hastie, brushing mud from his backside after an embarrassing fall. On his mud-spattered t-shirt could be discerned the legend "A GOOD LOSER WILL ALWAYS BE A LOSER" 'Sixth formers should be leading, not traipsing behind like a bunch of cripples.'

'We had to stop for Crichton, sir,' said Blair, 'He had an asthma attack.' Hastie approached Crichton and put a hand on his shoulder.

'Are you alright lad? Didn't know you had asthma. Nurse should've told me.'

Over Hastie's right shoulder where a group of the boys stood shivering, a laugh emerged — a slow two-note cynical 'Ha, Ha!' Had there been any talking it might have gone unnoticed, but from the silence it emerged clear and crisp. Hastie turned.

'Who was that? Someone think having asthma is funny. Was that you, Johnstone?'

'No sir.'

'Steele?'

'No sir. Think it was Yum...er... Tim sir. 'He nudged Tim who stood next to him and who had stolen three packets of Hannigan's 'flame grilled steak' crisps from his locker the previous Monday after prep.

'Pringle. Come here, lad.' Tim glanced at Steele and shuffled forward.

'Did you ejaculate there?' said Hastie, unable to resist the pun which he knew formed a comical bond with his charges. On cue they burst into cheering. 'Because if you did, lad, I'd really like to
know what the joke was. Wouldn't' we men?' The men mumbled their assent, and the focus fell on Tim again.

'They cheated,' he said in a soft voice. Hastie grasped him by the shoulders.

'What was that? Speak up laddie.'

'They cut the course, sir. He hasn't got asthma.'

Cutting the course wasn't the worst crime by Birchbrae standards but it was enough to attract a degree of shame on your House and a degree of attention from your tutor. Had that been it, perhaps the matter would have settled and been forgotten, but Blair was not a man to forget a snitch and young Pringle had snitched.

Two nights after the incident the three decided to repay him. After Prep they waited for him to emerge from West House accompanied by another boy called Dickson, both headed for their dorm. Simon called out to Dickson that he was wanted by the
warden and Dickson, though puzzled, returned to the main building
leaving Pringle to continue alone. A moment later an arm round his neck took the breath from him and he was frog-

marched up two flights of stairs to Blair's dorm — a three-bedroom plastered with
posters, a stuffed badger and a huge Confederate flag. He was flung to the floor and pinned by Blair's knees. Simon stood outside while Tom stood behind Blair.

'Now you little sod, we'll see how smart you are when you're on your own.' Pringle saw stars as a swift slap stung his right cheek.

Blair grabbed his hair and yanked it tight and with the action something broke in Blair Lithgow, as if a long-held anger had burst. All the wrongs done him, all the accusations, the recriminations, the false promises became a phalanx of demons demanding retribution. He struck Pringle on his nose once, twice, and the face burst in a spray of blood. Tom grabbed Blair's arm and shouted to stop, Blair's face red with rage now, Pringle's head beating a slow tattoo on the floor. And then he did stop. He fell off Pringle and curled up in a foetal position and whimpered like a baby. His head felt as if it would burst. Boom-boom-boom the blood beat. Pringle lay bloodied and still, his eyes open staring up at the ceiling as if he dared not move.

'Get up, Pringle,' said Tom. Simon had gone, his footfalls receding on the stairs when Pringle had begun screaming.

'Come on, Yum-yum. You're OK. It's nothing to cry about. Come on, get up. I'll make you some tea.' Pringle, still stunned by the suddenness of the attack, clambered to his feet and stood motionless, his cuff brushing blood from his face. He looked down at Blair's form and made for the door.

'No, no, don't go,' said Tom, 'Use the sink there to clean up. Go on.'

Pringle feared now that any attempt to go would make matters worse for him, so he splashed his face at the sink while Tom plopped two tea bags in the pot, the act a desperate

grasp at normality. As Tom moved to the door, he was met by the bulk of
the Housemaster, Eric the Red, (or Eric the Ped, as Blair liked to call him) a ginger-haired veteran of The Falklands who took no prisoners in his determination to maintain his love for the boys in
his care.

'What the hell is going on in here Birnie? And why are you lying there Lithgow like some half-wit who's lost his doll?'

'Just a bit noisy sir, were we? I know. We were having a mock fight,' said Tom, his fists playfully reprising the gestures of the fight. It was, in its painfully ineffectual way, effectual enough to defuse the situation without further questioning, for discipline in such a school as Eric knew all too well, relies more on negotiation
than on confrontation, the latter stance risking expulsion and the resultant loss of fees. The school motto "Fiat justicia, ruat caelu"— its insistence on justice being done should the heavens fall, was an ironic twist not lost on the governors whose heaven was built on fees of £15,000 per year per pupil.

'Well, get yourselves to bed and if I hear another peep from this room, you'll all be on detention for a week. 'Is that you, Pringle, skulking in the corner? You shouldn't be in here, should you?'

'No sir, 'came a muffled reply. 'Just came for some sugar sir. '

The Housemaster shook his head and left, clomping up the stairs to settle those above who'd heard the commotion. Pringle dashed out before Tom had time to say anything more.

'Shit. We're for it now, Blair, you stupid idiot 'said Tom, whose shock at Lithgow's violence had momentarily

overcome his deference, 'He'll blab, and we could be going home. What the hell were you doing hitting him like that. You might've killed him.' Lithgow had stopped moaning while the Warden stood over him and now slowly uncurled his long legs and lay as if dead on his back. Tom switched on the reading lamp by his bed and saw a smile
post itself on Blair's face. He felt a shiver run through him, a shiver of incomprehension that in the aftermath of such violence on Blair's face should appear a look as if he had been at prayer and seen God. 'Poverty is the worst form of violence' said Blair pushing himself upright, 'Ghandi was right. Pringle is an irrelevance.'

'What the hell are you on about Blair? 'said Tom, 'What's Ghandi got to do with beating up Pringle?'

'Just a thought. Wouldn't expect you to get it.'

The next morning at breakfast, Tim Pringle felt a strong hand on his shoulder and his bruised face appeared above a scarf too high on his neck. Questioning reduced the boy to tears and he told his story to the nurse. In the middle of their French class, Lithgow and Birnie were summoned to the headmaster's study. Mr Kinghorn removed his spectacles and let them dangle from his bony finger. Imbuing the action with the exaggerated precision of a Judge donning his black cap, he informed the pair in a calm voice that the goings-on involving Pringle meant their presence was no longer welcome at Birchbrae. Their parents had been informed and they should pack their belongings and report to the main hall where they would be collected in due course. The pair walked back in silence, Lithgow untroubled, Birnie silent, in the light of day, fearful that voicing his thoughts would infuriate his friend.

By itself, the assault on Pringle was worthy of a strong reprimand, had not the Head been warned for weeks before of the malign influence that Blair seemed to exert over his dorm mates. Housemaster Eric Dalglish however, tired of Blair's misdemeanors, was pushing for a more final solution to their problems and his influence finally drove the Head to act. The decision was not an easy one: Blair was a champion debater on the debating team and the team had made the quarter finals for the first time; he was a favourite with the English master Robin Reid who delighted in his protégée's insatiable desire to read anything from Dickens to Steinbeck; and he was also captain of the rugby team. With three months left before he would leave the school it seemed they were cutting off their noses to save their face, the Head believed. Put to the Heads of Houses for a vote, however, the result was overwhelmingly against him: Blair Lithgow was a danger to others and a succession of parental complaints regarding his behaviour could not be ignored any longer. He had to go.

Sir Digby Lithgow drove to Birchbrae himself that day, and now, angrily feeding the wheel left and right as they sped through the countryside towards home, he said nothing to his son. Bored of
foot tapping, Blair was texting Birnie.
For Digby Lithgow, days such as this, were not new. He had long since attuned himself to the notion that his younger son was sent by the Devil to plague his days. From his earliest years he mused, he had been nothing but trouble and with age the troubles took on more and more serious forms. He had been fully informed by the Head of the circumstances surrounding his son's expulsion and the Head saw in the eyes of this parent, not the usual pleas for reconsideration— the

shame on the family and so on—but a calm, almost resigned acceptance that this was how it would probably end.

'I'm very sorry, Sir, I really am. We hate this sort of thing as you can imagine, but the boy was badly beaten in what seems to have been some act of revenge and there have been other issues. His parents are very unhappy as you can imagine. Your son is very bright according to his teachers, but he seems... how can I put it... a little disturbed. What I mean is...'

'I understand,' said Digby, 'This is not the first time something like this has happened to us. Sadly, we give love, and we receive disappointment. But he is my son.'

'Of course. Naturally. This is never a moment I relish. We will of course, reimburse you for the rest of the year's fees.'

Blair's diary.

Shithouse. Hope that rat Pringle dies. Adios Birchbrae you sodding dump.

An hour and a half later, the black Toyota drew up in front of a large Victorian house by a river. Eastlea House had once been the holiday home of a famous novelist and since then had passed from family to family till Earnest Lithgow of Lithgow Steel, Blair's great grandfather, had bought it at the outbreak of The Second World War. Since then, Lithgows had been born there, had sported in the
woods and on the lawns, had courted and married and given birth in its chill rooms.

Digby turned off the engine and stepped out. A calm resignation had settled on him like a chill mist, sucking all energy and he couldn't wait to down a whisky and warm himself at the fire in his study. He made his way into the house and shouted up the curving stair 'He's here!' and promptly disappeared into his study to the right of the entrance. He slammed the door shut behind him.

Well, here we are again. The merry-go-round of Blair's education. More schools than an ocean of bloody fish. My son is just a bit of a nutter. How the hell did I spawn him. As if this place wasn't bad enough—falling apart at the seams—he has to reappear. I hated the look on that Head's face. The smug bastard.

Annabell Lithgow descended the stairs with her usual elegance, to stand on the third bottom step, arms folded, watching her son
enter the house. She was forty-five years old, tall and slim with long greying blond hair, tied back, and as always, she wore a floppy cardigan and jeans. She had once been a promising artist but had given up Art for motherhood, a decision subsequent events had
caused her to regret: a regret that had bitten into her soul and left a stultifying ennui that had estranged her from her once loving husband. Life had become a disappointment to her and any cursory
refuge she might have sought in her children had proved illusory.
The boys had grown to despise her it seemed, to varying degrees, ignoring any efforts on her part to shape them into rounded human beings. Robin, withdrawn, and living in his

own world, while Blair's indomitable personality constantly pushed against any normal rules it seemed. There had always been a streak of rebelliousness in the Lithgows she realised, her husband's brother a gambler and a drunk, his sister a chronic victim of marital breakdown, but genetic ill-disposition was little consolation. As Blair, struggling with his trunk, approached the steps, she opened her arms in a feigned gesture of delight and surprise to snap them shut over her chest a second later.

'Darling, you're home early! How lovely to see you,' she enthused, the exaggerated tone of her voice and her folded arms the metaphorical slap in the face Blair expected. Her disgraced son, head up, smiled, dropped his trunk and returned to the car for his guitar.

'Yeah, me too,' he offered over his shoulder, rarely missing the chance of the last word, even when it failed as a meaningful subjunctive to any previous conversation. He returned a moment later clattering up the stairway and disappeared, his jacket slung over his shoulder, his trunk left for others to carry.

Annabell knocked and entered the library to find her husband at his computer.

'This room is freezing,' he said, 'Why didn't you tell Sheila to light the fire?'

'Sheila wasn't feeling well this morning, so I told her to go back to bed. I'll set it for you if it'll change your mood.'
He didn't look at her but continued to stare at the screen. They hadn't discussed Blair's expulsion, for her husband had long since
taken responsibility for Blair's education, explaining that he understood the way the system worked better than she, and

besides her son needed strong handling which he did not consider 'her forte' as he put it.

If Annabell Lithgow felt excluded from the education of her son she hid her disappointment well, for since his birth, he had offered her nothing but tribulation. He had slept badly as an infant, destroyed it seemed any object within reach as a toddler, and made life hell for his siblings, lashing out at any opportunity, later lying when challenged as to his culpability.

Once, when he was seven, it became accepted in the lore of the family, his brother Robin had deliberately pushed him from the bridge over the pond after Blair had cut the latter's hand with a penknife. Blair had spluttered and struggled to the side to return to the house dripping and red with anger. Robin's gashed hand was stitched up at the local hospital where he admitted to his mother that he had pushed his brother over the bridge and hoped he'd drown. It became obvious to both parents that they had on their hands a child whose every impulse seemed to be designed to create unhappiness and harm. They could only hope that some hard schooling might help.

At his prep school he seemed to settle, developing a love of reading and a period of 'normality.' There was even a period in
which the young boy, sent home to convalesce after what appeared to be a serious allergic reaction to fish, showed a loving appreciation of his mother's nursing. Soon back at school, with stern warnings to avoid fish and to carry his epi-pen, he began to flourish academically. During the holidays he cultivated friendships with two local boys. The three together with Blair's beloved terrier Teddy would disappear

into the woods for hours to return at dusk full of stories for cook about what they'd seen that day. At table he
was quiet, while his brother would speak and both parents would exchange glances of relief when a new-found politeness such as asking permission to leave the table, suggested the child of the devil had become human at last. It was a false dawn however, for during the last term at Penhouse School a gardening shed burned to the ground and Blair Lithgow was proved to be the arsonist, an ignited spray-can having been thrown at some spilled petrol.

His attendance at Aspen Bank, a prestigious Fife institution came to an ignominious end when Blair was caught in flagrante delicto with a fourteen-year-old girl in the woods. Two years of calm followed at Strathtay School before four boys, one of whom was Blair, were expelled for desecrating a master's prized Morgan car.

Birchbrae had seemed the last hope that their son might behave himself but the swing doors of that saloon had now firmly closed. The leopard had not changed his spots.

Now at home again, Blair spent most of his time in his room reading and playing his guitar, appearing for breakfast and lunch as the others left the table. He had exercised a self-induced purdah which suited the others just fine. A manageable politeness sufficed instead. The silence, when by accident the family found themselves together, Blair took to be a planned campaign to assault his sense of guilt. Letting him stew, he imagined was the tactic — letting him stew till he apologised and then they'd have him where they wanted him.

The stand-off held till one morning Blair swore at the maid Sheila. Within earshot, his mother appeared on the scene and without hesitation slapped her son hard on the cheek.

'Don't ever use that language to Sheila, you lout,' she screamed. What the hell is wrong with you anyway? Can't you just treat people with a bit of respect for once? 'Sheila stood nearby; her lips tight in mock indignation but inside so inured to Blair's tantrums
that their sting soon subsided. Now, as the slap resounded down the empty corridor and a red blush appeared on Blair's cheek, she felt
a warm satisfaction. Blair shrugged with the pain and felt his knuckles tighten. His first impulse was to strike his mother, but that was a bridge he wouldn't cross, for on the other side lay a desolation that even he sensed with awe. Instead, he turned and kicked over a bucket of soapy water that Sheila had laid down in her distress. As the soapy water spread towards the stairs like some frothy amoeba, his mother invoked the Deity, though the Deity till now had shown little inclination to intervene.

There was no more school for Blair Lithgow, his days passed practising riffs on his guitar, reading, or shooting rabbits in the woods around the house. His dog Teddy had died and he missed the dog. Some days he lay in bed complaining of headaches, but sympathy was in short supply. Talk at the dinner table was of how the banks were foreclosing on Lithgow and Sons. Digby spat fire when he recounted the way he was treated by 'the money men' as he put it. How much had been spent on their son's education. How well Robin had done. What a waste of money Blair's schools had been. No wonder the family were skint. Blair listened, watching his father's confidence disintegrate as the days passed and a genteel poverty settled like snow.

For months he passed his days at Eastlea in a maelstrom of angst and frustration till it was decided to pack him off to a crammer in Edinburgh in a last effort to pass some exams.

It was a forlorn hope for the Lithgows but the only one to cling to. He would stay with his elder brother in his flat, an arrangement met with dismay by Robin, whose girlfriend Susy also lived there without the knowledge of his parents.

Blair's diary:

Edinbugh here I come. Maybe sleep better there. Can't in this dump. They can't hack me. Shot a fucking hedgehog. Just sat there while I pumped pellets in... Told Harry McFarlane to fuck off when he told me to get out of the wood. Fucking peasant. Camus is cool. I'm an OUTSIDER!!

A house Party. Four-by-fours in the drive and a bunch of strangers swigging our booze. Some of the women were OK. That one with the red hair that was in ma's studio. Would fuck her in a mo. Just smiled at me and like a fucking idiot I ran off. Shit.

4

The rain had stopped by the time Donald Leckie garaged the car. Megan was with Ricky watching the telly, the pair glued together as if an inch of space between them might seriously question their bond. He got a 'Hi, dad' as he made for the kitchen. In a moment she was at his elbow.

'How was your first day at school then?' said Megan, 'Did you make some nice friends?'

'I thought we had a couple of Lorne sausages left.'

'Oh, sorry. Ricky was hungry and it was his first time.'

'What first time?'

'First square sausage time. Thought you'd approve of me converting him.'

'Aye, well next time don't convert him at my expense. Think I'll go over to Liz's and see what's in her fridge. At least she's not into proselytizing.

'That's a very big word for an angry policeman.'

'Not angry and not a policeman. Nothing out of two, honey.

He'd taken to using the word 'honey' for her, avoiding the intimacy of her first name. Intimacy always a problem, as if emotions left him exposed. Blame the Force, he told himself. Megan seemed to like it. 'Now just you go back to lover boy and tell him he stole Pop's sausages. See you later, yeah?' She kissed
him on the cheek and skipped off. She was so damn happy these days he couldn't get angry with her anymore, it would be like breaking a beautiful spell.

Now the default position to domestic harassment for Leckie was time spent with Liz. While he loved his daughter, he was increasingly the fly in the loving ointment of her new relationship.

On nights he cherished, he'd return exhausted and find her absent, food in the fridge and something decent on the box. Sometimes he'd play a little Chopin or zip through The Brandenburg third, stumbling a bit over what would be the cello parts in the left hand but enjoying the lovely melodic right hand. When Rick was around, he'd rarely play — it was an indulgence of sorts he supposed, and few of his visitors ever seemed eager to listen to his playing. He found the same response to the few good paintings that hung in the flat. It was as if most people were blind to their surroundings, to beauty, hardly ever commenting on who might have painted them. Philistinism was a disease like the common cold: those suffering from the symptoms were unlikely to die and therefor the urgency of a cure was correspondingly lax. Liz liked his pictures, and she liked hearing him play, always a smile on her face as he'd finish a piece and turn to her for a response. To Liz he would escape, when the presence of Megan and Rick became oppressive.

Liz made him an omelette and they went to bed. He told her about the woman, and she laughed while she removed a piece of blue fluff from his navel. She was a picker, his Liz; if it wasn't his
navel, it would be a blackhead on his nose or shoulder or the hairs on his ears. She should have been a monkey with all the grooming Leckie thought, then wondered if perhaps we weren't all still monkeys. A doubt crept in about the accuracy of his anthropological speculations however, so he kept his thoughts to himself. If there was one thing Liz liked more than his dick and his blackheads it was putting him right about things. Everything. She held every woman's deeply rooted

conviction that men are supremely limited creatures, to be tolerated, even enjoyed at times, but were basically superfluous to the smooth running of the world.

'So, what are you going to do about it? The woman, I mean.'

'Just watch lover boy. Maybe he's shagging his mother, eh? Now that would be something. I'll speak to Ed in the morning.' 'He got out of bed with some difficulty, feeling an ache in his back from lying on creased sheets.

'You've got sensitive skin,' said Liz, 'Perhaps you're a Prince.' Leckie gave her a quizzical look.

'Don't you know the story of the Princess and the pea? Tut, tut. And I thought you were well educated.'

'What's a Princess needing a leak got to do with my sore back for God's sake.'

'Not that kind of pea, idiot. A green pea. It was meant to test how soft her skin was. I suppose in those days only a princess would be used to such comfort so any little hardness would be noticed.'

'Yup. I must be a fucking Prince then,' said Leckie, slipping on his watch.

He sat and rubbed himself, feeling her hand on his. His watch said twelve-thirty. Time to go.

'You OK?'

'I think you could do with a new bed. It's too soft.'

'Well, you may be right. It has a hard time. Sometimes.' Leckie laughed.

'Your bed is OK.' He belted his trousers and turned to look at her. She was lovely he thought. Every time he looked at her after they made love, in the half-glow from the bedside light, her flushed skin glowing and her eyes bright with trust, he wondered why he couldn't just say it, just let her into his life, heart and soul: his wife. But he couldn't. The scars of break-up and divorce were still raw even after all this time. Maybe, he thought, they would never heal; maybe he was fucked as a person. He was afraid to love her too much. Shit, he was afraid of everything really, but he knew too, that this woman deserved more than his occasional visits. Little by little he noticed her insecurity manifest itself in questions about Megan and Ricky and housework, even what he ate and drank. She was pushing at a door marked 'Leckie at Home' but he kept it shut. She'd been in his bed but when she began leaving her toothbrush and a couple of cosmetic jars, the possibility of her moving in triggered an avoidance strategy for a time. It was a game both realised was being played out between them but for one of the players the game was leading nowhere, and she wanted more.

5

Perched on a barstool of The Bridge Hotel, Sir Digby Lithgow (a Knighthood for services to the Steel Industry) stretched out his long legs and felt an ache in his right buttock where he'd argued with a tree. A tee shot into the trees had resulted in a cramped swing out and he'd slipped back against a pine trunk. A second whisky might just help he thought, as it trickled down his throat. He was a tall man, on the foothills of corpulence, with a full ruddy face and a bushy head of white hair.

He'd just completed eighteen holes at the course above the village and he told the barman he was knackered. A knowing smile. He had a few friends in the village but since he'd retired from the firm, gratefully selling out to a Chinese consortium as the balance sheet lost its equilibrium, he'd found playing companions difficult to pin down, so he often played by himself. They were all still working while he was now a man of leisure. He liked this bar: the dim lighting, the taped music, the warmth as the whisky took you and in Winter the heat from the log fire. It wasn't exactly classy, though it had been once, when the railway came and brought visitors from the South, toffs renting places for the summer. Now you noticed the edges fraying: bulbs that didn't come on, the ancient wallpaper uncurling above the skirting boards, sticky carpets and the burnt ochre stains on the ceiling from years of smoke and loose slates. Winter was coming. He thought of Edinburgh and a flat in Comely Bank where a certain lady would at that moment be preparing dinner. He whispered her name and the sweetness of it warmed him. Soon. Soon, Fiona...

As he stared at the optics opposite, he could hear the muted conversation behind him. Two women discussing a man. Was that all women ever discussed? He smiled to himself as he imagined Annabell discussing him with any of her friends. Poor Annabell. She'd once been so beautiful and kind and now she'd turned into a harridan. No, she'd become another person from the person she once was, cold, unloving, constantly criticising him. He couldn't trace the change though, pinpoint the moment. Perhaps, he mused, it was those unkindnesses that end in sarcasm, when every remark has a sharp edge.

That morning she'd shouted to him as he was shaving that they were off to Edinburgh in the Toyota. Blair was going to a 'crammer,' exorcised from their lives, if only temporarily, in the faint hope of redemption. Since coming back from Birchbrae he'd seemed like a poisonous presence around the place, appearing briefly for meals but otherwise invisible. Annabell was even more on edge than usual after the Sheila episode and now they hoped for some relief with Blair's absence.

As Digby stared at the oily insides of his glass his woozy head took him to places sobriety shunned — those nights when Annabell had been away, and the dark barn of a house had seemed to close in on him. He'd visit the warm pulsing black of his younger son's room. Sometimes he'd squat by his bed to stroke the soft hair on the pillow, before falling asleep himself. Sometimes he'd wake him...but that was their secret...

He returned home at five-thirty. Annabell had come back. A bit of food in him and he'd be OK to drive to Edinburgh. In his study he warmed his hands by the fire and checked his mails. One from his friend Bill Wyllie confirmed their meeting that evening at the Black Watch Club. It was a tartan-bedecked Georgian throwback whose celebration of Scotland's military past offered cozy solace to Wyllie and his cronies. Digby's father had belonged to the regiment and as a child he'd celebrated family birthdays, all sparklers and ice cream within its walls. Now though, the once proud regiment had been throttled by the politicians in London and rebranded as The Royal Regiment of Scotland Third Battalion— a name to trip from the tongue. Its motto *nemo me impune lacessit* a proud boast of stoicism in the face of danger, now as lifeless as the denizens of the place. Wyllie owned a chain of small public houses inherited from his old man and he and Digby had been at school together in Perthshire.

As a schoolboy Wyllie wielded a bat like no other and Digby, had revered his skill. They had shared a dorm and kept in touch ever since, Lithgow often staying in a flat above one of Wyllie's pubs on his visits to the capital. Of late however, Wyllie's business had faltered at the same time as his marriage to Sarah, a woman in whose company Digby Lithgow had never felt comfortable. She was a looker and a wit, but at dinner parties she'd avoid him, settling her attentions on younger or older men whose intellectual achievements were more obvious.

Digby Lithgow was a proud man and the notion that he was not considered important did not sit lightly on him. Now it seemed, Sarah was screwing a Professor of English at the University and Bill was taking it badly. That night Digby was set for one of those chats between men that never quite seem to meet the emotional needs of the moment.

6

Blair Lithgow stared at the little orange space-hopper alarm clock on the bedside table. It was three-twenty in the afternoon, and he could hear rain battering the Velux above his head. The cloying aroma of her scent filled his nostrils, and he breathed in deeply. A soft warm arm clasped his bare chest.

'It doesn't matter.' A head emerged from the duvet. 'Is something wrong? 'The voice of Tricia, his girlfriend of two months.

'Nope' He got up from the bed throwing the duvet aside over her head. A disappointing bout of lovemaking was the least of his worries. Today he should have been in College at an English class, but waking that morning, a dread had come over him. His expulsion from Birchbrae had stirred a self-awareness, dormant till then.

In the months of his lying-low he had reappraised his life and his possible future. He knew he was intelligent: could cleave open the motives behind every word and every action of others. He knew his father's thoughts before they were voiced; could read the look on his face, that just-discernible twitch of the mouth that presaged the sarcastic remark. His Housemaster he'd diagnosed as a paedophile manqué: a man whose touch seemed to linger too long, whose eyes sought places politeness should have avoided, whose voice went soft suddenly as if some invisible net had been cast over the unwary victim to ensnare rather than to reassure. Now his intelligence lit the way, but it was a path leading nowhere.

In Edinburgh he looked around his classmates and saw the intellectually challenged, the socially inept, the no-hopers whose fingers-up to authority had only rebounded in personal failure and who now sought rehabilitation in the last-chance saloon of academic achievement. None seemed his equal, which only emphasised the enormity of his own failure. He felt the same obscene discomfort he'd felt visiting his grandfather amidst the pervasive senility of his Old Folks Home: a house of shakes and tremors, of boiled veg and the stink of hopelessness. No, none his equal but Jack Dickens, at eighteen a self-styled artist who spent most of the time in lectures drawing caricatures of the tutors and yet who challenged Blair for top in almost every assignment. When he found out Jack's surname, the name 'Boz' came to him. Old Charlie Dickens and all that. *'Sketches by Boz.'* he came out with one day in the canteen and Jack liked it.

'Did Boz draw Dickens characters then?'

'No. Not the drawing kind of sketches. Snapshots of London life. Haven't read them. Bloody boring probably.' Christened thus by the posh boy whose wit and personality were so charismatic, he became an acolyte of the Church of Blair, a church of anti-authority reserved for those perceptive enough to pray with eyes wide open. Lip service in Excelsis Deo.

Boz, aware of the need to establish credentials, spoke up in class one day offering the considered opinion that Othello was 'a stupid wanker.' Much laughter and a strained smile from the tutor. The class continued, but every mention of Othello was met by a subdued murmur from a dozen voices and the play was abandoned.

The next day Boz was summoned and warned as to his future conduct--his ticket to ride the Blair train. The pair drank together at various pubs and spent evenings watching videos at Boz's house while his mother, a nurse, was on night shift. It was there one evening listening to a news report about the impeachment of a banker that Blair's idea was born. By now Blair's reading had stirred in him an irresistible urge to oppose any authority that he recognised as oppressive. Holden Caulfield's fight against 'phoney-ness' in *The Catcher in the Rye* had struck a chord and Blair's angst sought a target. Politically, it was a time of austerity and he knew how Eastlea was faring. He passed folk with Asda bags coming out of an old school and was told it was a food bank: on the News shares were rising. Something was wrong. He tried reading *The Wealth of Nations*, but after twenty pages decided that he had his own ideas. In Boz's flat he slugged his beer and shared his thoughts.

'Bankers, right? Why should those bastards get away with it while the poor have to go to food banks. Christ my old man's down to one bottle of whisky a day.' Blair took a slug from his can and wiped his mouth. The sermon was just beginning. 'Know why they get away with it? Because they're all in it together. The Old school tie. Well, yours truly would have one if they hadn't chucked me out. Blue and yellow diagonal stripes. Very fucking attractive.'

'Yeah, but you're one of them, aren't you? I mean your folk are well-off, yeah? 'said Boz. 'Fair do's. I'm working class and you're posh, man.'

'Wrong. Wrong. Like, I'm not posh, I'm with you lot. Distribution of wealth, see. Fair distribution of wealth. You can't blame me for my parents. See this jacket? Five quid from Oxfam. That's how fucking wealthy I am. That bastard that calls himself my old man won't give me a penny more than the fees, says I'm on my own. So don't call me posh or upper-class cos I ain't.'

'Well, no offence Blair, but you've got to admit you're not like me.'

'No, I'm not. I've got ideas and you don't have any.'

'What ideas?' said Boz, 'What can to open next, like.'

'Cheeky cunt. No, bankers — the final solution.'

'Final solution? Hydrochloric acid? said Boz, feeling very witty.

'Not a bad idea. "And we welcome you this afternoon gentlemen to our plastic surgery demonstration. Our patient is Sir Very Rich Wanker who has just experienced his face melt away after a young radical sprayed acid over it...'

'Christ, Blair, that's going a bit far, isn't it? Acid.'

'The redistribution of wealth. Heard of that? Banker gets a bonus of two million quid while your average worker gets fuck all. How fair is that? Work in a baker's and you get a bag of free rolls — work in a bank and you get armfuls of free cash. Are you kidding?'

Boz listened and nodded. 'No, you're right, Blair. But that banker makes money for the bank and the bank pays taxes doesn't it. He's only one man but there are heaps of workers.' He sat back against the settee as if he had delivered the coup de grâce to Blair's theories.

'Oh, the numbers game. Heard of The Crash, have you, you dick? The Credit Crunch? All those folk in America who couldn't pay mortgages that they shouldn't have had in the first place. Those bankers at the top caused that, no? Throwing money about, taking risks to make more money. People thrown out of jobs and houses. Debt. People that hadn't done anything wrong. And you think that's OK? And what about that guy Nick somebody who lost his bank millions in the nineties and caused it to collapse. One rogue trader. Shit. That's the numbers game for you.'

'No, it's not right, man,' said Boz.'

'I'm going to scare the daylights out of them; find out where the top guys live, then move in.'

'We burn down their rich homes. It's the People speaking their rage. If you're a criminal and you're jailed, they take all your assets: the assets of crime. So, whose taking criminal bankers' assets. No-one. But then maybe you don't give a fuck about any of this. Maybe you're happy to wallow in shit ignorance while everything turns to dust...'

'Don't know if I'm angry enough for this stuff Blair. Are you off your head? You can't go burning people's homes down. Christ man, people will die.'

'No, they won't. I'll make them regret what they've done, that's all. We'll warn them what's going to happen. Get everyone out, before the place goes up. Maybe when we've scared them shitless the government will act.'

There was silence in the room, only the tick of the clock on the wall and a passing bus could be heard while Blair's words, settled.

'I'll think about it,' said Boz.

Blair's diary:

Tricia's history. Cow. Boz thought I was posh. Fucking right I'm posh. I know a napkin ring from a cock ring. Felt good when I was laying off. Something to fight for. Can't wait. Didn't take him long...

What a hero. Now it's all-- 'Oh Blair that's a good idea lets firebomb a house!' One word from me and folk listen...Maybe I'll go into politics.

7

Leckie's dreams plagued him the night after meeting Paula Gilhooley, nothing erotic, but a series of scenarios in which he fails and is the object of ridicule or admonishment. Faces from the past inhabited strange rooms, voices shot at him from walls and paper bins and the jumble of images and sounds wouldn't let go even when he woke or seemed to wake and fell into a slumber again aware of the film of sweat on his chest. When he did wake fully, he stared at a spot on the ceiling and rubbed his gritty eyes. He hadn't drunk anything the night before apart from the oily dregs in a bottle of Amontillado that had lain about since before his wife left. It was nearly nine and he could hear a pan clattering in the kitchen. Megan was up. She wasn't home much these days, spending all her time with sausage thief in his flat off The Meadows. She seemed happy though, so that was fine as far as Leckie was concerned. He grabbed his gown and shuffled through to the kitchen where Megan was stirring some porridge in her very short negligée.

'My God, that's just over your arse and no more, kid.'

'You shouldn't be noticing. You're a father, not a pervert. Want some porridge? I can stick more oats in.'

'No thanks. I'm late as it is. Just wondered what you were up to. How is Mr. Megan these days, still cool?'

'The things you come out with. "Mr Megan" as you call him, is just fine if a little stressed with exams. That's why I came here last night, to let him get some studying done. Ok if I stay for a few nights?'

'It's your home honeybunch, remember? You don't need permission. Anyway, I'm off so I'll see you later. Fancy a take-away tonight and some telly?'

'That sounds divine darling. Can't wait. Will you be back by seven? I'll phone The Royal China for some deep-fried chilli beef and the usual sides yeah? '

'OK but ditch the prawn crackers for me. If I want to eat polystyrene packaging sprayed with fish piss, I'll let them know.'

In twenty-five minutes, he was in his cubicle waiting for Ed to appear, nursing a cup of Zoe's vile coffee. He craved a bacon roll but was afraid Ed would be in the office first so resisted the temptation from the bakery two doors away. He pulled out The Scotsman and flicked through the first couple of pages till a headline caught his eye 'Bruntsfield Death has Police Puzzled.' An old man had been found dead in his bed and the circumstances were suspicious. A post-mortem had revealed a healthy heart, and his elderly sister told police that he had been in good spirits. It was the second such death in the space of a few weeks where an elderly man living alone had died in his bed for no apparent reason. There might be a link between the deaths, according to the police but no more details. Typical, thought Leckie, no need to say a word but the hungry open mouths of the press needed feeding. Leckie shook his head, wished he were in on this. Sounded juicy.

He sipped from his cup and looked at his watch. After ten minutes of the sudoku he realised he had two 2's in one box. Shit. The usual. What rule of life meant he always guessed wrong? And why did it take so long to find out?

Twenty minutes later he heard Ed's voice greeting Zoe. He popped his head round his door and asked Ed if he could have a word. Ed was with another man that Leckie had seen in the office a couple of times—-a rough looking number in a leather jacket with a tattoo of some sort on his fingers. Not a bank manager then. After a few minutes the man had gone.

Leckie liked Ed. At first, like all men of his age he entered relationships with a bandana over his face. You see my eyes, but you don't see what makes me tick and I've been ticking this way for fifty-odd years. Women seemed to gel with each other or not very quickly, plugging into a sorority of shared victimhood and enforced caring, while men circled each other searching for some familiar ground. Leckie often wondered just why Liz seemed so fond of him. He didn't really talk much when they were together, but he supposed she wouldn't notice as she was always chattering away, and he was pretending to listen. Trouble was, occasionally it became apparent that she was playing a game of how much you care what I say, and she'd turn on him and accuse him of never talking to her.

It wasn't a new scenario between the sexes he realized, but it was never comfortable when it was being played out and that conversation killer "What do you want to talk about?" only led to a smouldering silence: any possibility of spontaneity hit on the head with a large hammer. Now he'd just had a chat with Ed, and it had been agreed that he should follow up his meeting with Paula Gilhooley and try to track down her old man. 'Sounds pretty routine Donald. He's probably shacked up with some woman somewhere and saying he can't get a signal on his phone. If you must go to the ends of the Earth that's fine with me, but make sure she understands what our charges are. Sounds like a good gig old son, just don't dip your rod on the firm's time will you. Ha.'

Leckie drove to Barnton and found Paula Gilhooley's house. It was a large whitewashed detached job with a multitude of leaded windows. Bit Arts and Crafts thought Leckie. Money wasn't an object then and kilty-boy had landed a good one. He pushed the bell, and a pretty maid in black opened the door and ushered him through a shiny dark-wood-floored hall into the conservatory at the back. It was a jungle of palms and climbers with a watering system too if the multitude of snaky pipes was any clue. She was smiley as ever, as she rose to greet him, her hair a brilliant gold in the sun.

'I'm really glad you're going to help Mr Leckie...'

'Look, call me Donald, it'll be easier on the tongue. Donald Duck. Donald.'

'Nice name, Mr Duck. Strong. Coffee or tea?' Leckie chuckled. Sense of humour too.

'Coffee will be fine. Thanks. Black.'

She sat down and ushered him to do likewise. He sat back in the cane sofa and pretended he was comfortable, though one of the cushion's hard corners dug into his back. She sat opposite him in a short print dress and cardigan. His eyes settled on the delicate veins in her naked foot as she crossed her legs, her peep-boo slipper dangling precariously from her painted big toe. He wondered if all his new investigations would be quite as pleasant. The coffee was strong with a hint of bitterness, but he declined the chocolate biccies in favour of business.

An hour and twenty minutes later Leckie sat in his Saab and scrutinised the notes he'd made. He had a cheque for a thousand pounds in his pocket. Easy come for some, he thought. He didn't go back to the office but parked in his lane and went to The Royal for a pint. The place was empty, Scotland's new Calvinism in full play. He'd done enough for one day. He settled in a corner below a blue-paned window with some obscure coat-of-arms on it and began reading a Scotsman that someone had left. As he turned to the Sport section, a waft of tobacco assailed his nostrils. He looked up and blinked.

'Well, well, if it isn't Mr Donald Leckie of that ilk, 'came a voice above his left shoulder. Leckie was staring into the beaming face of D.C.I. Hamish McBride. A barrel head with piercing hazel eyes, a broad nose, a sweep of thick grey hair and a moustache that Leckie had always envied. He'd put on weight. 'Mind if I...'

'It's a free country.' He didn't like McBride much. He was a man aware of his position and with a need to remind you of yours.

'Aye, well, free-ish I suppose. Needed a quick puff before I came in. Can't even smoke in this fucking country anymore. Can I get you one?'

Leckie had never refused the offer of a drink in his life and even the presence of a man he'd always been wary of wasn't going to break the habit. 'Yeah. Same again.'

McBride returned with two heady glasses of Guinness and sat down opposite Leckie. He was in his late fifties, a Shetlander who'd turned his back on twenty-five years of wind and squeaky fiddles and seasonal fat men in shiny breastplates for the cosmopolitan pleasures of Edinburgh and eventual promotion to Chief Inspector. Early hopes of a move to the Crime Division had been scuppered when Police Scotland was formed and the MITs were created. He didn't fancy a move to Glasgow.

'Christ, mind if I move the table a bit. Fucking legs get everywhere, not to mention the belly. Gave up smoking and now I'm a fucking balloon. Chocolate. Took a London flight last week and I couldn't walk when I got off. ' Leckie pulled the table towards himself, surprised by its weight, to give

McBride's long legs some room. He folded his paper realising he couldn't read it now anyway and pretending to do so was stupid.

'So how are things at the nick? Still fiddling your targets? Hear you've got a wee issue with elderly men. Probably wanking themselves to death.'

'Now we didn't think of that. That's that solved then. Well done. Anyway, Police fucking Scotland. Fucking joke. Don't blame us, blame the suits in The Executive who haven't a bloody clue about crime or criminals. Don't ever see a body these days, bloody Crime Division gets all the fun while we're left with the routine stuff. Anyway, never mind that, I hear you've got yourself a new job. A Private Investigator, that right? 'Leckie gulped down his whisky and took a sip from the Guinness.

'That's correct. ' Fuck it, Leckie thought, dismissing the 'for my sins' bit—why should I apologise for earning a living. Not to this guy.

'Very interesting work. Not a target in sight either. Free to come and go and a decent screw. ' He put down his glass and stared at McBride. There was a glint in McBride's eye that unsettled Leckie though, as if this chance encounter wasn't chance at all. McBride did come in here from time to time but rarely at this time of day. He should be behind his desk bawling out DC's and plods, not sitting here drinking.

'Come here often?' asked Leckie. McBride grinned, his generous grey moustache expanding across his cheeks exposing a good set of teeth.

'Only when a wee bird tells me you're here. We'll keep the identity of the wee bird a secret if you don't mind, but look, it's brought us together in a social setting. Isn't that great? ' He crossed his arms and stuck a huge black shoe into the isle.

'Grant.' he said.

'Grant?'

'The deceased Jim Grant and his employer Mr Edward Findon. ' Leckie was thrown. He wasn't expecting to hear his old buddy's name, let alone that of his new employer. He was intrigued. What the hell had McBride come up with? A conversation with him was an iceberg—one-eighth out of his mouth the other seven-eighths in his head, looking for a response, a twitch, a movement of the eye, a hand, to vindicate some theory. Leckie attempted impassivity. He wondered if this was about Stapleton and that business. Had something come up that could put him in trouble? He decided to force the conversation.

'Jim Grant is dead. Murdered by Finnegan. Now I work for his old employer. Is there a problem here?'

'No problem, Donald. Well, a peedie problem for you maybe if you don't mind me saying so. You see Mr Findon your employer is of interest to us. I mean the Police. Now you'll appreciate that I can't divulge any details, but I know you Donald and I believe you're a good man. You're a bloody nuisance at times, if you don't mind me saying so, but essentially a good man so...er...off the record and all that, I'm warning you not to get too involved with his business dealings. That's it. That's why I had to speak to you, if you're wondering. As I know you are. '

Leckie sat back. He didn't know what to say. It felt as if some rug had been pulled from under, as if someone knowing how grateful he was for this job had decided to unsettle him, whip the axminster and topple him into that abyss of nothingness again. That's how he had felt these last few months, as if nothing really mattered anymore apart from Megan of course. Nothing to get up for, nothing to interest him in living but reading the paper and drinking. Now he wondered if he'd made the wrong decision.

'You can't just warn me about the man without giving any more information. What the fuck am I supposed to do anyway — resign because the guy's of interest to you? 'McBride stood up, all six-three of him and offered his hand across the table.

'Can't say more, Donald. Sorry. Chust be careful, that's all. Cheers. ' Leckie shook his hand, an innate politeness overcoming any other feelings he had. McBride strode towards the door and went out with a raised arm to the barman.

8

In the hallway of a Georgian House in a well-to-do suburb of Edinburgh, a tall suave white-haired man was on the phone. The recipient of his call was Sergeant Colin Mabon of St Paul's Police Office. Twenty-five minutes later, James Mitchener's wife Elspeth and their two sons Rory and Jack were sitting in James's black BMW X6 outside their house. Sergeant Mabon and a constable appeared. Mitchener showed Mabon the note he had received that day at his office in The Dewar-McLellan Investment Bank in the city Centre. He believed it was a hoax and apologised for calling out the sergeant. It was composed from newsprint headlines and read simply:

'THE PEOPLE WILL SPEAK.
YOU'RE A PARRASITE
SUCKING THE BLOOD OF HONEST MEN.
YOU HAVE SIX HOURS TO EVACUATE
YOUR HOUSE BEFORE THE PEOPLE CLAIM IT.'

The sergeant assured Mr Mitchener that these threats should always be taken seriously and called the Station to speak to his Superintendent. Mr Mitchener drew his attention to the spelling of 'parasite' and suggested that this might be a hoax by some ill-educated idiot. Sergeant Mabon said he hadn't noticed that and anyway it wasn't a reason not to take the whole thing seriously. Some of his fellow officers weren't too hot at spelling either but it didn't mean they were all idiots. Mitchener shrugged.

Mr Mitchener was advised to find alternative accommodation that evening and to call in at the Station the next morning for further questioning. Mr Mitchener shook his head and drove off with his family. It was seven-fifteen in the evening.

On the same road, a hundred metres further up on the opposite side, a red Clio was parked. Robin had gone to London and Blair had borrowed his car. Inside, observing the arrival of the police and the conversation with Mitchener, were Blair Lithgow and Jack Dickens. Lithgow sat in the driver's seat, his eyes on the rear mirror. On the back seat two bottles stood swaddled in a blanket. He felt that old excitement rising. Boz tried to see through the side mirror but it was angled badly. Lithgow was nervous, enervated by the thought that one note delivered to a top executive could cause such a stir.

He turned to Boz. 'He's gone. I'll bet they've been told to clear off while the house is searched. They can't take chances, yeah. Might be true, and if they ignored it and anything happened there'd be hell to pay and maybe lives too.'

'What are the police doing, I can't see very well,' said Boz.

'They're back in the car just sitting. Maybe waiting for back-up.' Lithgow reached for a pan drop from the glove compartment, brushing Boz's leg.

'Heh. Watch it, Blair. My mother warned me not to go into cars with strange men.'

'Well, if your mother hadn't gone into cars with strange men maybe you wouldn't be here today, yeah?'

'Oh yeah, very funny. My mother was a gem. Is a gem. Christ she's only thirty-nine. Don't know what she'd reckon to this little lark though. I'd be told to pack my bags I imagine. Fucking criminal for a son. Wow.' Boz howked something hard from his nose and rolled it between thumb and forefinger.

'Don't even think about it buddy' said Blair, turning to face Boz. 'Keep your snott where it aught. This is Robin's car and he's very punctilious about things like that.' Boz opened his window and flicked the tiny ball away.

'When did you learn to drive anyway?'

'On my driveway, where else. Posh boys have always got driveways. The squad car's moving off. We'll give it thirty minutes before we go up the lane at the back, 'said Blair. He keyed the ignition and drove the car along the street, turning left at the end into a cul-de-sac off which was the lane.

Thirty-four minutes later the pair with balaclavas over their faces, edged their way on foot along the lane. There was no-one about. They'd already done a reccy of the house and lane, so they knew which gate led to the Mitchener's garden. Once in the gate, the house was about thirty yards across a lawn bordered by shrubs. A brick path meandered down one side by a summerhouse and a little pond. The house was in darkness and so were the houses on each side. There didn't seem to be anything on the wall, so they edged their way forward. About fifteen feet from the kitchen window Blair stopped, lit his Molotov and threw it. A second later Belling threw his, but it bounced off a wall and burst into flames on the patio. Blair's bottle had crashed through a window and burst into flames. The kitchen glowed dully then got brighter as the flames licked. The pair turned and walked back to the car.

'Bingo! The People've spoken! ' shouted Blair, as he turned to take a last look at the burning kitchen. Back in the car, they drove back to Blair's brother's flat.

Blair's diary:

Bingo. The peepel have spoke! We lit up their little house even if that pratt Boz couldn't even throw the fucking thing. How do I always end up with idiots. Can't wait to read the papers...

9

Leckie picked up the phone. It was Findon.

'Donald? Something wrong? Thought you were working for me, or have I been dreaming?'

'Ed I was about to phone. Feeling shit to be honest. Nose streaming and a throbbing heid and before you even think it — no, it's not a hangover, it's a cold. I'll be in, just give me time to get some stuff from the chemist...'

'OK Donald. We all get colds. No worry. Just let me know sooner next time. I've a wee problem this end, and I need to talk to you. Hasta la vista.'

Leckie put down the receiver and cursed silently. A new job and you want to impress and here he'd been chastised already. He'd gone to bed late after watching a film in the dark and couldn't sleep, waking up sneezing like billy-o. He got himself some Lemsip and forty minutes later he was face to face with Findon.

'Ah, it's the invalid. Have a seat.' Leckie sat down and felt another river forming in his nasal passage. He took out a tissue and wiped his nose. Findon fished in a cabinet and pulled out some papers. He turned to Leckie and gave him a buff envelope with the name 'Harris' on it.

'Read that through Donald and let me know what you think. One of the hazards of this profession is meeting dishonest people. And that's one right there. Anyway, how is Mrs Gilhooley? She phoned for you just as I got in. Seems quite excited but didn't want to speak to me.'

'Does she want to see me?' asked Leckie.

'She does.'

'Hubby is playing away she thinks and wants me to find out for sure. I'll tail him. She's tried but he only ever goes to see his mother, she says.'

'His mother? That's a new one. Usually, he's disappeared to Greece with all her money, or he's tried to murder her.'

'A new one? '

'Aye. Mrs Gilhooley is a regular. Pops up every year or so with some story or other. I think she gets off on us. Found out Grant was screwing her, the idiot. Strictly against the rules that. If I'd known at the time he'd have been out on his backside.'

'Grant? Screwing Paula? Jesus Christ, I'd no idea.' Leckie sat back in his seat stunned. He'd never imagined a 'regular,' but he'd had a spell as a Samaritan in his younger days when a chance meeting had sucked him into voluntary work on the end of a phone. Afternoon shifts in a grubby wee room full of smoke from two elderly ladies and two booths where the phones were and the supposedly suicidal regulars whose voices were immediately familiar. He learned nothing about suicide but a lot about loneliness and how some folk needed the crutch that a phone conversation would bring. So here too, there were regulars, folk habituated to need, who'd fabricate stories to involve them in human contact. Money no object.

10

The day following their bombing, Blair Lithgow didn't go into college, instead meeting with Boz at a pub in the Grassmarket called The Lucky Rope. The plaque said a Margaret Dickinson had survived being hanged there in the seventeenth century.

'Rope must've broken,' said Boz.

'Or she'd a fucking brass neck,' said Blair.

The pair scanned the red tops and The Scotsman for any mention of the fire but found none.

'Shit and buggeration. They must be hushing this up, ' said Blair, slamming the tabletop. 'Why am I surprised. The press is in league with these bastards. Always has been. Who owns the papers? The rich, that's who. OK, we go again...'

'Wait a minute, this might be it,' said Boz, holding up The Clarion. 'Just a few lines about a fire where we were. Just says "Kitchen Blaze" then "A fire appliance was called to a domestic fire last evening in a house in the Merchiston area caused, it is believed, by an electrical failure..."'

'An electrical failure? Fuck me. What about the bottle that hit the wall?'

'Yeah, I know, I know, and the warning. But maybe they're twisting it so that folk don't panic,' said Boz. ' I don't know.'

'No, you don't. Well, next time there'll be no mistake. We torch the fucking place good and proper and we let the press know it's happening.'

'Yeah, that's what we should do. We should've done that last time, yeah? ' Blair turned to Boz.

'Yeah. We need more names. Bankers.' Boz thought for a moment.

'There's a girl I know who works in an office in St Andrews Square. Banky sort of stuff…

Blair Lithgow walked back to Robin's flat and printed out a map of South Edinburgh. He drew a small circle round the area where the Mitchener's house was. More to come, he thought, and the thought comforted him as a dream of celebrity emerged. There he was being interviewed and there was his name in all the papers. The saviour of the working class —Blair Lithgow, the ne'er-do-well who changed the face of society. He looked briefly in the mirror and pulled a comb through his thick hair. He was looking good.

Blair's diary:

Rain again. Electrical fire my arse. They know what it was. Zilch about the letter. Arseholes. We'll be back.

11

Digby Lithgow parked his Toyota opposite the Club. He placed the Resident's Permit Wyllie had sent him on the dashboard to avoid the Gestapo that paraded with a smirk and a blue book around the bosky squares of The New Town. An icy rain settled on the windscreen. He sat for a moment and let out a loud fart. He smiled. He farted a lot these days, attributing it to rich food, his age and a delight in disgusting Annabell who was one of those annoying human beings who never farted. He pulled the collar of his Barbour up, crossed the street and mounted the steps just as Wyllie appeared round the corner.

'Digby! Well met, old man. Save you the explanations at the front door, ' said Wyllie, tapping Lithgow on the shoulder.

'Good to see you, Bill. Dreich night.'

'Nothing a few drams won't put right.'

They passed the smiling doorman and Wyllie signed Digby in before they mounted the stairs to the main lounge. It was a throwback to another age: the smell of leather from the Chesterfields, the tartan rug that held the scent of expensive shoes, the log fire, the ancient paintings of men being slaughtered under shredded flags, the little occasional tables with their Art Deco lamps. Three men sat in one corner by the drawn curtains and two others near the double doors. Women were allowed but were *rarae aves* in this land of Glenfiddich and Laphroaig and laddish camaraderie. Wyllie ordered two doubles of Highland Park and said he'd have a Becks for a wee chaser.

'Well, how are things in the outback Digs? Still fighting the Indians. Haven't seen you down here for ages.'

'Aye, well, I'm a busy boy these days with one thing and another.'

'And how is the lovely Annabell? Still painting?'

'Oh aye, she's splashing away at the birds and the flowers. It's the bloody walls that need painting these days though. Christ you're lucky you don't live in a barn like that. Soaks up the money like a sponge. Heating's a nightmare particularly in a summer like we've had. ' The young waiter appeared with their drinks, placed them on the table with a jug of water and a small dish of nibbles. He asked if that was all.

'Yes, that's fine,' said Wyllie, shoving a handful of nuts in his mouth.

'Nice in here. Bit of class, eh?' said Digby. 'So how are you?'

'Oh, you know. Up and down, up and down.'

Digby wasn't sure why they were meeting. It had been ages since he'd seen Wyllie. He wondered if Wyllie needed a sub. Between the two there had been a strong friendship from schooldays, but Wyllie's pub business had always seemed a little *infra dig* to Digby, bringing out a latent snobbery: steel was one thing—beer another.

Now here he was opposite his old friend who, he had to admit was looking good in the dim light.

Wyllie adjusted his position on the settee.

'Bloody Chesterfields may look good but they're murder on the back. So Annabell and you are ok? Just asking. Since Sarah's gone, I realise life goes on. You adjust, eh. Find new interests. No-one to nag you about pissing with the seat down and all that stuff. Women!

What would we do without them, eh? Well, who would we fuck without them eh?' Digby laughed as he knew he should, but a nerve had been touched and he couldn't resist responding.

'Well, a good fuck would be nice. To be honest Bill, I can't remember the last time Annabell and I had one. I think as you get older it just doesn't seem to matter. If Annabell started nagging me at least she'd be talking. Hardly see her these days to be honest. Bill shook his head in sympathy and swallowed more whisky. Annabell's behavior was just what Bill wanted to hear, and a sweet content settled in him.

The pair reminisced about school and cricket matches and the clock ticked time away. Another round of drinks and Digby looked at his watch. Time for up.

'Well Digs, it was good seeing you again. Keep in touch. It's been too long.'
Digby rose and made for the door.

'And keep taking the Viagra! 'said Wyllie, in a voice intended to be heard through the whole lounge. A titter over his shoulder confirmed the joke had worked. Digby had gone. 'Wanker,' thought Wyllie. 'Doesn't deserve a woman like Annabell.'

Wyllie ordered another drink and took out his phone.
'Annabell? It's me. He doesn't know…

12

Boz was excited as he showered. He'd met the girl and she'd told him about her boss, a man called Oxby who was a Hedge Fund manager. He'd spent three hours chatting to Beth Fielding in an old church that was now a chic meeting place for office workers. You could see steps that would have led up to the altar and the pulpit were still there, extended to accommodate two tables with views. The evening light through the original stained-glass windows cast odd colours on faces around him and Boz's pint looked almost blue. The Glory of God turned interior design.

Beth sat opposite him looking beautiful in the filtered light and he had to remind himself of his task as his eyes strayed to her cleavage. Most of the time he asked her about herself but as time wore on and the Polar Bears disappeared down her lovely throat, his questions turned to office matters. This was his Project he said and though he couldn't really get interested he had to find out as much as he could about Hedge Funds and that sort of stuff. Well, it turned out that Beth had been this guy's P.A. for a short time while his regular P.A. was on Pregnancy Leave.

She said she didn't know much about the technical stuff but someone else in the office told her his job was to invest in securities that sold at less than he thought they should be worth. He said analysts sometimes lost interest in these, or the markets did them down and he knew their value would come up again. That's how he made money for the bank. He told her one day that he supposed he was a hedgehog and then he told her a joke about hedgehogs, but she didn't get it. Boz

asked her what the joke was, and she said it was something about sharing. He laughed in an encouraging way then asked her if she knew where Oxby lived, and she said she did because he'd asked her to send a bouquet of flowers to his wife on Valentine's Day. Was he an old guy? Boz asked. Oh no, he was
he was in his forties, not bad looking in an overweight kind of way. Boz took her home and kissed her deeply outside the front door of her flat. She was tipsy by this time and desperate for the loo she said, and he said he'd be off then, and she looked at him a moment before saying 'OK. '

Boz felt good as he switched on the telly the next day. It was a political debate where the suits gabbled on, cutting each other out and never answering a damn question from the stookies in the audience who smiled as if a few seconds of their phizogs on TV was all that really mattered. He felt good in a mission- accomplished kind of way, though what would happen next began to worry him. There was something seriously wrong with Blair he thought, as if the normal rules didn't apply. He didn't seem to care much about what happened to himself or presumably him either. How would he react if the going got tough and something went wrong? Could he be relied on not to panic? Boz had come home from the bombing, his nerves jangling in a way he'd never experienced before. He felt alive for once in his life and wanted a re-run.

He punched Oxby's address into his phone and grabbed his coat. He'd show Blair Lithgow how useful he could be.

An hour later, as a light rain began to fall and his watch said ten-to-four, Boz found himself in a leafy square at the West End of the town. It was The New Town in all its glory: the elegant curve of the street, the black painted railings, the large lounge windows through which grand pianos and expensive paintings could be seen. In the Centre of the square was a garden with large beech trees and a tennis court. Boz mused on the trappings of the rich and how easy their lives were compared to his neighbours on the Estate and as he thought about it all his anger grew. There it was at last, number 16. 16a must be the first floor. A light was on in the large lounge, and he saw the grey hair of an elderly woman glide across the room. Was that Oxby's wife? He crossed the street opposite the house and observed it for a few moments as if looking for his car key. Bombing this would be tricky he thought, for it was a terrace and unless there was a rear entrance, he didn't see how it could be done. The street was busy. He found a lane and wandered along past numbered gates and dust bins and an old man walking his little dog till he came to a pair of garage doors next to a gate with '16' painted on it. Bingo! It seemed almost a replica of their last house as if the rich of Edinburgh always lived in the same sort of houses. He texted Blair saying he'd found the house. Blair would meet him there.

Evelyn Oxby was entertaining two lady friends as the clock in the hall chimed half-past four. One was an old school friend and the other she'd met at a writing group. 'My God, I didn't realise the time,' she said. 'This is so embarrassing, but I've to collect Neil from the dentist in five minutes. Look, just enjoy the cake and talk about me. I'll be back in half-an-hour.' A tall red-headed woman in a blue cashmere suit rose and folded her napkin.

'Evelyn it's not a problem. I told Peter I'd be back by five. We're going to a 'do' at the University tonight — some celebration for one of the History Profs who's got a chair at Oxford. As if Oxford was the Holy Grail or something. Peter plays squash with him though, so it's the "my mate" thing and we're expected.' The other woman, dark-haired, younger than the other two, rose also and smiled.

'Evelyn, I assume you've heard of First World problems? I think it's a left-wing invention to make us feel guilty about things we know are important. As if picking up the old man from the dentist wasn't just as important as collecting water from a well. Dental hygiene is bloody important. It's all relative as the niece said to her panting Uncle as he...well never mind, you get the point.' In the awkward silence that comprehension fills, the other two gathered themselves.

'Me too Marjory,' said the tall woman. 'Life intervenes as per. Michael will be home from school soon and I like to be there when he gets back. Who wants a latch-key child eh? Might sue me for neglect.'

'Where are you parked Sarah?'

'I'm bussing it. Never drive in town. Parking's a nightmare.' The other two laughed, shaking their heads in agreement and made ready to leave when the doorbell rang.

'Oh terrific,' said Evelyn, 'That'll be the plumber about the boiler. Perfect timing!' She moved to the front door, pressed the intercom button and told him to come up. There was a clatter from down below somewhere and steps on the stairs.

All three women stood by the door. Evelyn opened it and a fresh-faced young man with long hair stood there, a piece of paper in his hand.

'Are you the plumber?' said Evelyn, 'I'm afraid this isn't a good time. We expected you yesterday.'

'Er... no, I was looking for a Mr Smith.'

'Sorry? A Mr Smith?' A note of irritation had entered Evelyn Oxby's voice now and she told the man he must have the wrong house. He blushed it seemed, apologised and disappeared down the stairs. The women stared after him till Evelyn collected herself and made an ushering motion. 'Nice hair. Ladies, after you.'

By the time Boz had regained the street, the absurdity of his plan had dawned on him. There was no way the Oxby's home could be set on fire without the danger of burning every other flat in the block. He turned and saw the three women exiting and chatting on the steps.

Blair Lithgow was excited. Boz had done as he'd hoped and come up with another victim. He got off the bus at the West End and walked for five minutes till he saw Boz leaning against a lamppost.
'Hi man. How goes the crusade?'
'Oh, hi, Blair. Well, not too well really. This is where the bastard lives. Second floor...'
Lithgow stood as if he'd been hit by some extra-terrestrial beam. He stared at the house and said nothing. 'Second floor?'
'Afraid so, 'said Boz. 'Bit of a problem eh?'
'Not really, ' said Lithgow, 'We warn them, give the hundred folk in the terrace twenty minutes to evacuate and then we fire flaming arrows through the windows.'
'What if the fire spreads? We can't kill all these people. ' Lithgow grasped him by the shoulders and put his face close to Boz. 'Look at me. In my eyes, man. You think this is some kind of joke? You think I'm having fun here or something. This is deadly serious and if you're not up to it you can fuck off you little shit. These bastards are stealing from the poor. Look at the rooms in that place. You could hold a fucking dance in that living room. You could house

twenty Paki families in there and that's only one room. You think that's OK? You think that's fair?'

Boz squirmed out of Lithgow's clutches and stepped back a pace. Words wouldn't come, but in his head the enormity of what they were planning overwhelmed him. He was afraid of this person who stood before him and yet he understood Lithgow's message. He too felt that the rich treated the poor abominably but had never found the words to explain why. In his staring silence, Lithgow saw fear and the possibility of conversion.

'You get it, don't you. How important this is? ' He waited for Boz to respond. 'Yes, or no? Yes, or no? Come on!'

'Yes. ' said Boz, searching Lithgow's face for some sense of acceptance.

'In that case you're just a fucking idiot. You bring me down here to a fucking terrace, and we're supposed to fire it? Jesus Christ man.'

Lithgow's eyes widened and his head tilted offering a response but Boz had been wrung inside out by now and something in him slumped and died. He turned and walked away along the street throwing a piece of paper into the gutter as he went.

Just then, from the entrance in question three women turned into the street voicing their various goodbyes. Blair Lithgow brushed the arm of one of them, a tall red-haired woman who apologised in that reflex way folk do. She wasn't young but she radiated an aura that struck Blair. As a lock of her hair fell over her right eye. Something deeper struck him, deeper than attraction: it was as if he knew her. Did he know her? Had he seen her before?

'Sorry' he said, ' Clumsy me.' She smiled, turned, and waved goodbye to the other two, making her way along the leaf-strewn street. She seemed to float rather than walk. Blair Lithgow never could explain why he followed her. Perhaps it was the idea that she was rich: perhaps he was still thinking of rich banker's wives and their cosy lives; perhaps in some perverted way she reminded him of his mother. She reminded him of something. Who knows. He had nowhere to go and no-one to see, so his curiosity took him after her.

He followed her to a bus stop and waited. He couldn't take his eyes off her hair: it mesmerized him- that tumble of red held by a blue clasp. She got on a number 33, and he followed her; it was something he'd done before when he'd followed Tricia, suspecting she was meeting another man, and it gave him a strange frisson of excitement. Following someone who had no idea they were the focus of your attention put you in control.

She sat inside and he sat further back, opposite an old man with a young child. Twenty minutes later she rose and alighted on a busy street in an area Blair knew well. Where would she live, this stunner?

This was student land near the university frequented by his brother Robin and his friends. It was an area of little specialist shops and restaurants and behind the main drag, the quiet residential villas of Edinburgh's bourgeoisie. He followed her, the faint click of her shoes like a trail as she left the busy road and turned left then right to enter the front door of a detached villa. He watched her disappear into the house and felt as if something precious had been taken from him. Later he remembered that he found his right hand shaking as he returned on a bus to Robin's flat.

It was empty, thank God, for he didn't feel like talking to anyone. He was missing Tricia. He heated up a Chinese ready meal from the fridge, took it to his room and clicked the iPod. Taylor Swift was singing 'Love Story 'one of his girlfriend's favourites. As Swift sang, all he could see was that strand of hair that had fallen. He flipped over the duvet of his unmade bed and lay down. Was this love? Was this sickness? Was everything he'd ever felt now suddenly trashed, an irrelevance? Finding religion must be like this, he mused, a sudden shaft of light that takes you by surprise and changes things forever. He had to see her again. He had to talk to her. It didn't matter if she told him to go to hell, he had to act on this feeling. He wondered what her life might be. Would she be married? Yes, of course, a woman like that would be married and she'd have children that would call her 'mum' and who would see her in her intimate moments sitting on a sofa, her legs out, her lovely feet bare, clutching a coffee cup maybe, watching the TV, not knowing how beautiful she was, not knowing the effect she'd had on him on that street. Yet he knew her. He knew her. But how?

BLAIR

Shit. I'm in love, man. That hair. That face. Got to find out about her. This is how it works. Love at first sight. Fuck me. Won't sleep tonight. Old man sent me fifty quid.

13

From the window above the study, Sheila watched Annabell disappear down the path into the woods. It was raining again, the grass beaded and bent with it, and thick where the mower's blades slid ineffectually over it. Wilson had attempted to cut it before he'd left after an argument over wages. The garden was in mourning: the fruit cages which she could see to the left of the main path looked redundant, their dark netting limp and awry and the beds by the path rusted, each crisp and colourless, redolent of death. She hated this season, the decay, trapped as she was here inside, placing buckets to catch every new leak through the ceilings.

Robin's room held two containers which filled constantly and even in Digby's room a bucket stood by the window. Annabell constantly bemoaned the incipient dereliction which she knew was coming, but Digby seemed deaf to her pleas. Sheila knew that the failures of the house itself were mirrored by the neglect, the rot that had increasingly set in between the inmates themselves, though perversely, she remembered the frisson that ran through her as she witnessed Annabell strike Blair that day. That feeling lingered as the water trickled down the stairs and the bloom appeared on Blair's cheek.

As she lay in bed later, his face swam in her head, that beautiful face as it turned from rage to resignation and his hair flopped, defeated. She felt such pity that this beautiful boy should be so lost to himself. Her only wish was to hold him close, to stroke his hair, to show him what love could be. Housemaid here for four years now, she had developed an intimate understanding of the politics of the Lithgow family: the comings and goings; the rows that resonated through the faded rooms which must once have been rich with laughter. Sheila knew there was no longer love in this house, only a crass functionality oiled by the polite acceptance that this was the way it was, and the best had to be made of it. There was no escape for any of the prisoners here, only a sentence to be served till some unseen event might intervene. Sheila was going. She couldn't stay now that Blair had gone and her visits to his room, where she would open his books to see his handwriting and hold his clothes to her nose, came to an end when Annabell caught her there one day wearing one of Blair's pullovers. Annabell was her favourite: a kind, elegant woman who was trapped here with no children to love her and a grumpy husband who never seemed to offer a kind word.

Sheila wondered where Annabell went in this weather. Surely she couldn't paint in the rain? Was it just to walk away from the house? What was she thinking as she walked towards the river? Was there escape? Was there a life better than this, and if so, how would she attain it? Digby's strident tones came from below and she touched her hair before going down.

Two days after Bill Wyllie's conversation with Digby in the club, his Nissan X-trail turned into a side road bordered by woods. It led to a small dam that once served as a conduit to refresh the fishponds of the estate and was rarely used now. His hand on the wheel trembled a little. He smiled. He was excited. He was always excited as he waited for her to emerge from the woods on that path. At the sound of her name a fire had been kindled. For months now they had met here and driven to a cottage on a nearby estate. Wyllie had known

Annabell since her marriage to Digby years before and though there had been periods when the families had met infrequently, on their twenty-fifth wedding anniversary the Lithgows had thrown a party.

The house buzzed, the July sun blazed, and the striped marquee swayed to a jazz band that played into the night. His memory was a little blurred now, but what he did remember was the face of Annabell as she sat at the table listening to Digby give his speech. It isn't difficult to know a true smile of happiness from the forced smile of duty, and Bill Wyllie, ever an admirer, knew Annabell was unhappy. The day before, in an intimate moment made more intimate by several glasses of a good Chateau Neuf Du Pape and a Cuban cigar, Digby in response to a joke about sex and marriage had shocked Wyllie by remarking that he and Annabell slept in separate beds. 'She's a fine woman I suppose Bill, but fuck me they squeeze you dry sometimes.'

'How do you mean, Digby?'

'Oh, you know; nothing you do is right. Constant fucking nagging about the house and money and all that stuff. Can't seem to relax unless she's doing her painting. Misses the kids, I suppose.'

'Well, you can't expect love's young dream to last forever, can you? I've been lucky I suppose. Sarah and I get on fine even if it's not like it was in our younger days. She gets off on this arty stuff too, I suppose it's just the way women are.'

'All this party crap. My idea Bill. She didn't want it. Christ there's such a thing as keeping your end up though. People expect some sort of acknowledgement after twenty-odd years, eh? We owe it to our friends.'

'I know what you mean, Digby. Anyway, I'm glad to be here. Haven't seen you for ages. Garden's looking good.

You're bloody lucky to have all this, I must say. Where are the kids?'

'The kids? Packed the little buggers off to Edinburgh. You know what kids are like. Oh, not a party! Well at least they're not around to embarrass me. Any idea of the upkeep of this place Bill? Steel isn't what it was either, the Chinese are taking over, subsidised to the hilt, the fuckers. Can't see me going on for much longer if you want to know the truth. At least you're in the right line. Punters will always want a swallow, eh? ' Digby refilled his glass and drank. He had filled out in the months since Wyllie had seen him last and his complexion had taken on the florid look of the drinker in middle age. Annabell, he pondered, had grown more beautiful as she aged, a new grace enshrouding her. He hadn't spoken much to her since arriving, she and Sarah chatting in her studio with plans for an exhibition of her paintings in Edinburgh, but later that evening the party in full swing, Wyllie found himself alone on the terrace.

The deep silence of the woods seemed almost enhanced by the buzz of voices and conversation inside. He walked down the ten steps and across the lawn to a raised gazebo from which an avenue opened up through the trees. There were two cane chairs and a table on which lay one of Annabell's straw gardening hats. Some impulse made him put it on and he sat quietly in one of those moments when peace comes dropping slow and a delicious calm falls: no thoughts, only the hoot of an owl somewhere and the party reduced to a distant hum. Then a sound, a soft sound of footsteps...

'Annabell, it's you.' He swept the hat from his head.

'Don't. It suits you. Perhaps a tad gay. Are you escaping my party you horrible man.' The hat remained on the table.

'Oh, not escaping, just enjoying a bit of country quiet. And why are you here? Aren't you the hostess flitting like a butterfly from group to group keeping the fizz going?'

'Well, this butterfly is nectar heavy just at the moment, thank you very much.'

'Isn't this terrific. A wee hut away from everything. You're so lucky.'

'Yes, lucky old me, Bill. The girl who has everything.'

He turned to look at her sitting in the other chair, bent forward a little, her long legs stretching the blooms on her dress, her hands clasped in her lap, staring ahead into the night. The posture seemed to him the epitome of sadness; a thought no doubt triggered by Digby's earlier confidences.

'You're so beautiful, ' he said, staring straight ahead himself as if the words had been uttered as a challenge. ' I mean... ' Now he regretted them and the silence that followed filled him with trepidation. He was about to retract in some way when she spoke...

'I know, Bill.'

He turned to her. 'You know?'

'I know. ' He stretched out his hand and she turned to look at him and took it. He felt its fragility, each bone, the long fingers with just a hint of sharp nail pressing his palm. He let go and stood up, bent to her and kissed her gently on the top of her head. She smelled so new. She looked up at him and their lips touched. Nothing like this had ever happened to him: no teenage fumblings in the woods, in the backs of cars or at parties, no time even in his courtship of Sarah could he remember his heart doing somersaults. Suddenly she had filled him full of something that felt warm and good. They agreed to meet in Edinburgh the following week, he, fearful that the moment might never return, she, wary but excited that someone seemed to care for her with a tenderness she had forgotten existed.

14

Leckie was at the piano when his Don Giovanni ringtone interrupted him. He hoped it was Liz. It was Paula Gilhooley. As agreed, she would let him know when her husband left the house in the evening. She'd asked where he was going, and he'd said he would pop in to see his mother on his way to meet a friend. Leckie hadn't eaten and the thought of beans on toast began to torment him as he struggled into his jacket.

He revved up the Saab and eased out from the lane on to the main road. This was his first assignment, and he would make it quick and make it good. Findon would be impressed not to mention how disappointed the lovely Gilhooley might be that their association was at an end. He did wonder for a second as the lights changed what sex with Paula Gilhooley might be like: imagining her face flushed and the sounds she would make and felt a stir below, but the thought that Grant had been there brought reality back. Grant had been a bastard and where bastards have trodden is not where you want to tread. He reached in the glove compartment for some mints but there were none. Shit. Now the glove compartment door came away in his hand as it did occasionally. This had better not be the way the evening is going to go, he thought.

Ten minutes later, the traffic lights kind for once, he drew up opposite an imposing sandstone building set back from the road in the Blackhall area. The sign cut in the gatepost said Craigcrook Care Home. He drove in and drew up in a car park to the left of the building. Bingo! There, three cars away was the Jag which Gilhooley drove. What the hell is going on here, Leckie thought. Is he fucking his mother? Do zimmers and cabbage turn him on? Leckie sat in his car and tried to fix the glove compartment door. Finally, it clicked into place. Something to do with the angle at which he opened it caused it to slip out of its housing. He half turned the ignition and caught Classic FM. If the fucking announcers said 'Relax ' once more, he'd be forced to listen to the posh up-your-arse Radio 3 instead.

Then two figures emerged from the main door. A man and a woman. The woman skipped lightly, hugging her coat around her as if she'd hardly buttoned it and the man put his arms around her. The man was Duncan Gilhooley: the woman was the prize. They drove off in the jag and Leckie followed, excited in a way he hadn't been for ages. It was predator and prey and this predator had better not fuck-up.

At a set of lights, a white van got between him and the Jag and he thought for a moment he'd lost them, but there they were still ahead turning right again. The Jag drove through the gates of a park and drew up alongside two other cars. Leckie followed and parked at the far end where he could observe the car. He waited a few minutes and then opened his boot. He took out a piece of metal and made his way to Gilhooley's car. Gilhooley was still seated in the driver's seat and the woman in the passenger seat. He knocked on the window. The driver's window slid down.

'What's the problem? ' said Gilhooley irritably.

'Oh, nothing really. I thought I heard something falling off your car and I found this. Is it yours?'

Leckie now saw Gilhooley clearly in the light from a lamp near by. He seemed relaxed. He couldn't see the woman's face, but he saw her hands and a flash of blue under her coat. A nurse.

'Oh, right, thanks, ' said Gilhooley, ' I didn't hear anything. Can't see where that would come from. I'll keep it. Cheers. ' The window closed and Leckie walked away. It was a piece of metal that had opened many a car window. Well, fully clothed occupants and clear windows had established that car parks weren't the couple's chosen place for lovemaking. He wondered why they'd gone there. Just to talk? It wasn't his experience that lovers seeing each other just wanted to talk. Now he was curious about the woman. He sat in the Saab and decided to go back to the Care Home. He felt hot now, in that way he did when pieces of the jigsaw seemed to reveal the picture, to offer up the picking and the placing one by one.

He parked where he'd parked before and braced himself. He was an actor going onstage, the heart racing, just a hint of moisture in the armpit. Up the steps with just enough urgency in his stride. He pressed the bell push. A nurse came from the front desk and spoke through the inter-com.

'Can I help you? Visiting time is past I'm afraid.'

'Oh, that's alright, ' said Leckie, ' I was walking down the road a bit when a woman fainted. She's being tended to now. A nurse's uniform under her coat. She said she worked here, just left about half-an-hour ago. Would you know her name? She seemed very vague when I asked her.'

A look of concern filled the nurse's face, and she opened the door to let Leckie in.

'Half-an-hour ago, you say. That must be Lucy. Wasn't she with anyone? She was off then. I'll just check the book.'

Leckie didn't want to mention Gilhooley. Too risky. She moved back to reception and pulled out a blue ledger. Her finger trawled the page.

'Yes, it's Lucy. Where is she now, Mr...er...?

'Oh, er...Park. Mr Park. Do you have her second name? It's for the hospital, in case she's taken in.'

'Graham. Lucy Graham is her name. Look, I think I should get the supervisor on the phone in case it's serious.'

'Ok. Good idea. Or maybe give her a phone. Who knows she might be at home by now. Does she live far away?'

'I don't know. I'm new here. Yes, I'll do that first. Make sure she's OK.'

Leckie buttoned up his coat and leaned forward.

'I know it's silly, but as I found her, I'd really like to talk to her myself to make sure she's OK. Can I have her number?'

The young nurse, flustered and red now but taking a lead from Leckie's calm, scribbled the number down for him. He took the paper and said he'd better scoot as he was supposed to be meeting his wife. She let him out and shook his hand.

Leckie never failed to be impressed by the concern ordinary folk showed for others in these circumstances: the passer-by who sits the roadside drunk in his car only to be vomited on; the middle-aged man who plunges into ice-cold water to rescue the lagered-up teenager who's fallen from a bridge; the stranger who plunges into a burning car to haul out the unconscious driver. And it's that same selflessness and trust that enables men like him to establish the name and phone number of Gilhooley's mistress. A good night's work, Leckie thought, and he'd enjoy sharing his dastardly skill with Megan. Unfortunately, that was one Care Home that wouldn't care to see his face again. Oh well.

Leckie texted Paula.

Hi,
Found his girlfriend. Details tomorrow. Ten o'clock?

He drove home and parked in his lane. Half-an-hour later he was sitting watching Arsenal beating Southampton, on his lap a rapidly cooling fish supper that he'd picked up on the way. He took out his phone and trawled 'contacts.' Liz. The number. Just one call and they'd be back again. The silence from her was killing him.

'You don't know what you've got till it's gone…' That song came to him as he stopped outside her flat and sat watching her window. What the fuck was he expecting to see—a man? He didn't know. What he knew was that he'd fucked up. She wanted more of him. And now in the distance between them he desperately wanted more of her. Before his fingers gained the courage to press, he heard Megan calling from the hall.

He told her what he'd done at the Care Home. She wasn't amused. She said it was nasty to frighten that young girl; she'd probably get into deep shit when they found out there hadn't been an accident. Leckie, sniffed, rolled up his last few limp chips and told her it was his job. Finding out things was his job and sometimes you couldn't just ask, you had to be a little inventive. She shook her head and disappeared into the kitchen.

There was mail, she told him, and she recognised the writing. It was from her mother. Leckie moved to the dresser and opened the letter with some trepidation. Nothing good ever seemed to emanate from any communication from his ex-wife.

'Donald,

I didn't want to text as you never seem to respond anyway so I hope you read this. Susan has been having very bad headaches for a few weeks and went to the doctor. She's been taking the usual painkillers, but they've had no effect, so she was referred to St John's for tests. The specialist thinks there may be a problem. We've discussed it with him, and he wants her to go in for more tests on the 15th. He assured me that there is every possibility that it isn't serious, but they can't take a chance when the brain is involved. She didn't want you or Megan to worry but I know you'll want to see her.
You can get her on her mobile number which I know Megan has. Haven't seen Megan for a few weeks. Tell her I miss her, and we should have a drink soon.
Marjorie'

As Leckie read, he felt his face chill. He was stunned. "Brain" The word burned into him. My God, his daughter might die... He shouted for Megan to come and read the letter and stood watching her face as she read. Her face crumpled. Tears welled in her eyes.

'Oh my God, dad, Susan might be really ill. It might be…'

'I know, honey. But let's not jump the gun. These people know what they're doing. Anyway, it may be nothing. Could be migraines or something like that. Let's go to the Royal and have a drink, get out of here.'

'No, I must talk to her. I haven't seen her for ages and now she's ill.'

'Fine, fine. Give her a buzz. We could all go for a drink and talk this through. 'Leckie sat down in his favourite chair and switched the TV off. The silence as Megan keyed in

Susan's number was palpable. Leckie shivered. The room held its breath. He knew he was in a state of shock. There was no answer from Susan, so Megan left a message to call. The situation hung in the air spinning on thin wires that seemed unable to hold. Leckie went to the pub while Megan stayed by her phone trying to study.

15

The next morning Leckie was seated in Paula's lounge. A log fire burned in the stove.

'So, we know who she is then. ' Leckie drank some orange juice then pulled out his notebook.

'I know how painful this is, Paula. He came out of the Care Home with a Lucy Graham. She's a nurse at the home. They drove to a park and sat talking for a while before driving off. I spoke to them in the car, that's how I know nothing was going on, if you follow me. I went back to the Home and established who the woman was.'

'Do you have her number, Donald?'

'Yes, as a matter of fact I have. And her address. ' He passed a piece of paper to Paula who got up to retrieve her glasses from a table.

'Well, I suppose it's mission accomplished. She offered her hand, and he stood and shook it. The suddenness of it all slightly surprised him. He'd imagined some scene where the cheated woman bursts into tears and bemoans the fickleness of love that has turned something beautiful into something ugly. Nothing. Just a wry smile and a handshake. As he walked down the drive, he wondered about the money she'd paid. Surely she was due a refund or something. It had been too easy.

He drove back to Portobello and got there around eleven. A weak sun poked out between the clouds. Findon was out somewhere. He drank a coffee and decided to go for a walk along the front. If he sat at his desk, he'd only beat his brains out over Susan. The night before he'd had little sleep, imagining the horror of a dying daughter and one who'd been living without him for so long. He'd never been a man at ease with his duties as a husband and father, but the present situation had undermined what he felt to be a growing acceptance of what he was as a person.

He loved his daughters, though Susan had chosen to live with her mother. He had come through a hard time with Megan and the affair with Stapleton. Anything he'd done he'd done in good faith through love, and he had nothing to be ashamed of. Now though, he realised how separated he was from Susan; how little he could comfort her; how little perhaps he meant to her; how little his love might mean now. He stood and watched a woman playing with her two kids on the sand. A family. A husband at work who'd return and kiss them all. They looked so happy it seemed almost an affront to him then. He moved on, bought a burger from a van and sat in a shelter looking at the grey sea while a sliver of onion snailed down his wrist.

Back home, with Findon nowhere to be seen, he struggled with The Scotsman sudoku at his desk. Megan appeared with the news that Susan was not in any danger. She didn't know the details, but her mother had phoned to say things were going to be fine with Susan. Leckie took off his jacket and hugged Megan as if she were the one that had been in danger. It was one of those rare moments for Donald Leckie when his cynical view of the world fell from him to expose another being—a creature alone and vulnerable to all the winds the world could blow. His chest heaved and he cried into Megan's hair. She clasped him firmly and made no move to break from him knowing how embarrassed he would be with tears in his eyes. 'Ach,' he said at last, 'What an old daftie I am. Sorry.'

She pulled away gently and went to the kitchen again without turning to look at him, a movement that seemed to him almost cruel as he stood there abandoned, rubbing his eyes. Don Giovanni played in his pocket. 'Leckie.' It was Findon.

'Donald. Missed you at the office. Where were you?'
A scolding. 'There was nothing doing. I went home. What should I do, just sit there watching the clock?' This felt wrong somehow, as if something good between the pair had been jolted, but Leckie, already bruised from the day, was in no mood for a scolding. There was a long pause and then the call ended. Fuck him, thought Leckie.

This wasn't what he'd signed up for— the old nine-to-five routine. If there's work, I'll do it— if there's nothing I go home. He went through to the kitchen where Megan was preparing a pasta bake with tuna. She was becoming a decent cook, old Megan: perhaps it was a female thing preparing for domesticity with her man. Sometimes Leckie became fearful when he contemplated her leaving. She was untidy as hell and a pain in the arse sometimes, but her very presence gave the flat a sense of a home with its emotional ups and downs.

Now more and more he looked forward to returning to a meal in the evenings. Some nights Ricky joined them, and the guy was OK Leckie thought, though why he never used a knife was a source of mild irritation. Ricky stayed over some nights and Leckie could hear them from his room. He'd lie there listening to his daughter having sex and think back to the times when he'd throw her in the air to hear her squeals as he caught her. Now she was a woman with the body of a woman and the assurance of a clever confident one. 'Autonomous' Yes that was a word he'd heard a lot when feminists described strong women. He smiled to himself and felt glad to be a man relieved of the interminable effort women seemed determined to make to establish themselves as equals in the eyes of men.

Now they played rugby and football and battered each other in the boxing ring. Leckie had seen how women were treated in The Force: the innuendo, the locker room jokes, the dirty posters that would make them blush, the banter that most of them accepted as the norm. But slowly times had changed. His last superintendent had been a woman. Pam Wilson. He could see her now sitting behind that neat desk, a handsome woman with strong features, a photo of her son staring at her as she bawled you out. At first, she'd been a novelty, a kind of freak that had slipped through some net unnoticed, but she was good at her job and took no shit. Some couldn't cope with being told what to do by a woman and gradually they left to be replaced by a new generation of bright-eyed bobbies whose mothers were younger than Leckie. More women gained promotion and they became the norm.

Leckie had always loved women, even some of the poor souls that became regulars at the Station. There was always a trace of the mother in them, no matter how faint. Behind the frightened eyes you could imagine them clasping a child to their bosoms while the other held the needle…He began to think of Liz and as she stroked him, he drifted off into a deep sleep.

16

Sarah Wyllie picked up her violin and played 'The Ashokan Farewell' in the attic room that her partner used as his man-cave. It was a room that drew her: its cozy warmth and the smell of books comfortingly male. It was so much him, that she felt closer to him here than anywhere else in the house. She'd received money from her husband but had now moved into the Morningside home of her new partner, Professor Peter Wells. The room's walls were book-lined, the floor white-painted boards with a Persian rug in front of the stove. An antique French leather armchair and a saggy beanbag were the only seats apart from Peter's Captain's chair by the writing desk under the Velux window. Peter had written 'A Dip into Will S.' up here, a book that had made his name and brought him the trappings of a celebrity he found difficult to deal with.

He was a quiet man with a scholar's diffidence yet with a sardonic humour that women found attractive. They had met at a wine and cheese in honour of the Traverse Theatre, and he'd made Sarah laugh as he teased a TV editor earnestly attempting to tap his knowledge of present thinking about Shakespeare as a political activist. He had been on his own since his wife died three years before, and although tall and strong-featured, he became nervous at social gatherings and had been known to flee the scene to the consternation of his hosts. She wasn't too keen on bald men, but somehow, she was intrigued by this one. He had met Sarah three days later by accident in a bookshop and had hesitantly invited her for a coffee. While they chatted, a Beethoven piano piece came on the system, and he stopped speaking to listen. 'That bit there,' he said, 'I always play that much too fast.'

'You play?'

'Yes. Well, a bit. I'm no genius.' He paused and sat back. 'And so do you, I hear.'

'Who told you that?' She said, leaning towards him, interested.

'Oh, someone or other. I can't remember.' She knew immediately that he'd been asking about her as she had about him. For a woman increasingly ill at ease with a husband who was rich but had the cultural interests of a stick, the rest as they say…

She finished playing and looked at her watch. They were invited to supper that evening at eight and it was six-thirty now. She heard the faint music from the radio in the kitchen downstairs and wondered if Peter's son Michael, had come home. Sun through the Velux made an oblong of light on the carpet, and she thought of Spring. She bedded her violin, pulled a strand of hair from the bow and went downstairs. As she passed the window on the first landing she glanced out as she always did. Opposite, against the railings of the park, she saw a man looking at the house. He was wearing a hood over black clothes. Why was he just standing there? Waiting for someone probably. She shrugged and made her way down to her room to change for the evening.

Peter returned soon after and she poured him a gin. He kicked off his shoes and sat in his favourite armchair in the lounge. Sarah stayed in the kitchen preparing a chicken salad. He shouted through

'What a bloody day, darling. They're cutting my budget. Two bodies to go.' There was no response, so he rose and joined her in the kitchen, his socks leaving moist prints on the flags.

'Did you hear me? Two bodies for the chop. Will they listen to reason? No. "We're confident present high standards can be maintained in a leaner environment." My God who are these people? Not a bloody clue how it all works. Now I have the delightful task of deciding who goes.'

'Well, you know one of them already, don't you? Winslet. You've never said a good word about her, have you?'

'No. I suppose you're right. She's a brilliant scholar but she's like a fish out of water with students. Mind you, she's a tartar too. I can just imagine how she'll take it…'

Two days later, Sarah sat down on a bus and as she settled, looked up into a hooded face. That dark hood. She began to see hooded men everywhere now. A closer look and she saw it was a young girl.

She alighted at her stop and went into a store for some milk. As she paid at the till, she thought she saw someone disappear behind a shelf. She was becoming paranoid.

Later she opened the blinds of Peter's room and peered out. There he was. This time sitting on a bench in the little park opposite. He was talking on his phone. Sarah pulled the blinds down again and sat in the captain's chair, the evening sun slatting her face. She was being followed. Stalked. That was it. She was being stalked. Peter wouldn't believe it— he was a fireman always ready to douse any spark that her imagination struck. She stood up and looked out again. Still there but then he rose and with a glance at the house made his way out through the gate till he disappeared into the avenue. She would say nothing to Peter, rather she would wait to be certain that she was right. Wait and be sure. She went downstairs and made a cup of coffee.

As she sat there, the past returned. A twenty-two-year-old girl walking by The Water of Leith on a bleak December day suddenly grabbed and dragged into bushes where she was violently raped. It was as if unbidden, the past had returned with the full panoply of horror that it held. She fought the memory, but it stayed. The cup shook in her hand as she remembered the aftermath: the police station; the examination; the questions; the nights without sleep. They never found the rapist, but the trauma of her intimate life ransacked stayed with her for years. She would never go near a police station again. Ever.

17

Blair Lithgow felt oddly lost. The energy and buzz of his fire-bombing crusade was in limbo. The headaches had returned, and he couldn't sleep, waking as tired as he was, going to bed. Boz's reaction to the newspaper report had indicated that he might be up for something more serious. But as he thought of Boz, she came back to him again. She wouldn't leave him: wouldn't let him rest.

He'd seen the woman close on the bus after tracking her route that morning. She'd left the house at ten and got off in Princes Street. She'd walked to the West End then disappeared up some stairs. It was an Art Gallery. He pulled down his hood and went up the steps, but the glass doors were locked.

Back home he decided to make a chart of her whereabouts. Days along the top, places down the side, times too. He didn't ask himself why he was doing this. Somehow the act was more important than any outcome. A nice house in Morningside. He looked her up on Google: short and sweet-- she was a poet and played the violin. No picture. She wasn't on Facebook.

As the days passed a pattern emerged. She'd leave the house in Morningside, take a bus into the city. She'd go towards the cathedral and disappear into one of the adjoining houses. It said 'St Mary's Music School' on the door. Sometimes she'd be with a man, the same man, but often she'd be on her own. She took buses. Always the same number where she'd sit downstairs. It was about ten stops from Princes Street to her house in Morningside. At night the act of following became a dream of meeting her. He'd say

'Hi,' and she'd smile at him and say 'Hi.' Then he'd tell her his name and she'd say what hers was… The dream always ended in them having sex in bus shelters and in parks. Waking was a disappointment. He had been skipping college for a while, but he was neglecting the struggle for justice. He phoned Boz. Might as well give him another chance. Two heads and all that, even if one was full of cotton wool.

'Hi Boz. How's it going?. See U tomorrow morning in English. Cheers.'

The next morning Blair sat in English near the back, signed in and took some perfunctory notes: Indian police. Hassle from peasants. Elephant gone apeshit (with a drawing of an elephant with an angry eye) COLONIALISM fuck this…. Down the left-hand margin, he wrote 'Sarah.' In block letters that he then filled in. Then underneath, '18, Chilwell.'

It was Orwell shooting a fucking elephant. Imperialist pig. Had to shoot it because the natives expected it of a white man. Blair wondered where Boz was. As the class ended, he was summoned by a gesture from the lecturer, a Mr Watson, a small bespectacled guy with a tremulous voice and unlimited enthusiasm. He knew Blair's father.

'Mr Lithgow. Long time no see. Have you been called away on family business?'

'Nope. Just couldn't be arsed coming really. Don't see the point anymore.' Mr Watson's face stiffened with anger.

'Oh, you don't see the point of education. Is that it? Do I sum up your feelings accurately? Your essays were good. You want to throw everything away. Is that it?' He sat back on the edge of the desk as if he'd landed a left hook to finally dispatch his opponent.

'Well, if education turns me into a plonker like you, who needs it. See you.' With his final riposte, Blair strode from the room. If this meant the end of college then he didn't give a toss. He'd had enough of classrooms and idiots like Watson droning on about things that didn't matter. He was at war now: with society, his father, with his mother too, though he did feel some sympathy for her, being married to his father. There were dreams coming now involving his father—dreams he didn't want. His brother he rarely saw, and when he did, he felt patronized. A fucking lawyer is what he'd turn into. Another type who knew how to make money. Though his little car was useful, license or no license.

He spied Boz in the canteen talking to a girl. He waved. Boz came across with a tray. A glass of coke and a teacake in its shiny, red-striped wrapper. Blair snaffled the teacake and ate it. Boz laughed.

'You missed the Orwell. My favourite. Can't resist these. I'll get you another,' said Blair.

Boz was sipping his coke. 'It's OK. We Ok?'

'Yeah.' They found a seat by a window and sat down. A young guy came across and put his hand on Blair's shoulder. 'What was that about mate? Did you give squeaky Watson a run for his money?'

'Oh, yeah. Just personal stuff. You should've seen his face.'

'This place, eh? Fucking shithole. College? Don't make me laugh. Place is full of no-hopers. Present company excepted of course. Who's interested in fucking elephants?'

'Give's a look at your notes eh,' said Boz. Blair passed them over. There was a woman's head with scribbly red hair and underneath an address— 12 Chilwell Road. The young guy gave Blair a final pat and walked off, slinging his sac over his shoulder. Boz glanced at the notes and returned them. 'Didn't know you were friendly with him,' said Boz.

'Nah., He comes into The Lucky Rope. Total wanker. Likes to keep in with me.

'How about we hang around a Bank car park and take number plates. Then we go to posh neighbourhoods and check out cars. We might strike it lucky. Just an idea.' Blair stared at him for a moment till a smile crossed his face. 'You're not as stupid as you look. It might work. But can we get access to car parks?'

The plan was agreed. Blair would make a list of Banks and the pair would attempt entry to car parks. They agreed to meet in four days to discuss any progress. Blair strode off while Boz finished his coke.

Blair's diary:
Sent Watson packing, the fat shit. Wait till Daddy hears about it. Boz is a wanker. Fuck me they're all wankers. Just see the bugger crawling about car parks taking numberplates. Did the frogs have this much trouble starting a revolution?

18

Leckie picked up his mail.

'You are cordially invited to the opening of The Joseph Gallery, on Friday the 12th…'

An invitation from his old friend Eric Pyke. He'd owned a gallery near Leckie's old one and the death of his son Joe in a motorcycle accident had completely derailed him. The gallery had gone bust and Eric sold up. Now two years later he was back on his feet again and ready for a fresh start. He and Leckie had been drinking buddies for a time before the accident, but Megan's kidnapping had so consumed Leckie that the pair had drifted apart. Now Leckie smiled at the re-emergence of his friend. Though he hated parties, he would go for Eric's sake. Eventually he'd phoned Liz and invited her to join him, said he'd missed her. The silence her end seemed to last a long time. She was good at these affairs, always at ease with new people and unfazed by middle class bullshit merchants. If she didn't like you, she'd take the piss. Or worse.

'I adore the tissue-thin line in McIntosh's dialogue between the opaque and the real, don't you? So witty and yet deeply visceral.'

'Yes, I know exactly what you mean,' said the tall thin man cradling his Chardonnay, his old school tie beaming like a beacon.

'Oh quite' Liz would say, smiling knowingly, 'But for me they lack the elegance of a Bridget Riley, don't you agree? Nice tie, quite serviceable but I'm not too sure it goes with your eyes.' Leckie would stand and watch the stuttering response as the victim's emaciated wife, bangles clacking, would drag him away from this interloper who didn't know the drill. Liz said maybe, she'd think about it.

Three days later, on a Friday evening, Leckie pushed open the heavy glass door of The Gallery Joseph. It wasn't in the fashionable Old Town but on the tram route West in an old warehouse up a stairway. To Leckie, it smacked of something across The Pond. It was a huge glaringly bright space humming like a hive. Leckie fought his way to the table with drinks. A glass in their hands like a badge of acceptance, now a part of the crowd, they skirted the room glancing at the paintings against the green hessian walls.

'Good stuff. He always had an eye, Liz. Did you spy that Connors as we came in?'

'Where is he?' She asked. I don't see him anywhere.'
Leckie scanned the room and spotted Eric chatting to a group of two men and a woman. Almost by telepathy, at the same moment Eric looked across and beamed. He excused himself and made his way to Leckie.

'Donald.' They hugged, Leckie spilling a little wine in the process. He wasn't a natural hugger.

'Oops. This is great, Eric. Back on the road, eh?'

'Well, it's been a struggle, but I suppose it's all I know. Too bloody soon to be sitting by the fire, and this must be…'

'Oh, this is Liz, my…friend.' Liz looked at Eric and then turned to Leckie.

'A bit more than a friend really. Not sure friends sleep together, do they?' Eric laughed, a genuine laugh from the belly, amidst the heady posturing and polite smiles of the evening.

'I like you,' he said, 'I'm sure we've met before, haven't we?'

'You might have. A while ago,' chirped Leckie. A call came from nearby.

'Eric! Eric! Where are you?' It was his wife desperately trying to bring some focus to the party.

'Oh, I hear a bird calling. She's right. I'd better do my thing. Speak later, yes?'

He made his way to the far wall and delivered his speech of welcome. Much applause. Much raising of glasses. Much praise for his new venture. Much fumbling for credit cards at the desk as pictures were purchased. Such an investment. Leckie was always amazed at the effect of a free drink and some chat with artists had on the flight of cards from wallets. Something about an opening that cast magic dust over sane minds.

Leckie and Liz stood surveying the scene when a group caught Leckie's eye. Two men and two women. One of the women laughing loudly at some remark. A tall red-haired woman that Leckie recognised from his time as a gallery owner. He couldn't remember her name but as he looked, she happened to glance his way. She excused herself and made towards him. Leckie knowing what was coming, felt that male ego swelling. Here was a beautiful woman seeking him out in a crowded room. He turned to Liz who was on her phone to her son.

'Hello. Mr Leckie isn't it? I shouldn't be surprised to see you here.' She swivelled, her hand indicating the walls. 'Pictures.' He smiled and looked at Liz. Time for intros.

'Hi. Mrs Wyllie. I'm Donald. Sorry I've forgotten your first name…'

'Sarah. How are you?' Another quick glance at Liz who had put her phone away and was nervously sipping her Chardonnay.

'Oh, I'm fine. Sarah, this is Liz. Liz, Sarah used to buy pictures from me.'

'Hi Liz.'

'Hi. Nice to meet you. I'm his friend.' Leckie laughed.

'I'm not in the picture business anymore,' said Leckie, 'Too much competition these days. Retired now. Man of leisure.'

'No, you're not. You're busier than ever,' Liz quipped, happy to join the conversation and play the part of the caring partner.

'That's what you all say when you don't have to get up in the morning,' said Sarah, laughing.

'Oh, he gets up alright,' said Liz. 'He's still working really.'

'Oh? What keeps you busy these days then…er…Donald?'

'You got me. I'm a private investigator now. I take money for looking through wardrobes. Make sure adultery really is adultery. Dresses and suits hanging together. That sort of thing. Very exciting.'

'Well, I'll expect you any day to check my status. I left Bill, my husband for another man. I mean I left him for someone with intelligence and feeling. That's him over there with the green bow tie. Peter's his name. I don't think you ever met Bill, did you?'

'Not guilty. But I'll bet he's glad you've gone. He's probably got a nice-looking woman now.' For a micro-second Sarah hesitated, wondering if she'd just been insulted then it clicked that this man had a sense of humour. She laughed.

'He's probably got a dog now. He always wanted a dog's body.'

Now it was Leckie's turn to laugh. He turned and looked at Liz to see a weak forced smile cross her face. Sarah noticed

Liz's sudden chill and knew the reason. Time to go. Sarah touched Leckie on the arm and said her goodbyes. 'Time we were off. We've done our duty. Bought that one there. I love it. Well, I hope to see you both again sometime.' She turned and her hair turned after her.

'Nice lady,' said Leckie.

'Yes, lovely. You noticed. Nice bit of flirting there.' Leckie nudged her and she laughed. That was Liz— so much a woman in her instinctive reactions and yet she could be nudged back into love so quickly. In his head he just wanted to leave now and get into bed with her. 'Go and get your coat, Liz. I'm just going to have a look at a picture over there. Not buying. Honest. He moved off and she watched him as he made his way to the desk where a couple were paying for a picture. He waited till they'd gone, then spoke to the girl.

'That picture over there. He pointed to the one Sarah had bought. A friend of mine painted it. He asked me to let him know if anyone bought it. Red spot?' The pretty girl smiled, a little discomfited by the request but in compliant mood. She looked at the sheet. 'Er... yes. It's been purchased.'

'Look, he's old school. He always thanks his purchasers. Could you give me the name and address?' She frowned.

'I'm not sure Mr Pyke does things that way. You'd have to ask him, I'm afraid.'

'Eric's a pal of mine. I asked him. It's OK.' She shrugged her lovely shoulders in surrender.

'It's a Mr Peter Wells. Do you want the address?'

'Yes, and the phone number. He'll give him a call.' She gave Leckie the number.

'Have you had a drink?'

'Yes, thanks. Perfectly serviceable plonk. Tell Eric I was asking for him.'

'Who should I say...'

'Just Donald.'

As he made his way across the room, he wondered why he'd done that. Why had he felt the need to know where she lived? Yes, she was attractive but so were lots of women. He had a woman. What devilry was there in him that made him do this? Then he knew. Curiosity. Just a simple need to know that had been a part of him since forever. That part that had pushed him on when others had given up. No harm in talking to her again.

He met Liz at the door, and they made their way home along Princes Street past the late-night shoppers. As they walked, he realised a silence had fallen between them. He wanted to say something, but words wouldn't come. Here she was at last after he'd missed her and yet something wasn't right. The usual ease had stiffened. For both, it seemed. He turned and looked at her as they walked but she didn't turn to him. The barriers were up for the road works to bring Edinburgh into the twentieth century with a tram system, but the street looked a mess. Over George Street and Queen Street they strolled hand in hand, though her hand felt dead. As they approached the door of her flat in Stockbridge, she kissed him on the cheek and told him she was tired. No coffee tonight. He laughed; thought she was joking, but her face was firm. This was a first.

'OK,' he said, 'That's fine. I'll give you a ring tomorrow.' She knew he wouldn't. Settling in her now, was the conviction that this relationship was going nowhere. He wanted her when he wanted her. It was all about him: the jokes, the teasing, the tender moments. She knew in her heart that he didn't love her the way she wanted to be loved. He never would. And it wasn't enough. She saw how he was with women, the easy way he had of teasing them, flirting really. And something in her broke this evening. A heart string that had been pulled, had snapped. He'd turned the peg a twist too far.

19

Blair lay on his bed and tried to read 'Words' by Jean Paul Sartre, but the small print and the self-analysis irritated him. Here was a man who from an early age was conscious of playing a part. Blair related to that — the difference was that Sartre wanted to please and Blair wanted to be hated, or rather didn't care that he was hated. We consciously meet the characterisations others place on us, and Blair Lithgow rose like a fish to the bait as a sower of discord.

From the sitting room next door came the muffled voices of his bother Robin and his girlfriend. He'd been here for four months now and the strain of living with his brother was telling on both. Robin was studying Law —- a man in love with detail and order. He had stopped looking into Blair's room for it resembled a war zone: discarded clothes, books, papers thrown down when the urge to discard struck. The walls now covered in posters and paper of all kinds: drawings of naked girls, ships, heads; a chart with dates and times; a map of Edinburgh; two posters —- one black on red saying 'Turn Control into Chaos' the other for the film 'A Clockwork Orange' depicted four characters in white and their extended shadows. Faint hint of cannabis, chewing gum and sperm. Blair kept himself to himself, usually disappearing when Robin appeared, but his absence seemed to make his presence felt more strongly and Robin had promised his girlfriend that Blair would be gone soon. Tricia had bagged off with a bouncer at Mojo's nightclub and Blair had felt relieved. He'd convinced himself that they were sexually incompatible though she did have luscious tits.

The chart was filling. Times, places, buses. Luckily Sarah rarely took taxis or drove. Mostly she was driven. Though patterns were emerging, Blair found it difficult to pin her down and difficult to follow her. For two weeks in shifts he'd stood for hours outside the house in Morningside till his legs ached and he'd begun to chill. It wasn't working. She seemed to lead a random existence that took her all over the city. As the days passed, his obsession grew, however. She was never far from his mind at college or in the pubs that he frequented. He lived in the fantasy of meeting her and going somewhere with her. She would laugh, her hair flying as they sped along the beach at Cramond or climbed together up Arthur's Seat as the sun set on the city to sit and watch it before falling into each other's arms.

He bought her a scarf from The National Gallery—a John Bellany scarf, all yellows and blues with a funny pelican woman on it. It was arty, like her. He posted it to her but decided against any message. If she thought it was from a friend she might wear it. If she wore it, she would be wearing him. What he now knew though, was her favourite places: a French restaurant in Broughton Street; The National Gallery; The Cameo Cinema; a pub in The New Town called The Spectacled Hen and oddly enough—the Zoo.

He'd followed her there, up the hill, watching as she stopped at the large cats and then at the Budongo Trail where the chimps hang out. She spent ages watching the chimps just leaning on the rail as they wandered about eating bananas and fucking. Not a bad life, he thought. He stood close to her and saw her sweep hair from her face as a puff of wind blew. He could smell her scent he was so close. He wondered if he should speak, say something funny, anything, just to get her to look at him, but just as he was about to speak, she moved off. He followed through the panda enclosure and on to a large building which he took to be the headquarters of the Zoo. There was a card entrance system. She went in. So, she had a card. Maybe she was a member or a 'friend' or something like that. She would be. He went back to the chimps' enclosure but bored by the inane comments of the watchers who thought the chimps were 'monkeys' he decided to call it a day. Tomorrow he'd go back to Morningside again, maybe see that bald prat opening his umbrella in the rain.

Bair's diary:

Saw RED at the zoo. Christ, I want to touch her. Must be a member or something.
What about MY fucking member!!!!! I still smell her.

20

Blair was angry. He'd hoped for some acknowledgement that a group were out to get rich folk but there was none. It had to be a house not a fucking flat. Back to square one. What if the Mitchener house was done again? This time in another way? No little articles in the papers suggesting a house fire but something the papers couldn't ignore. The People had to speak, to shout, to get their message of justice known.

That night Blair and Boz agreed on a plan. 1) a letter to the press-cut-out and pasted. 2) they would break into Mitchener's house when the family were out. 3) they'd smash everything 4) daub walls with slogans so there's no doubt about their motive. No fire this time, but in the heart of the bastard's home they'd put the shit up him and his family. There would be no ignoring it. Boz would watch the house for a few days to learn patterns. When they were safe, they'd do it. An hour would be long enough. In and out.

Blair outlined the plan. No fire this time. Just a smashing time to be had by all, was Blair's way of putting it.

They stayed until thrown out. Both were drunk but Boz was finding walking a problem. Supporting him, he and Blair staggered along Kings Stables Road and cut through the multi--storey car park, Boz shouting incomprehensible gibberish all the while. As they mounted the stairs to the upper level, Blair tripped, releasing his hold on Boz who fell backwards, six steps or so, ending in a heap. The pair fell six or so steps to end in a heap. Boz had split his head and was bleeding badly while Blair had damaged his knee. ' 'What the fuck, Boz!' said Blair. He stood unsteadily a moment till he heard a voice from above.

'What's going on down there?' Blair limped back down the steps and hared it back to the Grassmarket where he vomited in a lane. Further along a couple were against a wall, the woman's face pale in a streetlamp, her eyes shut. As he passed, she groaned as if on cue. 'Slag,' he shouted, and made his way up Victoria Street.

An ambulance was called by an elderly man who had heard the commotion on the steps. Boz was taken to the Chalmers Hospital. Boz was treated for a head injury and a broken leg and kept in for observation.

Blair texted Boz the next morning.

Hi,
Where U?
Had to run. Needed a crap.
Tebilly sorry.

He wasn't sorry. He didn't care much what happened to Boz. But he didn't want to be involved in any outsider's questions. He had decided after the West end fiasco that Boz was a liability. He would do the job on his own with a thoroughness that an accomplice would only spoil. When he'd released Boz, he knew he'd fall but didn't realise how far and how he'd injure himself.

21

He dressed in his favourite black leather blouson and jeans with a neat new sky-blue shirt. Room for his balaclava too in the deep pockets. He was going to find his lady today and see if she was wearing his scarf. Robin was out. Blair raked through his clothes and drawers for some money. His father's cheque was due in two days, but he'd spent a lot in the pub. In a drawer by the bedside, he found sixty quid. He'd pay Robin back before he knew it was gone. As he mounted the bus towards Morningside he decided that he'd had enough of this stalking lark. Somehow, he had to contact her. He needed to text her. Let her know how he felt. He got off the bus and walked the two streets to the house she shared with the bald man.

It was ten-twenty in the morning. An April chill. Birds chirruped. He took up his usual position pretending to read a book in the little park. A woman pushed a pram past him on the path, smiling, and he smiled back. Not bad, he thought. Back to his Rankin. Baldy left at eight-thirty, and she usually left the house at about eleven, sometimes with a violin case as well as her handbag, sometimes with a back sac. Sure enough, at ten fifty-two she emerged, pulled the door to and descended the steps to the path. The violin as usual. But today she stopped by the gate and looked across at him, a long stare that might have been called rude. He dropped his head to his book. She knew. She knew he was looking for her. What now? He looked up again as if he were digesting a sentence from the book, dreamily, unfocussed. She had gone. The urge came quickly. He hadn't planned this, but he wanted into that house. He wanted into her life. He wanted to smell her life, her clothes, her perfume, the bed she slept in, the chairs she sat in…

He looked at neighbouring windows, saw no-one. He crossed the road, walked up the path. No sign of an alarm. He pressed the bell. A buzz somewhere in the bowels of the house. No answer. Again, a firm press. No response. He pulled up his balaclava and walked round the back, his feet crunching the gravel.

No problem. He's an innocent lad looking for a Mrs Anybody. Oh, wrong house, sorry.

This was the first time he'd done this, but he'd seen films, was sure he knew the drill. A side window on the first floor. Round the rear up some steps to the back entrance. To the right was a large bay window. It would have to be the door. He mounted the six or so steps and knocked hard. One-two-three. One-two-three-four. His knuckles complained. He tried the knob. It turned but the door was locked as he knew it would be. He checked for any alarms. None.

He went down into the garden and picked up a stone from the rockery. A heavy stone at least four or five pounds in weight. He'd give the handle a go. That's what the police do. One of those battering rams that splinter most doors to buggery. This was different but it was a good weight to bash the handle with. He was concerned by the noise, but the neighbours were a good few yards away on either side. He hefted the boulder and with arms bent threw it at the handle. It bounced off with a dull thud on the step. The handle had gone squint which was a sign of progress. He picked up the stone again and repeated the action but as the stone toppled from his hands, the door opened. A young man, half asleep and in pyjamas stared at Blair. There was no time for words. Blair charged him, forcing him back into the kitchen, toppling him over. As he lay, bewildered, Blair bent and punched him in the face. The face turned with the blow and blood ran from his nose. Blair repeated the punch with more force this time, and the boy's head turned again and hit the flags. Pringle. Pringle. He lay still.

'You stupid fucker!' Shouted Blair. 'What the fuck are you doing here! I rang the fucking bell. You deaf or something?' OK, this was going wrong. What to do? Was there anyone else in the house? Jesus. He grabbed the boy by the lapels of his pyjamas and shook him conscious. 'Who else is in the house. Divulge! Who else?' The boy was scarcely able to speak for fear and pain. He shook his head. 'No… nobody.'

'Nobody else in here? If you're lying, I'll batter you.'

'No. Please…'

'Ok. Calm down.' He caught the smell of the house now, a faint odour of toast and coffee and detergent. He was in. Christ he was in, but it was all ruined by this bastard. Who the fuck was he?

'Who are you? What's your name?'

'Michael. My name's Michael.'

'Are you her son? Are you? The woman's son.'

'No. He's my dad.'

'Baldy? He's your dad?' He nodded. There was no chance of exploring now. Couldn't trust this kid to just lie there could he, not while he ransacked the place for her things. That was it. Done.

'I'm going, OK? You stay here for ten minutes before you move. If you disobey me, I'll come back and kill you. You understand?' He nodded. Wiping the blood from his nose. His long blonde hair was tacky now with blood.

Blair backed down the steps and strolled up the path, ripping off the balaclava, and out to the street, looking back now and then. He walked for a half mile or so in a zig-zag manner till he came to the Meadows. His fingers were raw from the stone and his knuckles were bruised with the punches but as he walked a sense of elation took him. He was flying inside. It was as if the danger and the violence had released endorphins that drugged him now with a crazy joy. He punched the air and yelled as he passed walkers in The Meadows.

He'd smelled her house; the smells she smells every day. Close to her. He'd beaten that boy who wasn't hers but who would have talked to her. He'd smelled her breakfast. But he knew now that his days observing her from the park were over. She'd be scared now. He imagined the boy, battered and bruised phoning his father or maybe her, telling her what happened. She'd put two and two together. Him on the bench. He hadn't wanted to scare her, not really. That idiot had ruined everything. How would she ever speak to him now? He went to The Lucky Rope and settled in a corner with his pint and a packet of cheese and onion crisps. He texted Boz.

Hi,
You home? Better now?
Silly bugger.

22

As Blair had predicted, Michael texted his father and Sarah:

Guy broke in. Punched me.
He's gone. Asked who I was.
Knew about you both.
I'm OK. What now?

His father texted back:

My God Michael. Phone the police.
I'm coming home now.
Hope you're fine.

Sarah texted:

Let your dad know.
Wait for me.
Don't do anything.

She texted Peter:

This is awful. Can you get home?
I'm coming.

    Peter got home first. Michael was dressed in a sloppy pullover and jeans. His face had swollen, and he'd wet his hair so that it fell dark and sticky to his shoulders. On seeing his father he'd cried against his chest. Violence was new to him. The police arrived soon after, then Sarah. She was shaking. They asked if Michael had seen his face. No. He was wearing a balaclava. She told them she suspected it might be the man she'd seen in the park—leather jacket, hoodie, early twenties. Yes. That was the guy. Two constables, a man and a woman took notes. They examined the door; said they'd check to see if they could get prints from the stone. Sometimes you can, sometimes you can't. Depends. They suggested they get the door fixed as soon as possible. Did they have an alarm? You should install one. Puts burglars off. Sometimes. Lots of questions. They left saying they'd call later. The trio settled down in the lounge. Peter poured a whisky while Sarah had a gin. Michael was lucid one minute then broke down the next. Sarah held him, patted his back.

'It's OK. It's a horrible thing. It's over now, Michael. They'll get him.'

'Wish I could be so confident,' said Peter. 'We'll get an alarm fitted though. You saw him, you think?'

'Yes. I'm sure it was him. Remember I told you recently that I thought a man was looking at the house? It could have been him.'

Peter swallowed his drink and poured another. 'I'm going upstairs to get some work done. I'll phone around for a new door and an alarm.'

Sarah held Michael for a few more minutes then released him.

'How about a wee whisky young man? Might settle the nerves. But don't tell your dad I'm trying to get you drunk, will you.'

Michael laughed, for the first time. He took the glass, sniffed it then tipped it down his throat. It wasn't his first whisky, Sarah realized when the effect she'd anticipated didn't come.

'Well. That disappeared quickly. Maybe there's more to you than meets the eye, mate.'

The door was replaced in the afternoon. Peter and Michael were invited to St Paul's Police Station where Michael made a statement about the assault. Later that evening they all went out for a meal and returned at ten o'clock. At three a.m. Sarah crept downstairs and made herself a hot chocolate. Her brain was racing, and sleep was impossible. She turned on the TV and watched white horses galloping in the Camargue.

23

Leckie wasn't feeling too bright. A lusty curry and three Cobras had kept him awake till his bowels cried 'Enough!' Megan and the sausage thief had told him they were moving in together. He'd laughed, then decorum had set in, and he congratulated them on what was a big step. The sausage thief was a man of means of course, and his old man had promised he'd buy him a flat somewhere in the city. Sausage had told him it was a no-brainer with property prices in Edinburgh going up and up and the old man was convinced of his investment. They'd found a small flat up Nicholson Street and hoped to close the deal in a few days.

Leckie was privately delighted that Megan was going to be a grown-up at last. Oh, he'd miss her mess and her invasion of his privacy by dashing into the bathroom as he was taking a dump, but he liked Ricky and knew how happy she was with him. 'Cheers! Here's to a step on the creaky housing ladder!' was Leckie's cynical toast. He was a child of his time—a pre-Thatcherite left-wing Labour man who hated the 'home-owning democracy' of the Neo-liberals who delighted in selling off council houses for peanuts and destroying the power of the Unions.

There was a message on the answerphone.

Hi Donald, Findon here. Just thought I'd let you know we had a call after you left today from a Sarah Wyllie asking for you. I know her vaguely, but it seems she wants to talk to you in your professional capacity. Nice looking woman. Make sure it's office work and not a homer won't you. We need the money.

Leckie put down the receiver and smiled. Well, well. This was Christmas early. He drank off a huge tumbler of water and took two paracetamols. Jesus, that curry had done him. Must be getting old. He sat watching a political programme for a few minutes and woke to a vision of a twenty-stone man with the bulk of an elephant seal being hefted into an ambulance. He'd been asleep for half-an-hour.

Next morning he's dry shaving when Mozart calls.
 A text message from Findon:

Mrs Wyllie.
Today 3.pm
U a babe magnet or something?

He gulped down a mug of coffee and ate a banana. At the office he said good morning to Zoe and took off his coat. He got Sarah's number and rang.
It was 9.37. It rang and rang, and then was picked up.
 'Hi, is that Sarah Wyllie's residence?' A young male voice answered.
 'Hi, who's speaking please?'
 'My name's Donald Leckie. I believe Mrs Wyllie wanted to speak to me.'
 'Oh, right. Just a minute.' A call off. 'It's a Mr Leckie.' Phone down. Noises off.
 'Mr Leckie? Donald. Good of you to phone. Yes. I was coming at three o'clock. Is there a problem?'
 'No. That's fine. Just confirming. Look forward to seeing you.' And how. Just hearing her voice sent a warm glow through him.

Leckie walked along the corridor to Findon's room and knocked. No answer. He asked Zoe where Findon might be.

'Oh, he plays golf today.' It was news to Leckie.

'Golf? I didn't know he played golf.'

'Oh yes. He's keen on golf. He's on some committee or other.' Leckie was intrigued.

'Which course does he play at?'

'I think it's called Donmuir. Something like that.'

Leckie's brain did a flip and landed on its frontal lobe. Donmuir. The Committee. Noel Stapleton... What the hell does Findon have to do with that crew? These were the very men whose hands steered the dark ship that was Edinburgh's illicit dealings in drugs, sex and bribery of all sorts. He remembered the conversation with McBride that day. The warning not to get involved with Findon's business dealings. Leckie went back to his cubicle. He picked up a pen and tapped his desk. Nails knocked in. He knew Findon was a man of the world; he knew right from wrong and knew that sometimes wrong can be quite attractive. He'd sold his safety in Iraq for money. And now here, why might he not sell his soul for more? And if he was a crook? What was that to Leckie? He was paid to do a job and he did it to the best of his ability. End of story. Fuck him. Let McBride root out the Committee—it wasn't Leckie's bag now. Noel Stapleton was in jail in Saughton and maybe the others would soon join him. Leckie was done with all that stuff. He asked Zoe for a coffee, and she brought him a tea.

'I thought I asked for a coffee?'

'I know, Donald, but there's none left. Mr Findon wants us to economise. He sent me out to get a jumbo bag of tea bags that'll last us for about a hundred years.' She shrugged her shoulders.

'What kind is it? Lapsang Souchong?'

'No, it's just tea.'

'Just tea. Well, that has to be good doesn't it. Better than unjust tea anyway.' Zoe stared at him as if he'd just spoken in tongues. She turned and left, and he sipped the scalding liquid, which drowned in milk, had no discernible taste. The word 'economise' stayed with him for the rest of the morning. He interviewed a man at ten o'clock. Wife had taken up Judo. Sex life was fucked. She'd started painting her toenails and gone on a diet. Can you find out if she's having an affair? Leckie took all the details. He'd do what he could.

At twelve he sauntered down to the prom and bought a sandwich. It started to rain, squadrons of bruised clouds whipping in. Gulls wheeled and screamed. From a café Paolo Nutini sang about the lead in his pencil. Lucky him, thought Leckie. An ambulance siren slashed the air.

Back in the cubicle he began to read a book Megan had given him. 'The Children Act' by Ian McEwan. A female judge. Hard life thought Leckie. All those complicated cases. His back hurt, then the old leg joined in. The woman in the book was having trouble with her husband. For his birthday she'd learned a Bach Partita to play for him. She must be bloody good, thought Leckie, who didn't know what a Partita was till he googled it. Then he listened to it on You-tube. He smiled at the thought of the woman learning this piece. So difficult. Not by heart then, if she's a Judge. How long would it take to learn this? His reverie was broken by Zoe's knock. 'Mrs Wyllie to see you, Donald.'

She was as beautiful as he remembered, her long hair tied back in a blue scarf, her waxed jacket busy with pockets over a camel skirt and dark green tights. Handshakes, explanations. She'd phoned the Private Detective firms in the book and asked for him. Findon had told her he worked there.

Nice seeing him at the opening. But down to business. She was being stalked. She was sure her stalker had assaulted her stepson trying to enter the house. She was frightened. She hadn't informed the police about the stalking as she couldn't prove it and didn't want to sound like a helpless female. Not too keen on the police anyway she said, which puzzled Leckie. She wondered if Leckie could stalk the stalker if he reappears. Probably wouldn't now though as he'd be on guard. Leckie asked if she liked tasteless tea and she laughed. No, she was fine.

He agreed to pay her a visit to see where she lived and from where the so-called stalker would watch her. After she left, he listened to the Bach again. A slow opening then the pace quickens, and the runs begin. That lovely single note bass counterpointing the treble. He'd get the music, give it a go.
Her scent lingered. Sarah. Liz. Go away Liz…

24

The Wyllie residence in Warriston was a red sandstone five-bedroomed house set in an eighth of an acre of garden. It was seven-thirty, and the radio-alarm had just kicked in. Dim light through the thin curtains. Bird-cheeps outside. A familiar voice spoke the news as a hairy arm stretched out and met a tangle of fair hair.

'Morning.' No response. He turned round and nuzzled the hair. A hint of oil paint and flowers.

'Morning, beautiful.' She turned to face him, and her eyes opened. She smiled. He stroked her cheek and moved his body close to hers. His hand reached down and felt the slight damp in the high split of her buttocks. A light kiss that became stronger, more urgent and her hand clasped his head. He shrugged off his shorts and lay on her, her leg angling to receive him. Their lovemaking was short for he began wheezing.

'Bloody chest. Sorry.' He slipped off and lay staring at the ceiling.

'That sounds bad, Bill. You should go to the doctor'

'Nope. I'm fine. We'll try again tonight, eh?'

'You're so romantic.'

The pair had been lovers for a couple of months, Annabell and Digby's relationship having sunk so low that neither questioned the other's lives. Both disappeared from home for days at a time, leaving the house in the desperate hands of Sheila, who knew about Bill Wyllie from a letter she'd found, but knew nothing of Digby's affair.

It seemed to Wyllie now that the talk he'd had with Digby had been unnecessary. If Digby had his own little affair going, why should Wyllie feel it necessary to divert his attention from Annabel.

He shaved and went downstairs to the kitchen where he prepared scrambled eggs for them both. Annabell loved scrambled eggs. Twenty minutes later she appeared in a sloppy red cardigan and jeans, her hair tied in a headscarf. She worked in one of the bedrooms which had been cleared to make a studio space. She was happy and more productive than she'd been for ages. Five galleries were taking her work now from Inverness to the Borders.

25

The more Blair thought about his botched episode in Morningside, the more he resented what had happened. Michael had cheated him of something he'd dreamed of. Now, he realised, having been seen face to face, the police would ask Michael for a sketch. He was in trouble if he appeared near there again and yet he wasn't finished with Sarah Wyllie. She still haunted his dreams, and he was determined to talk to her. He'd keep a safe distance from the house and see her in her favourite places. Now however, he needed to change his appearance. A hat would help and maybe a tan. He was lucky that he had a strong facial growth for his age so a week without shaving would also help. Meanwhile, young Michael was going to pay…

From 'Today's Scot' Newspaper:

Merchiston Home Attacked for Second Time
A private house in the Merchiston area of the city has been vandalised for the second time in a month. Two weeks ago, the family returned to find the Fire Brigade dousing what appeared to be a kitchen fire. A police spokesperson later acknowledged that the circumstances were suspicious. The family returned from a night at the theatre on Wednesday evening to find their house ransacked and valuables taken. The homeowner Mr James Mitchener (58) said he and his family were shocked by what had happened. A police spokesperson said that several lines of enquiry were being pursued but no further information was available at present.

Michael Wells spent many hours at his computer playing games. He had left George Heriot's school a year before with a good clutch of Highers but a proposed 'year-out' with his pal had fallen flat when Tony decided to go to university instead. He was too late to apply and prompted by his father, had taken up a series of jobs each of which he hated. When Sarah moved in, he found a mother figure again and the pair enjoyed each other's company. She teased him and he loved it. He teased her and she loved it. With her connections at the Zoo, she got him the job of volunteer animal keeper. No pay, but he loved animals, and it was better than a sweaty day in a stupid cafe frying burgers somewhere. Pops had said money wasn't the issue so he should take it.

Two days later, after his induction, which included a tour of the zoo and a lecture on conservation and daily maintenance, Michael pulled the green sweatshirt over his head and filled two rubber buckets from the rack in the food room under the direction of keeper Jo Wilson. He filled them with the usual grasses and fruits and vegetables. There were two one-horned rhinos in the enclosure, great lumbering beasts whose bulk awed him at first as they sashayed across the stinking concrete to be fed. But later getting accustomed to them and the acrid smell of urine and dung, Javid, an Indian rhino became his favourite. He loved apples and pears and cabbages and Michael threw some into his cavernous pink mouth before hosing. The inner enclosure was shut while it was hosed down so Michael was alone when the blow came.

An hour later Jo, the keeper appeared, wondering where Michael was. What she saw was a crumpled body lying inside the bars. Javid was swaying in some distress as if the body was something he didn't understand. Luckily neither he nor

Quasif, the other male Rhino had touched Michael but apart from the head wound he had broken his left arm and badly bruised his shins. He had been lifted and dumped over the bars in an obvious attempt to cause him injury and perhaps death from the rhinos. The Zoo authorities quickly ascertained that Michael had been struck on the head and deliberately placed where they found him. The police were called, and an ambulance took him to The Royal Infirmary where his condition was said to be 'comfortable.' Sarah and his father sat by his bed, Sarah holding Michael's hand while Peter poured a glass of water. Michael knew little of what had happened, just a sudden shaft of pain and blackness. He did remember the sound of the door opening behind him though, which seemed to convince both the police and the Zoo authorities that this was a callous and unprovoked assault on one of their staff.

Michael was released from hospital after two days and told to rest. He was shaken by the incident, which together with the previous assault, was a serious blow to his self-confidence. Video games were back on the agenda. Both Peter and Sarah had played down the possibility that the same hand had struck him twice, but Sarah was convinced it was the case. Now she had a stalker who was intent on violence against her loved ones. Leckie had positioned himself in her street for three prolonged periods without noticing anything unusual, but with this second assault on Sarah's stepson, a new seriousness had taken him. He was determined that come hell or high water he would find this man.

Findon was surprised at recent events and told Leckie to be careful. To his mind repeated acts such as this were perpetrated by dangerously damaged individuals who were likely to become even more violent. 'It's a fucking drug for those bastards' was Findon's take on the matter. If Leckie was perceived as an enemy, then he should be vigilant.

26

Blair was homeless. His brother Robin, increasingly irritated by Blair's lack of respect for the flat or Robin himself, had contacted his father to urge that Blair had to go. Blair's nocturnal wanderings often woke Robin and his work was suffering. Digby was at home when the call came. He'd recently learned that Blair had left College — news which had infuriated him — but now the latest catastrophe to befall his errant son was the last straw.

'Pop, he's out of control. His room is a mess with these ridiculous posters and things everywhere. Empty bottles and cans and a floor littered with books and paper. I've spoken to him two or three times and he just laughs. He sleeps till lunchtime some days and he's chucked College. Says it's a bourgeois institution for half-wits. You get the picture. I can't take any more. Louise, my girlfriend, liked him at first but even she hates his guts now…'

'Ok, Robin, I get the picture. If he appears back home at least I know what's been going on. Has he gone yet?'

'Yes. Last night. There's something else— it's not pleasant. I phoned in and took the day off to clean his room. Dad, he'd shat on the floor. He'd shat on the floor, deliberately.'

'My God. What is he turning into?'

'He needs help dad. Really. He's really disturbed. Hates everything and everybody. Maybe himself most of all. And he stole some money from my room.'

'Right, Robin. Thanks. You get that room cleaned and don't let him through your door again. Have you got that? Do not let him back in your flat on any pretext. God help me, he's my son, and I'll deal with him. OK. Got to go. Work going well? Louise you say? Nice girl, is she? At least one of my sons is decent. Love you.'

'Love you, pop. Ciao.'

Blair had some money now. He'd ransacked the Mitchener's home and found two-hundred and thirty pounds in a drawer in Mitchener's study. He would go home to Eastlea. His clothes, some books and some toiletries; all his rucksack would hold. He left his guitar, thinking it would be a good excuse later to return for it. He'd defecated as a final act of rage against his brother, knowing the smell would linger. If he wasn't good enough for the flat, the flat wouldn't be good enough for Robin either, for a time anyway.

It started to rain as he left the little station in Dunbrae and began to thumb for a lift the ten miles or so home. Car after car passed before one slowed. A blue BMW. A woman. Blonde. Fifties. Smiling.

'Where are you going?'

'Eastlea House, it's just the other side of Broomfield.'

'Yes, I know it. Hop in. I'm going that way.' He got in the car and threw his rucksack on the back seat.

'Are you a student?' She asked, turning to him and smiling. Blair watched her slim hands on the wheel and began to fantasise.

'Yes. Edinburgh. Just coming home for a bit of peace and quiet.'

'What are you studying?'

'Er… Medicine. I'm doing medicine.'

'Ah. I'm a doctor for my sins. Went to Edinburgh too. Many moons ago, of course. What year are you in?' She drove fast, the car taking bends effortlessly, the upholstery still new with that chemical smell, the trim a dark shiny wood. He took out his phone and punched in his code, got the thumb going, then to his ear. If you get into a sticky with your lies, just make a diversion. He was an old hand. He pretended to have a conversation with his friend.

'Oh, Boz, yes, I'm on my way. Look, are you going to manage to come up on Saturday. Emily will be there and Harry. It'll be a break from the grind…Yes, the dog is fine, she caught her left paw on some barbed wire; you know what she's like when she sees a rabbit… vet said it would heal nicely…' He continued his mock conversation for a few minutes as the road sped under them. Then the car slowed at a junction where huge pillars led to a driveway.

'Well, this is you, I think. Eastlea. Are you part of the family?'

'Oh, no. I'm just a friend. Wish I had folks that owned a house like that…' She laughed. He leaned back, lifted his rucksack and got out. Just as he was closing the door, he leaned in and said 'I would fuck you, but you're a bit old. Sorry.' The woman's face passed through disbelief to anger. 'What did you…' Was all she could muster before he slammed the door. She sped off, her breaks screeching. He smiled, shouldered his sac and walked up the rough driveway which had once been smooth tar but was now deeply pock-marked.

Blair's diary:
Home again. Alone. Left bro a wee present. This dump is a shitheap. Leaking like a sieve. Might give old Sheila a go. Need a shag. Never fuck the maid, eh Mummy!!!!

Boz hadn't been to College since the day he'd taken Blair's notes. Now at home, he lay on his bed and listened to his young sister dancing to Beyonce's 'Crazy in Love' in the next room. Yeah, he thought, that's Blair Lithgow — crazy in love with that red-headed woman. What if…

27

The sitting room at the Well's house. Sarah and Peter sitting on the sofa, Leckie in an armchair. Peter and Leckie each have a glass of whisky and water.

'You're not on Facebook. Any other platforms? Information someone could pick up on-line. No. And you've had no communication from anyone? Good. I'm thinking about the zoo incident. What's puzzling me is how he knew Michael was working there.' Leckie sipped his drink, looked at Sarah. 'If he's stalking you, Sarah, why turn his attention to Michael? And at the zoo?' Sarah glanced at Peter.

'Well, I'm involved with the zoo as a member of the fund-raising committee. Maybe he followed me there.'

'Right, I want you to think hard about the last time you were there; in the zoo, I mean.'

'Last week. Thursday. I walked around a bit then went into the offices. I'd arrived too early.'

'And where did you walk?'

'I went up the hill to the Budongo Trail. Bonobos. I love watching them. Oh, and I stood by the black jaguar for a bit. Love him too.'

'Melanistic aren't they.' said Leckie.

'Well, well, I'm impressed.'

'Had a painting of one once in my gallery. Loved it. Anyway, did anyone talk to you? Stand close? Anything unusual?'

'Not really. There was a young guy watching the chimps and two young girls.'

'Right. Is it possible that that young guy might have followed you to the main building?'

'I'm sure he was still watching the chimps when I left.'

'But it is possible?' Sarah felt she was being pushed into a corner and was reluctant to be led to a place she felt might please Leckie but be a false trail.

'Donald, what does 'possible' mean? Even if something is possible, it doesn't mean it happened. Aren't you trying a bit hard to make connections that aren't there?' Leckie closed his little notebook. He smiled.

'I've been at this business a long time, Sarah. Believe me, you'd be astonished at how many possibles are actually very likely. No, I'm not pushing you, but I need you to remember who you've spoken to, or who might just have been in your company more than you'd expect. You saw the guy watching you. Can you give me a rough idea of his appearance? Height?'

'I didn't pay much attention, but I'd say he was quite tall. Well built. He had one of those hoods up so I can't tell you about his hair or much about his face. They all wear hoods these days.

'Hood again. Like the man watching from the park. You didn't see his face then. But Michael spoke to him, yes? Where is he? I need to speak to him.' Peter Wells said his son had gone to stay for a few days with his mother. He'd given them a statement.

'Oh, how could I forget,' said Peter, there was something Michael said…'

'Yes?'

'Michael said he sounded posh.' Leckie opened his book again, wrote. 'Posh. Good. That's something unusual. Why 'posh?'

'It was a word he used. Er…Oh what was it…Oh yes, he said 'Divulge.'

Leckie nodded sagely. 'Good word. "Divulge." Not "tell" but "divulge." Unusual is what we're looking for.

Thanks. If he's not posh, he may be educated. Anything helps.' He stood up. Sarah stood also. She glanced at Peter. 'There's something else. I haven't told you. Last week someone sent me a scarf. I thought it was maybe one of the St Mary's crowd, but no-one admitted to it. Now, I'm wondering.'

'A scarf? What kind of scarf?'

'A silk scarf. Yellows and greens. A Bellany scarf.' There was no message. It's upstairs. Do you want to see it, Donald?'

Peter stood up. 'My God, Sarah. Why didn't you mention this to me. It could be him.'

'I know, I know. I didn't think it was important. It slipped my mind. I've a lot on my mind you know.' Peter patted her shoulder.

'Let me have a look, Sarah,' said Leckie. 'Everything is significant. I know how you feel. Really. This stuff leaves a bad taste. Er… not the scarf—that's quite good taste. If you like Bellany.'

Leckie was shown the scarf. He asked if she'd handled it. Yes, she had. Still, he would hold on to it in the meantime. He looked at the label. The National Gallery of Scotland.

'When were you there last, Sarah? It may be important.'

'Oh ages ago.'

'Before all this business?'

'Yes.'

'OK. Let me think about all this. I'll give you a ring tomorrow or the next day. In the meantime, keep vigilant. Wherever you go, keep a keen eye for who is nearby. If you see the same person in different places let me know. Look out for a hood — he seems to think he's safe with his hood.'

He put down his glass, shook hands with Peter and kissed Sarah on the cheek. Chanel No5. Leckie knew his perfumes.

Two days later Sarah phoned Leckie.

'Donald, I've just received a letter today. You asked about communications. It's about my stalker.' Leckie punched the air and his coffee left its cup to soak the file he was reading.

Within the hour he was sitting with Sarah reading the letter. The envelope with a first-class stamp simply read: Sarah, and her address; 12, Chilwell Road. No postcode.

'BLAIR LITHGOW IS STALKING YOU. HOPE YOU GET THE POLICE ON HIM.'
HES A MAD BASTARD.'

'Well, somebody doesn't like old Blair then.'

'But he…or she knows about him following me,' said Sarah. Her eyes had taken on a glow of excitement that Leckie had seen before when an issue seemed to have been resolved in one fell swoop. He was more cautious.

'I know a family called Lithgow' said Sarah. 'Can't remember the sons names, but I doubt it's him. They live in Perthshire. Nice family. Haven't seen them in ages though.'

'Of course, the person who would know you were being stalked might be the stalker himself,' said Leckie. Sarah frowned.

'You mean this could have been written by him?'

'That's possible. It's equally possible that this guy is real. There is a real Blair out there and he didn't write this. Leave this with me. If this Blair exists, I'll find him.'

'And if you find him Donald; what then?'

'If I find him, I'll kill him.' The colour drained from her face.

'Donald, that's not…'

'I know. Sorry. Bad joke. If I find him and get evidence that it's him then the police will move in.'

Leckie finished his tea and the chocolate cake on offer. He kissed Sarah on the cheek.

Still heady with her perfume, he made off in the Saab.

Back in Portobello he trawled the phone book for Lithgows. Fifteen. Bugger. Where did she say that family was? Perthshire. One by one he dialled and asked if he could speak to Blair. Seven replied and said there was no-one of that name living there. Three didn't answer. Five wanted to know who he was and almost immediately cut him. So much for the beauty of cold calling. He'd bumped into Simon the IT man in the corridor a few times with a cursory 'Hi,' the cramped nature of his 'cubicle' still rankling, but now he saw the need for the wider net that Simon might offer. Then he remembered Michael's remark that the intruder sounded 'posh.' A posh boy breaking into a house and assaulting someone? 'Posh' could mean anything of course and was an idiosyncratic response to an accent. Michael was a bit posh himself of course, so if someone else sounded 'posh' then that might mean even posher than Michael. He knocked on Simon's door and went in.

'Oh Hi, Donald, isn't it? I've knocked at your door a couple of times, but you've been out. Good to see you at last.' Simon was thirty-ish, balding, with a chubby face, small eyes and glasses with blue legs. He had that intelligent geeky look that suggested a man more at home with screens than human beings.

'Yes, busy man me. Simon. How goes it?'

'Oh, fine. Just tracking down some court records.'

'I've a wee job for you.' Simon smiled.

'Well, that's what I'm here for. Shoot.'

'I'm looking for a guy called Blair Lithgow. Might be from a family with money. Perthshire is a strong possibility.

If you can get me some addresses, I'll take it from there. Can't be all that many in Scotland. That's if he is Scottish. He's a bit of a toe-rag this one and I need to find him. See what comes up.' Simon made a note on a post-it and stuck it on the side of his Mac. It fell off and he stuck it down again more firmly.

'Damn things keep falling off. Give me a couple of hours and I'll get back to you Donald.'

Leckie patted him on the shoulder and returned to his cubicle. He searched Facebook for Lithgow as a surname but came up with nothing, apart from two young women called Barbara and Belinda Lithgo both of whom looked like they could give you a good time for two hundred quid.

He phoned Megan and asked how she was.

28

Blair Lithgow was alone at Eastlea. He'd expected his father to be home, but the house was deserted. Upstairs, the airless rooms sent their share of damp to the stairwell. His room was as he'd left it— a shrine to teenage angst and debilitating boredom. Clothes lay where he'd left them, neither his mother nor the maid permitted upon pain of death to lift them.

He pulled on his multi-coloured pullover and thought it smelled faintly of perfume. Funny. Now he lay on his bed and stared at the shifting patterns of shadows on the ceiling from the oak outside. His head spun, a tangled churn of thoughts that swung from satisfaction to despair like a washing machine's relentless spin. He thought of the Mitchener place and remembered the fun he'd felt trashing it: he thought of Sarah's stepson and how he'd squealed when he hit him: he thought of Boz tumbling down the stairs. He picked a crust from his nose and flicked it on to the carpet, then pushed his hand into his pants. Sarah was there again smiling, in stockings and suspenders, her hair down about her white shoulders as she strode towards him, her arms out. She touched his cheek then stood by the bed before turning and offering her behind…A leisurely wank sent him to sleep, and it was the crunch of wheels on the drive that woke him. He yanked up his trousers and crossed the hall. The black Toyota was parked outside. The old man. He went downstairs and met his father struggling to carry a case of wine.

'It's you. When did you get back?' The face was not happy.

'I'm back. Tough.' His father glanced away then proceeded into the kitchen area. Blair was not in the habit of apologizing, but somehow the look on his father's face elicited an unbidden response. He followed his father in the hope of some food, but bottle by slow bottle, labels examined, the case was emptied.

'Need a hand?' said Blair.

'Is Sheila back?'

'Didn't see her. Is she still around?'

'Of course she's still around. Who the hell would look after this place if it wasn't for Sheila? You?'

'Where's mater?'

'Mater, as you call her, has left. I texted you. Don't you read my texts?'

The question hung in the air for a moment then died as some questions do. Blair caught the anger and returned upstairs wondering how he could stay here with his father. His father heard the steps with some relief and poured himself a glass of water. He wondered what he could say to his son that hadn't been said a million times before. Words that changed nothing. Now there were no words left. All paternal affection had dried, shrivelled in the searing heat of his son's waywardness. He was a disgrace to the family and to decent standards of behaviour.

Digby Lithgow went into his study and switched on his computer. Upstairs there was a stranger— a son no longer. No longer a responsibility, for that implied caring. Would he just say that? Would he just say to Blair 'I don't care what you do anymore. I'm finished with caring.' No. No more words. Only the silence that comes with ineffable disgust. He sat and examined his right hand. The liver spots seemed to be spreading and the veins pushing to the surface. Fucking old age. He stared at the rug and found himself swimming in a pond. He was struggling to breathe, breaking the surface now, then sinking, gasping for air which came at last. He was twenty again and a woman's strong hand pulled him to the bank. Annabell. He felt his chest swell and tears welling. Why had everything fallen apart? He'd worked hard for his family, dashing here and there to meetings, smiling when he had to smile, standing his ground when it was necessary and it had all gone well until the tide turned against steel...

That evening Sheila returned. She'd been away for three days at a cousin's wedding in Orkney. As the taxi spun away Digby greeted her at the door.

'Ah Sheila. At last. Blair's here.' He found himself whispering as if this news was not for broadcast. It was the significance that bore down on him. That Blair was not to be served, not to be obeyed in any way. Blair was to be treated like a stranger that is not welcome. Sheila seemed puzzled at first, till Digby told her he'd fucked up in Edinburgh. Sheila was used to his language and responded as he hoped she would. 'Whatever,' she said, which meant 'whatever you say, Sir.'

'I want you to ignore him. Want him out of this house as soon as possible, so don't do anything that might encourage him to stay. Got it?'

'Got it.' She lifted her bag and Digby took it from her, smiling. They entered the house and Sheila unpacked in her room.

It was eight o'clock and Blair hadn't eaten since noon. He opened the large fridge and peered inside. A packet of fish fingers, a couple of burgers and a small bag of peas. He fried the burgers with an egg and sat at the kitchen table to eat. Sheila came in, jeans and a top with 'Hell is Other People' in gold on black. She asked if his father had eaten, but he didn't know. I bought him the fish fingers. He likes them. Simple tastes, your dad.

'Jean Paul Sartre,' said Blair.
'What?'
'The words on your top. Jean Paul Sartre.'
'I know.'
'You know? How do you know? Did someone tell you? Some bloke looking at your chest?'

She turned and glanced at him, noted how tired he looked, how washed up somehow and felt a pang of sympathy. No-one loves him. Not even his own family.

'They told me in the shop who said it. They had lots of famous sayings and a book about them.'
'And do you believe that?'
'That hell is other people? No, of course not. I like people.'
'I don't. I fucking hate people. I like you though, Sheila.'
'That's nice to hear.'
'Do you like me?' Sheila took a carton of orange from the fridge. The door pinged shut. She poured it into a glass. She stood, one arm resting on the table and sipped, her eyes on him. Since Annabell had left, Sheila had found a new freedom.
'Well? Do you?'
'Why wouldn't I.'
'Oh, very non-committal. I like you, if you want to know.' Inside Blair's head he knew this girl liked him. He had known for a while that she thought him good-looking. Now, cornered, she couldn't admit it. He'd let it go, but he would be back.

'Well, I'm off for a wee stroll. I've got a key.' He stood up and noticed that his belt was not properly fastened. He slowly pulled it tight while her eyes were still on him.

'Dad likes fishy fingers. Yum, yum,' he said, smirking.

29

It was May and the air was warm as if Summer had come at last. It was a week since Leckie had tasked the stalker's name. Leckie had been out that morning on a case and returned to the office at twelve-thirty, hungry and thirsty. Findon was out and he could hear Zoe clicking away at her computer. There was a knock on his door and Simon's head appeared.

'Hi, Still interested in that Blair guy? Sorry it went completely out of my head. I've had this for a week, but I've been doing Findon's stuff. Looks like I might have something. Perthshire helped.' He passed a print-out to Leckie.

Blair Chisholm Lithgow, youngest son of Sir Digby Lithgow and Annabell Lithgow residing at Eastlea House by Inverden, Perthshire...

Leckie read on. Schools, membership of a gun club, rugby for Perthshire Colts.
Edinburgh College...There was even a picture of him from the local paper. Mother, father, and sons in front of a pair of stone lions.

The Lithgows of Eastlea at home.

'That might be your man there,' he said pointing to the fair-haired boy in the photo.

'Tall. Big lad.' When was this taken?'

'No way of knowing.' He turned to Simon and nudged him.

'Good work mate. Last week would have been nice, but better late than never. Maybe you're worth a wage after all.'

Leckie phoned Sarah and arranged to visit. That evening he sat in their lounge and watched as Michael scanned the photo.

'That him Michael?' Michael screwed up his nose.

'It could be. But I can't be positive. We can't see his eyes clearly. He had blue eyes.'

'Yes, fair enough and we don't know when this was taken. Could be a year, maybe more ago. I want to know if it could be him. Yes, or no?'

'It could be, yes.' Sarah looked at the photo again.

'My God. That's them-the Lithgows. She nodded her head.

'Yes. You know Donald from what I saw of him in the park there, it could be him, the younger one.' She sat down, folded her hands in her lap. I'm being stalked by Annabell's son. My God. Why?'

'Because he's obsessed with you,' said Leckie.

'He must be in Edinburgh.' she said, 'I should phone Annabell.'

'No. Don't do that. That'll only complicate things,' said Leckie.

'I'll track him down, sort it out. Don't suppose his family really want to know. This guy is dangerous.' This wasn't an avenue he wanted to go down. Where the blighter was, was best kept to himself. He'd experience of folk taking the law into their own hands, and it wasn't a good idea. If you're a decent citizen you're a fish out of water in the world of the bad guys. And we all know what happens to fish out of water. He glanced at Sarah, made a placatory gesture with his hand. 'Leave this to me. Please.' Sarah nodded.

'What do we do now? Get the police involved?' she said.

'I don't want that.' Leckie grunted. He didn't want to get the police involved either, if they were wrong. Didn't want egg on his face. That guy Leckie the Private Dick with the gammy leg who sends them on wild goose chases after innocent wee boys. That's what they'd say. No. He'd have to be sure. He stood up.

'With your permission I'm going to follow this one up and see where it goes. We've no proof of anything yet.'

'What will you do? Go and speak to him? Ask him if he tried to kill my son?'

'Not exactly. But I'll find out more about him. Speak to people. Find out where he's been. If he's got any friends. The note might have been written by someone who's trying to get him caught. Trust me, I'm a pro.' He smiled at the last words and looked at them sitting there.

'That's good enough for me,' said Peter. 'To be honest If we never see this bugger again, I'll be happy.'

'I won't,' said Sarah. 'I want this boy behind bars Peter. He tried to kill Michael. How can you sit there and just let it all go? Bloody hell.'

'She's right, dad. He's an evil bastard,' said Michael. 'I'd like to kick his teeth in…'

'Ok. Let's keep calm,' said Leckie. 'I want him locked up too. Believe me. But we must be clever. I've seen folk like him walk away because of sloppy police work before now. That's not going to happen here. That is, of course, if it is him. We don't know for sure. But I'm going to find out. If it is him, then he must be staying in Edinburgh. I'll find out.

There were nods all round and Leckie slipped out more determined than ever to catch his man.

Sarah didn't sleep that night. Something deep in her had been stirred. She wasn't a woman to sit by while things happened around her. Wrapped in one of Peter's dressing gowns, she sat in front of a heater in the kitchen. She stared at the red glow of the element and felt that same heat within her burning with hatred for the man who was threatening their lives. She didn't believe it was all over. She believed he wanted to destroy them and wouldn't let go. Leckie might make his enquiries, but she wanted to be a part of it, to see him in the flesh, to tell him what harm he'd done to her family. As the heat burned her bare legs the urgency grew in her and she knew what she had to do: she had to stalk the stalker.

Leckie went home that evening, the picture of the young man burning a hole in his brain. He went over the sequence of events as clearly as he could remember them— the stalking episodes, the attack on Michael at home and then at the zoo. This character was dangerous. Should he report him? Maybe he should. No. Where's the evidence? Michael as a witness? No. A hooded figure outside the house. That could be a thousand men. Useless. He held the print-out and read it over and over. It was obvious what he should do. He'd pay a visit to Eastlea House. He poured a Laphroig and ate some crackers from a tin in the kitchen. But who wrote that note? Who wants this character caught? He switched on the TV and watched a discussion programme but as the words droned on, he fell asleep in the chair.

Next morning, he shaved and laced up his shoes. The lace broke. He shortened it and tied it. It would do. As he passed the long mirror in the hall, he caught sight of himself and stopped. A man in a dirty Barbour. A man with hair sticking up and sideburns that were too long. Not an impressive figure. Megan never ceased to nag him about his appearance and sometimes he got it, saw himself as others did. Then Sarah came swimming into his head. He remembered the previous evening: he in the middle of things, in control, the professional while they listened to his advice. He knew all about her and for a moment a sense of unease took him. He wanted her to be safe. He wanted her looks to be a gift and not a curse. He wanted her to like him, to admire him as the man who could make her safe.

She was beautiful. By fuck, she was beautiful.

Findon had to be told about this. He wasn't in his office when Leckie arrived. Zoe's face had lost its normal bland happy look, replaced by a troubled demeanour. Something was wrong.

'Donald, the police've taken him away.'

'Taken him away? What do you mean Zoe?'

'They came about nine this morning. There were two men in coats and a uniformed officer. They handcuffed Mr Findon and took him away. He said when you got in to phone. He gave me this.' She gave him the address of the Station that Findon had scribbled down. Walker Road.

'He said you'd know what to do. I can't believe this. Why are they doing this…' He put an arm round her shoulder and told her not to worry, they would sort it out. But as he tried to reassure her, he remembered McBride's words in the pub. Was Findon up to something?

Leckie knocked on Simon's door and went in. Simon was staring at a screen littered with words and lines.

'Donald. What the hell eh? They took him away so fast I didn't have a chance to say anything.'

'Yes. They do that. Eastlea House. Any details for me? How do I get there? Can't work the damn phone the way my daughter can.'

'Sure. Give me a minute.'

'I'll be next door.'

An hour later Leckie was sitting in a bleak interview room in Walker Road Police Station. Opposite him a young woman DC wrote down his name and address and asked if he'd like a cup of something. No, he wouldn't.

'Look, I used to be Police. Donald Leckie. Is McBride around?'

'D.C.I. McBride?' She began to tap her pencil on the desk.

'I want to speak to him. Now. If that's OK.' Leckie stood up. The Policewoman asked him to sit down. He remained standing. He took out his car keys.

'Look. I'm here as a friend of Findon. I just want to know what he's being accused of.'

'Would you like a lawyer to be present?'

'What? What the hell are you talking about? Why would I need a lawyer. Are you arresting me?' He leant over the desk close enough to smell the soap she used. She smiled, but she was nervous.

'Right. If McBride won't see me, I'm off.' He strode to the door and went out, passing an old colleague on the way.

'Tom. Is McBride about do you know?'

'Donald. Good to see you're still upright. No. He's at Cromwell Road. Big stushie there. Some character brought in over the killing of these old guys.'

Leckie patted Tom and found his car opposite the Station. North or here? Findon would be fine, he thought, my job is to find Sarah's man. Back to basics. North it is.

30

Blair woke suddenly. A thud on the window. A bird. They were always doing that. Never seemed to harm them. He lay staring at the big blue paper shade that dangled from the intricate plaster rose. To the right, a foot away was a brown stain. Brown stains everyfuckingwhere now. Shit hitting the fan. Water, water, everywhere. One day it would all go. The whole fucking ceiling—just woof! The room a shambles of plaster and lathes like pale tongues. He smiled. Sometimes in his head he'd imagine the future when his folks were dead. He'd imagine Eastlea rotting in its grounds and Robin trying to sell it as an old-folks home or some damn thing. Fuck this place, he thought. His time here had once been happy but latterly it held nothing but pain and boredom.

Outside a car drew away. His father off to play golf maybe. Sheila would be around somewhere hoovering or dusting or washing. He imagined her in the kitchen bending over the butler sink, how he'd shove his hand up her skirt and the little jump of surprise she'd do before settling to her washing again, pretending he wasn't there, while moving subtly to the caress of his hand in her. She'd be wet and he'd paddle her to little gasps of pleasure as he leant on her shoulder and whispered 'You little whore. You're just a little whore, hot for it…' Then she turned and her face morphed into the face of Sarah. Hair flopping, her face flushed, smiling, grateful that at last he had her, for she'd been waiting so long. 'Why didn't you speak to me you handsome boy. I wanted to speak to you, but you kept hiding from me under that hood…'

It was nine-thirty, and he was hungry. In the kitchen he found some eggs and made himself an omelette. He'd been here for three days, and the rain had been incessant, every leaf heavy with it, the paths soggy, filling up. Every room cold, every surface chilled.

At night here he'd lie trying to sleep and when the room faded the demons came flying and whispering. He'd wake screaming, but there was no sound. His legs were cold. and blankets didn't seem to warm him. He was dressed in two rugby shirts and a chunky green polo which his mother had knitted yonks ago but still he was cold as if the walls were giving it out. He unpacked his rucksack, throwing bits and pieces in the corner. He cast one last glance at his jotter and laid it down thinking he'd get Sheila to come and tidy his room and she'd be impressed by his notes. He'd walk and walk then read for a bit. Later he'd wander along to the village for a pint.

Driving North over the Bridge, Leckie listened to Dougie McLean and tapped the wheel to the rhythm of 'Turning Away.' The rain was heavy, and the washers swept the screen as best they could, though the spatters like big pebbles seemed to be winning, the car ahead wavering. He was happy now, flushed with the thrill of the chase. In his head he pictured a house, lawns, trees, maybe gateposts that harboured this little shit that thought it OK to break into the quiet contentment of a decent family. He was stoking his fires, charging himself for the task ahead— the stalk, the confrontation. Just let me get a confession, just a fucking confession and I'll get him back to Edinburgh to face the music.

Leckie turned into the drive through the gateposts, the old car jolted and splashed by the pooled potholes. He pulled left and switched off the engine. A moment's thought before he got out and retrieved his Barbour from the back seat. He'd walk up to the house, suss things out. What cars might be there. Who he'd be. Certainly not Mr Donald Leckie Private Investigator at Findon Investigations. Have you a young man called Blair living here please…

Leckie was nervous. He was always nervous on the trail. He told himself the day he was no longer nervous would be the time to chuck it. Nervous was good. Nervous was what kept your senses tingling. He remembered being in a play once at school and the stomach-churning nerves that grabbed him as he was about to go on. He'd asked the boy next to him if he was nervous and he's said 'Nah.' Afterwards Leckie was praised while Nah fluffed his lines and almost brought the whole show to a stop. Nerves are good. A crow exploded from a cypress and Leckie jumped. Fuck. I am nervous, he thought.

In three minutes, the drive turned a sharp left and the house appeared beyond the lawns. An impressive light stone Victorian pile with bay windows on either side of the entrance. Almost symmetrical apart from a wing on the right which seemed to be a conservatory. There were no cars in the drive and no-one in the garden. Leckie walked between two stone Lions, up the steps and tugged the bell pull. He heard a voice shouting inside but no-one came to the door. Leckie tugged again. The heavy door was opened by a young man with long hair in a striped pullover.

'Yes?' It was him. Leckie's felt his skin tingle. Calm. Calm.

'Good morning. My name's Watson. I was driving past, and my car started acting up so I drove a bit up your drive to get it off the road. Would you know of a local garage that I could call?'

'Er…No. I'm a visitor here.' The young man stepped back as if he was about to shut the door. Leckie moved forward.

'Is the owner around? Perhaps he would be able to help.'

'Nope. He's out.'

'The owner's wife maybe?' Irritation spread like a rash over the young man's face.

'Look, just fuck off will you. Go on, fuck off.' He shut the door with a thud. Leckie smiled. Nice chap, he mused. Sort of chap that just might bash your face in if he felt like it. Leckie turned down the steps walking purposefully back down the drive aware of the possibility of eyes on him. He turned out of sight of the house and found a bush that offered shelter and a view of the front door. He perched on a fallen tree. He'd give it some time to see if his guy left the building.

Twenty minutes later, as Leckie finished a Wordscape on his phone, he heard the door thud and Lithgow emerged. He stood and looked around then pulled his hood up. Leckie grinned. He grabbed his camera and zoomed in. Click. Another and another. The man walked into the woods to the left of the house. He carried a stick with which he swiped something that Leckie couldn't make out. Leckie moved from the bush towards the house keeping cover in the trees. He'd have to cross a lawn to follow the man and he had no way of knowing how far the man had gone. It was too risky. He went back to his car and sat at the wheel. He texted Sarah:

I have your man.
Spoke to him.
He doesn't suspect.
Be in touch.

Leckie phoned Digby Lithgow. Perhaps they had a land line. Big place like that. They did. It rang and rang and then a voice said 'Eastlea House. Who's speaking please.'
'Oh hello. My name is Mr Wilson. I'm phoning from the College in Edinburgh. I need to get in touch with Blair about an exam but he hasn't been in college for a few days. It's very important. Is he there? Is that Mrs Lithgow?' There was a long pause.

'No, I'm the housekeeper. Is it important?'

'Yes. He can't miss this exam. Can you give me his mobile number?' Leckie's heart raced. He sensed success.

'Wait a moment please.' Sheila went into Digby's study and found his contact book. She returned and gave Leckie Blair's mobile number. Leckie thanked her. He drove to the town and parked. If he met Blair, he'd just say he'd had his car fixed. In the bar of The Station Hotel he bought a whisky. The bar was quiet: two men in Barbour jackets like his own, a young family of four and a young woman on her phone.

'Terrible weather for the time of year.'

'Too true,' said the barman, a young man with an attempt at a beard on his face.

'Eastlea House,' said Leckie. 'That far from here?'

'No. Just a mile along the river. Big place, you can't miss it.'

'Don't suppose you know who lives there do you?'

'Yeah. The Lithgows. Digby comes in here for a snifter.'

'Digby?'

'The father. He owns it.'

'Any family?'

'Two sons. And his wife.'

'Lucky kids eh, place like that to run about in.' Leckie was digging and the hole deepening delightfully.

'Oh, they're not kids now. All away from home.'

'Lithgow. God. I just realised, that must be Blair's family…'

'Blair. Yeah. You know Blair?'

'Yes, friend of my son. To be honest, I don't think much of him. Nasty piece of work.' The barman stuck a rag in a glass and twisted it. He lifted the glass against the lights and placed it below the counter. He looked at Leckie and smiled.

'Well. Kid's got problems. Are you a friend of the family then?'

'No, just up here on business. I knew his mother. Thought Blair's place was near here. Well, back to the drizzle eh. Thanks for the drink.' Leckie knew when to stop. He wondered where Blair would be. Didn't want to bump into him here. He walked a few yards up the street and looked in the window of a shop. Deerskin moccasins. He imagined his feet in them. Lovely. He went in and bought a pair. £75. Robbery, but as he tried them on his feet back in the car it felt like he was wearing clouds. They'd do for those days when his feet throbbed and he just wanted to get out of his shoes.

31

Blair pulled his hood up from the rain as he made his way through the back woods to the town. A bird shot from a bush, and he turned. He was jumpy. Something about the encounter at the door worried him. The story seemed far-fetched. The road was a quiet one and there was plenty of room to stop a car. There was a house opposite the gate where he could have phoned for a garage. He'd wondered about going to the front gate to see if there was a car but couldn't be bothered with the extra walk. He'd had a text from Boz asking where he was and now he was wondering about going back to Edinburgh.

He sat in The Station Bar and sipped his Cider. A new barmaid had served him and now he glanced at her as she pulled a pint for an old man. Not bad, he thought, one of those blunt-featured faces that dingbats have, but he wasn't interested in a conversation about politics. Nah, he thought, can't be arsed saying nice things to her. She's probably got a boyfriend anyway. In a few moments the regular barman Gary appeared and nodded towards Blair in recognition.

'Hi Gary. I'll have another. Strongbow.' The barmaid made to pull Blair a pint, but Gary told her he'd see to him. He looked up as he poured.

'Someone asking about you earlier.'

'Me?'

'Yeah. He seemed very interested in your family.' He passed the pint to Blair.

'Was he a big red-faced guy in a Barbour?'

'That's him.'

'A friend of your mother, he said.'

Blair returned with his pint and sat down. A friend of his mother was bollocks. If he was a friend of his mother, why didn't he ask for her first off at the door. No. Who the fuck was this guy? He decided to walk to the front gates to check that he'd gone. Outside, he scanned the street. No sign of him. At the gates and up the drive there was no sign of any car. Back in the house he went to his room but couldn't settle.
He texted Boz:

Coming back. Can I stay with you?

A mile from Eastlea House Leckie sat in his car and ate a Mars Bar. He wasn't going back to Edinburgh without knowing for sure that that boy was Blair Lithgow and that that boy was stalking Sarah. He couldn't get in the front door but there had to be another way. He wanted to see this boy's room. There might be something to link him with Sarah. The sky was clearing, and a glint of sun shone off the bonnet of the Saab. Leckie parked outside a cottage on the side of town nearest the house. He scrunched up the chocolate wrapper and put it in his pocket. He put on his bunnet to complete the countryman look and set off once more for the house. If Blair was out, then there was another opportunity to get in. There must be servants of some kind if the parents were away.

Blair was half-way down the staircase when his phone beeped. It was Boz.
    I'll have 2 ask the keeper.
    We've a spare room but sis
    Comes back now and then.
Cheers

Wanker. Now he'd have to hang on here. Sheila was in the kitchen. She was avoiding eye contact, pretending to be busy polishing a piece of silver.

'Fancy a drink?'

'No thanks. Are you going out?'

'Do you want me to go out or something. You got a young man coming? That's it isn't it. You've got a lover who comes when we're away…'

'Don't be cheeky, Blair. Now I've got work to do.' She lifted the piece and moved past him. He grabbed her round the waist and spun her round.

'Let me go.'

'Oh, come on, you know you like me.' He released his hold.

'Your breath stinks. Go and brush your teeth. And then do something useful for a change.' She strode out. He stood for a moment then cupped his hand over his mouth and puffed out a breath. 'Not bad. Not great, but not fucking bad. Bitch.' He went back upstairs and packed his sac. In the bathroom he swigged some blue mouthwash.

Downstairs he passed the silver cabinet. He stopped. It was open. Of course, she was in polishing mode. He took three pieces and put them in his sac. He looked for money in his father's study but found none. The thought that there might be money in the house plagued him. In his mother's studio he ransacked some drawers, pulling out invoices and some letters from galleries long since gone bust. As his eyes ranged round walls which were plastered with postcard reproductions of famous paintings and some photographs, his eye stopped him dead.

It was a group photo of guests at a party; here, by the look of the terrace. Among the smiling faces of men and women one stood out—a smiling face that he recognised. It was Sarah

Wyllie. He pulled the photograph off the wall and looked more closely. He felt cold with excitement. Her arm was round that Wyllie man that his father knew from way back. She's been in this house! Jesus Christ. He pocketed the photo and looked at his watch. Time he got a move on.

Outside his father's study he gobbed on his hand and rubbed it over the handle. 'Enjoy,' he said. Sheila appeared from the kitchen.

She was about to tell him about the phone call but he swore at her and said 'If you don't love me, I'm going back to Edinburgh to kill myself. Then you'll be sorry.' He's probably going back for his exam, she thought. It won't matter.

He pushed the heavy door behind him and went down the steps. From a bedroom window she watched him walk down the drive.

Leckie saw Blair leave the house and walk towards him. He was in the same bush as before and quickly retreated behind a huge oak. Blair passed; his stride determined as if he knew exactly where he wanted to be. It occurred to Leckie that a rugby tackle from behind would be enough to bring Blair down and then he could grab him by the throat and face him. The thought died as quickly as it had come. He was big, young, strong. What would happen when he regained his composure? He'd throw Leckie off and kick him. Maybe in the head, who knows, with someone like him. A kick anywhere was not what Leckie wanted at this time. No, he'd let him go. He'd follow.

Annabell Lithgow sat in the front of Bill Wyllie's car and doodled on a notepad that she always carried. She was shaping petals this way and that with a biro till a pleasing pattern emerged. Wyllie glanced over and smiled. He touched her right knee with his hand, and she glanced up.

'Always on the job, eh?'

'An artist never sleeps, Bill. Besides, it passes the time till we get there…'

Her words were cut short by the sight of a young man standing at a bus stop.

'That's Blair. I'm sure that was Blair.'

'Should we give him a lift somewhere or what?' said Bill slowing down.

'No. Just drive on. He's OK. In fact, it's good that he's not at home. We can collect my stuff and go back to Edinburgh without meeting him. I wonder why he's come back. You know I don't miss him at all. Isn't that bad of me?' He said nothing.

Wyllie drove on the quarter mile or so to Eastlea House. He parked and the pair mounted the steps. Annabell rang the bellpull. She'd misplaced her key but expected Sheila to be there. The door opened and Sheila greeted Annabell warmly. She smiled weakly at Wyllie as someone whose face was vaguely familiar.

The pair went to Annabell's studio and filled a box with paints and took some old canvasses. Then they disappeared upstairs into Annabell's room. Sheila heard the opening and closing of doors and assumed Annabell was taking clothes. Fifteen minutes later Annabell and Wyllie came down the stairs with two suitcases and several carrier bags. Annabell asked if Blair had been home and Sheila said he had, but he'd gone back to Edinburgh about an hour before. She told Sheila that she'd be away for some time, but she'd be in touch. 'Look after the old man, he needs you.' As Sheila watched Wyllie's car drive off, she remembered seeing her mother drive off with her second husband after the wedding. Sheila knew now, if she had ever doubted, that her time here was at an end. She would speak to Mr Lithgow when he reappeared.

Blair hadn't seen his mother with Wyllie, nor did he see Leckie in his car parked fifty metres behind the bus stop. As the bus pulled out Leckie set off hoping that Blair would be going directly to Edinburgh and not stopping off anywhere else, but it was a local bus going to Dundee and he lost it in the traffic. Damn it.

In Edinburgh Boz answered the door and was surprised to see Blair.

'Geez, man, didn't expect to see you this soon.' Blair barged past him.

'Desperate for a piss, man.' Boz listened to Blair's gush. He was unsettled. Hadn't had the time or wit to forestall Blair's request for a place to stay. Now his mother would be angry. She'd met Blair a couple of times and had made her feelings known. He'd smoked a joint once breaking house rules and the return of mother had been met with a stern stare. 'I don't want that boy in my house again, Jack.' Now Jack had about an hour to persuade Blair that staying here wasn't a good idea. He went to the kitchen and pretended to be making tea. Blair plonked himself down on the settee and Boz heard a clatter as Blair's bag fell.

'I'll have a cup if you're making one.' Boz got two cups. He heard the radio.

'Let's hear the News, eh? Someone might've been killed somewhere.' Boz came through with the cups.

'Blair, there's a wee problem.'

'Oh? You haven't killed someone?'

'No. It's my mother.'

'Your mother?'

'She doesn't want anyone here apart from us.'

'I thought she liked me. You told me she liked me.'

'It's not about whether she likes you. She likes Robert De Niro, but he isn't moving in either.' Blair gave Boz one of his long stares which was intended to unsettle and inject an element of trepidation.

'You do realise I've been kicked out of my brother's place. Been ejected. Now I'm fucking homeless Boz.' He lifted his rucksac. 'Bit of the family silver to keep my head above water. Look, I only need a settee or something to sleep on. Fuck me, is that asking too much of a friend? How's the head by the way?'

'Oh, I'll live. Thanks for caring.'

'Look, just a couple of nights, eh? Your old woman will understand. I think there's a guy after me. Fucker came to Eastlea. Big bugger.'

Boz was cornered. His distrust of Blair had morphed through adoration to hatred to fear. He convinced himself that he could talk his mother round. Two nights only. Two nights…

BLAIR

Can't stay here in this shithole. I need a bed. His mother's a bit of alright. Maybe give it a go. This guy's shit scared of little old me. Ha ha.

32

Leckie texted Sarah that he had located Blair at his home and had learned his mobile number. She was jubilant, wondering what else Leckie would have to do to get him to confess. Leckie didn't reply. He wasn't sure himself how to proceed. Why would Lithgow use his own name on that note if he knew Sarah? Didn't make sense. No, someone doesn't like Blair Lithgow and that someone might be the only chance he'd have of stopping him.

Back in Portobello Leckie was surprised to find Findon at his desk. He offered Leckie a tea which he declined. There was however an indefinable change in the man. He seemed uneasy, edgy, his eyes not engaging Leckie.

'How is the Mrs Wyllie case going? Tracked down the little shit? Simon gave me the gen. Posh boy making a damned nuisance of himself.'

'More than that Ed. Apart from stalking Sarah he broke into their house and beat up the son. Then, crown it all he heaves him into a rhino enclosure at the zoo…'

'A rhino enclosure? You been reading Rankin? Are you kidding? Why didn't you say?'

'You were away. Otherwise engaged. 'The kid was working at the zoo. He must have tracked him down and whop! Over he goes. Christ knows what would have happened if the rhino had had a go at him.'
Findon shook his head. He stood up.

'And you're sure it was the same guy?'

'Pretty sure, yep.' Findon clasped his meaty hands together on his desk in a gesture that meant business. 'Let's cut to the chase, Donald. As you probably know, I had a wee visit from the Fuzz. It seems somebody at the golf club didn't like the way I putt. I'm out by the skin of my teeth but they don't let you go. I'll be frank, Donald. One or two of my colleagues are not as law-abiding as myself and if you swim in a muddy pond, you can't be surprised to come out dirty…'

'As long as it doesn't stick, Ed. I know about The Committee. Had some dealings with a Mr Stapleton who thought it was a good idea to kidnap my daughter. He's slopping out at Saughton for a few years. Fucking arse.'

'I wasn't on the Board then, Donald, but I heard about it. Good for you. That's why I phoned you. I needed a good man here—one that could get the job done quickly and quietly…' There was a knock on the door and Zoe's head popped round.

'It's Mrs Gilhooley to see you Mr Findon.' Findon smiled at Leckie.

'Never stops, eh? Must be my turn.' Leckie raised his right palm in sympathy and went to his office. He passed the entrance area and saw Mrs Gilhooley sitting waiting. Elegant as ever, she looked up and smiled.

Leckie stared out of the window in his room. In front of him were grey tenements their early evening lights flickering on like waking stars. A gull perched on a satellite dish was screeching and below a man carried a crate of something from a white van into the pub opposite.

He saw all this, but his brain was elsewhere. It was in Barnton where a woman's shoe dangled, where that pretty smile glowed and those thin hands poured tea. He was feverishly trying to untie a knot of puzzling circumstances. Why was she here to see Findon? He said she was a regular. Fine. But Leckie had tracked her husband. There could be no reason to be back, surely. And Findon? The police had taken him away so quickly according to Zoe that it didn't sound like a traffic offence. From what he said they might be back.

Leckie felt on the periphery of things. A child on the stairs while the parents squabbled. Understanding nothing but expected to just accept it all. Fuck it, he thought, I'm pissed off with this. He strode along the corridor and after a perfunctory chap on the door, entered Findon's office. In front of Findon's desk his boss and Paula Gilhooley were in a tight embrace, Findon's large hand on her right buttock where her skirt had ridden up.

The couple separated. The woman turned her back and adjusted her skirt while Findon approached Leckie.

'Donald,' he offered. Leckie was struck dumb. He stood for a second or two, his eyes moving between the pair. 'It's not what I think eh? 'He turned and closed the door behind him. He left the office and drove home, his knuckles tight on the wheel. He poured himself a large one and sat by his window.

Findon and Gilhooley. Leckie couldn't believe it. Now he began to wonder about the police taking Findon; the whole Committee thing and Findon's relationship with Gilhooley. Was Findon just following in Grant's footsteps? Perhaps she just didn't fancy me, Leckie thought. What was all that about her husband? Was this all some game? He poured another and then another. He played 'St James Infirmary Blues' on the piano and tears began to fill his eyes. Drink and music did it to him. Drink and music and Megan made him cry. As the tears fell, he continued playing, feeling renewed in some way, washed clean for a moment or two. Keep playing. Keep playing, let the music take you away from here, he told himself. His phone played. He ignored it.

As he played, he became aware of a background sound. He stopped playing and a cello up above stopped soon after. He started again and the cello played with him, its resounding bass in counterpoint with the piano. He smiled; the tears still wet on his cheeks. There is a God. There is a God in this mash of lies and deceit and he plays the fucking cello.

It was Saturday. Leckie went to watch Hearts play St Johnstone. He hadn't been for ages, and he liked football. Findon had tried to phone him and then texted.

Leckie, need to talk. Can explain everything.

He ignored the text message and made his way to Gorgie where he sat for two hours and watched his team win. Two scrappy goals and a penalty was enough. He ate a luke-warm pie and drank some watery Bovril. The hubbub, the shouts, the taunts, the tribal chanting touched some deep atavistic seam in him, and he joined in. On the way back to his flat another text message. It was from McBride. Leckie wondered how the hell McBride knew his number…
Donald, need to see you urgently.
Serious stuff.

Then he remembered when Grant was killed, they'd called him on his land line, and he'd given his mobile number. He didn't have a landline now.
McBride left a number and Leckie called.

33

Next afternoon he was sitting opposite McBride.

'Glad you came in Donald. Have a seat. Something's come up, old man.'

'"Old man?" Fuck me if I'm anybody's old man. What's up?'

'In a nutshell, it's your boss, Findon. He's not what he seems, Donald. We've been tailing him for weeks and he's in with some murky boys. You know about The-so-called-Committee. Well, we've just lifted someone, and he's fingered Findon as a key player. People-smuggling. Leckie took an extra breath.

'You're kidding, right?'

'Wish I was. No. We're still working on this, and it isn't easy, but what we know is when he got back from Iraq the contacts he made out there were some bad asses that were shipping poor wee lasses from Fallujah and Mosul up to Lebanon. From there they go to North Africa and France.'

Leckie sat silently listening. He'd never seen McBride in this ultra-professional mode. There were no jokes, no little insinuations about Leckie's devotion to the Police—no, this was serious.

'I'd no idea about any of this,' said Leckie. McBride sat back and sighed deeply.

'We know that, Donald. This isn't about you, though. Have you seen anything unusual working with him? Any visitors? Any sign that he was on edge or looked anxious?'

'No. Nothing. I've just seen him with a woman I thought was a client though. Very pally.' Leckie gestured that this was all he could come up with.

'How "pally?"'

'They were necking in his office, and I walked in.' McBride smiled, nodded.

'Mrs Gilhooley would that be?' Leckie jolted upright.

'Christ Almighty. What the fuck's going on with you guys. Yes. Mrs Gilhooley. She's not…'

'Afraid so. We've been working on her for as long as Findon. She's the financial brains behind this little caper. And you did a bit of work for her, I hear.'

'Yes. First job I got. Hubby was being a bad boy.'

'That was all a set-up to test you. She hoped you might say something about Findon. Remember you and Grant were buddies. He might have told you about their wee racket. Did the good lady come on at all? She's an attractive woman.'

'Nope. She is, but I'm sworn to chastity, so she knew there was no hope for her.'

McBride shifted in his seat, a little irritated that his serious demeanour had not persuaded Leckie to adopt a reciprocal tone. Here was the old Leckie being disrespectful.

'Donald this isn't funny. Did she try to seduce you in any way? I'm asking a reasonable question.'

'No. She did not. And I didnae try anything either if that's what you're thinking.'

McBride told Leckie that there were two brothels, one in Edinburgh and one in Glasgow where women were working. Promises of a new life, a passport, a nice train journey and then the passport taken away. No money up front, for these girls had no money, only bodies. Families are glad to see them taken away to safety from the poverty they face at home. Romani families in Slovakia too. Little do they know what's waiting for them. McBride offered Leckie a coffee and the two chatted for some time. It was the first time Leckie felt any affinity to this man who till now had only ever treated him as a failure—a cop who had to get out for he couldn't stand the pressure anymore. Leckie toyed in his mind with mentioning Blair Lithgow but resisted the urge to share what he knew. Blair was his business, and he would settle the Blair issue if he could. Leckie wondered what he should do about Findon, and McBride told him to lie low, keep all this to himself but keep an eye on goings on. If their investigations progressed, he'd be lifted some time soon.

34

Digby had just been told by Sheila that she was leaving. He stood looking out of his study window at the rain. He could hear the Hoover going upstairs and the sound of it irritated him. She'd stay another week she said, till her stepfather moved out. Digby found out that Blair had come back and according to Sheila had taken some silver from a cabinet in the West lounge. She was sorry, she said.

There was no reply from Blair's phone nor from Annabell's. The previous night he had spent in the lounge of The Station Bar and his head held the memory. He had never felt so alone. Annabell had gone. Sheila was going, Blair was a liar and now a thief. Paris with an aunt and Robin, held any hope for his future. He checked the cabinet and sure enough some valuable Georgian silver pieces—the Wakelin and Gerrard sauceboats and the Hester Bateman tray had gone. Of late, Digby, with poverty looming, had taken a careful inventory of anything valuable which he possessed and there was no mistake— they'd gone. Worth thousands, and they'd gone. 'That's all you'll ever get from me you little bastard.' The thought consoled him. He needed a loan. Then he thought of Bill Wyllie. Yes, Bill would help him out. He'd go and see him. Yes, man to man was better than phoning.

He went upstairs to his bedroom and lay below the duvet in his cardigan and trousers. Above him there the plaster was flaking. That was new. God. The hoover was silent. Sheila must be in the kitchen. He opened his bedside cabinet and took out an old Playboy magazine. He opened it to the centrefold. There she lay, a dark-haired beauty, her legs wide, her shaved vagina a pink promise. His hand found his penis and he turned towards the window. As he stroked, nothing was happening, the head fallen out with the groin. Three minutes later he threw the magazine down and zipped himself up. Not like me, he thought. He fell asleep soon after and woke in the dark. It was seven-fifteen. He'd been asleep for five hours.

Bill Wyllie was mowing the lawn. It was May, warm with a few scurrying clouds in the blue sky and his garden had been neglected. What with Annabell and the two pubs he was running, there seemed no time for anything these days. Every time he thought of her a warm glow still held, but the first throes of infatuation were fading to be replaced with an acceptance that Annabell was not the ideal he'd once made of her. A woman in her forties. who is clinging to a fading beauty is a woman who needs reassurance, and Bill Wyllie was not skilled in that department. If everything was fine then he could be kind and loving, but when things were less than fine, he turned inwards and began to smoulder.

Annabell had a temperament that the word 'artistic' was invented to describe and perhaps forgive. Since moving in with Wyllie, she had basked in the glow of his attention, but her years with Digby had hardened her, had made her suspicious of affection. Now her paintings were a struggle. She had decided to change the focus of her art from flowers and still-lives to a semi-abstract style which went well at first but had now hit the buffers. With her struggle came frustration, and with her frustration came moodiness and sometimes downright anger. Wyllie was the only one there, and Wyllie became the target.

Upstairs, as he mowed, he heard her curse and the clatter of a canvas being thrown. He stopped and cut the power. he'd made a mistake with Annabell. He felt as strange in Annabell's world as he had in Sarah's. Why the hell did he go for artistic women? Why not a wee quiet woman who'd be happy to shop for shoes and cook him a nice meal. Provided she looked OK of course.

35

'Leckie. I've been calling you. Why no answer?'
'Sarah I'm sorry. I don't want you involved any more than you are.'

'Tell me where he's living in Edinburgh Leckie, or I'm no longer your client. I've got enough hassle here without you adding to it.'
'What hassle?'
'Nothing to do with you. Now am I still your client?'
Leckie was sitting by his window watching two crows on the roof opposite. His mind went blank. He simply didn't know what to say to this determined woman. The crows were joined by another that settled a foot away. It sidled up to them and they flew off. Poor lonely crow.
'I need more time. Be patient. I'm getting closer…' The phone went dead.

Leckie switched off his phone. He sat a moment, thinking. He had things to do in the office. Two clients to satisfy. He'd been out most of the morning tracking the activities of a young boy who'd left home to live with a friend. Parents were beside themselves when they discovered his 'friend' had been in trouble with the police for using. Now this. His leg hurt. That old injury tended to reappear from time to time just when he needed two good legs. He hadn't been sleeping and was missing Megan. Shit, he was missing Liz too.

He had established a routine in the last few weeks: home by six; stiff one; something from the fridge; stiff one; watch the news; stiff one; nod off for half-an-hour; wake and try to read something; nod off again; end up in The Royal till closing. He'd make his way back to the flat burping and farting and go to bed. By two o'clock he'd be wide awake again. And she'd creep back into his head. That fucking hair. He'd lie and look at the curtains, lit by the streetlight outside. In the morning he'd pull himself out of bed and shower. He'd shave trying not to look at himself too closely. He was tired. He was so fucking tired. By ten he was feeling better. Who needs sleep, he would tell himself. But by two or three the tiredness hit again and all he wanted was to lie down. That was when Sarah phoned.

Findon was rarely around these days. Leckie wondered if he'd been lifted, but there would have been word. From Findon himself or McBride. Nothing. As he sat and thought about Blair Lithgow, a searing anger rose. He hadn't felt like this since the Stapleton affair. He imagined a young face, a fist, the face fracturing in an explosion of blood till there was no face. And another face appeared. It was the face of Sarah, a smile spreading, her eyes gleaming as she moved towards him, her hair on his face her lips on his…

His reverie was broken by his ringtone.

'Hello. Findon Investigations. Donald Leckie speaking. Can I help you?'

'You certainly can. McBryde here, Donald. Can we meet? It's urgent. I mean fucking urgent. I know he's not there nor is his buddy. That's why I'm calling.'

'You've got him?'

'I wish. But we know where he is. The McDonald's at the top of Leith Walk. Fifteen?'

What could he say? 'I'll be there.'

Leckie sat back. Three balls to play with. Two too many. He phoned the parents of the boy and said he'd need more time to investigate further. They weren't happy but what could they say? Done. He phoned Sarah to say he'd be at her house in the morning. Now it was McBryde and Findon's wee caper. It suddenly stuck him that if Findon was canned there'd be no Findon Investigations any longer. Oh well. Time for another rest. The thought was comforting

36

The shiny, non-descript banality of a burger franchise hit Leckie as he opened the door: the cloying stink of frying meat, of deep-fat sizzling round doughnuts and onion rings. He knew enough about the Amazon's deforestation to hate this culture. He glanced round at the families munching away; the kids with their 'kiddie-cartons' and funny hats on as if shit food and baubles was all it took to make them happy. He rarely frequented such places unless he was tramping dark streets when decent folk were in bed. Near the wall he saw McBryde guzzling a huge burger. There was mayo on his cheek.

'Enjoying the Amazon?' said Leckie.

'What?'

'You're eating the Amazon.' McBryde smiled.

'You watch too much TV old son. Have a seat. Want something?'

'Just a reason to be here.'

'Leith. You know Leith, I believe.' McBryde smirked between mouthfuls. Leckie decided not to mention the mayo. McBryde sucked his coke through the straw, and it sounded like a drain being unplugged.

'I know Leith.' Leckie was playing it straight. He wanted home but he suspected this would probably keep him awake even longer tonight.

'He's holed up in a guest house near the front. We've tailed him for the last couple of weeks. Where he goes, who he sees, the times. You know the score. We've enough on him to make an arrest, but we need him out in the open. We need files. He knows we're keeping an eye on him and The Committee, but he doesn't know we've got him for trafficking. So...'

'He doesn't know you've got him for trafficking?' Leckie was puzzled. 'Why wouldn't he suspect that? If you were after me for GBH one day, would I go and beat up my wife the next? If you've scared him, he's going to wipe away every trace of his dealings. And that means his files too. Come on.'

'Maybe. But how do you get rid of ten girls from a house? He's got them trapped in there and the fucker's in there with them. So we break down the door and he says "Oh come in gentlemen, these are my friends…"'

'You've spoken to some women?'

'One. Girl called Sonya. She ran away in Glasgow. Went to Bridgeton nick. Social Services got in touch with us. We got the whole story. Poor lassie was petrified that he'd find her.'

'If he's trafficking then he's using them. There must be men going in there day and night. Send one of yours in.'

'We did.' McBryde's face clouded over.

'And…?'

'Hasn't been out.' Leckie shook his head.

'You sent a man in, and he didn't come out? Are you serious? What the fuck are you playing at? Go in there with AFO's and sort this out.'

'Too risky. He's known to have weapons. These girls could be collateral damage.'

Leckie shifted in his seat. The conversation and the smell were getting to him.

'Why the fuck am I here? I've got nothing to do with this. Go get the bastard. Good luck.' He stood up.

'Leckie, you know him. He likes you. Talk him out. It'll save lives…'

Leckie turned and left McBryde to his burger and his smeared face. As he hit the street though, something clung to him and it wasn't the stink of grease. "You could save lives" was a stain that wouldn't go away as he walked. He'd been a cop for twenty-odd years through good and bad. Sometimes he hated it. Sometimes all he saw of humanity was its dark underbelly—the scarred faces, the pallor of poverty, of bad housing and bad parenting, of existences mastered by drugs that sapped meaning from life. Sometimes he went home and cried for the world that he was faced with daily. And sometimes he felt a warm glow as the bad was replaced by the good: the bravery of some colleagues; their love for their families; the rough camaraderie; the peace that his work brought to those who'd been victims. He was a plasterer, plastering society's cuts, but he couldn't prevent more cuts and that was what did for him: the endlessness. He wanted an end, and he made one for himself before he gave way under the weight of it.

McBryde finished his burger and slurped the last of his coke. He dabbed his mouth with the red napkin and felt the smear go. Fucker never told him. He knew Leckie. He knew Leckie's type. Once you were a cop you were always a cop. Unless you were a shitbag like Findon of course. But Leckie was a good man. Leckie wouldn't let this go. A man in there? There wasn't. It was a gamble worth taking. Leckie couldn't let that go. Leckie would be back.

Leckie went home and gulped down a Bowmore. He sat back on his armchair and looked out at the slates of the opposite roof. Through a dormer window he could see a woman brushing her hair. He'd never noticed her before. Sixty yards away a woman brushing her hair had never heard of Donald Leckie. Never took drugs. Had never been poor. Had never gone hungry or felt a father's fist on her jaw. She looked happy. She stopped brushing and shook her hair before reaching behind her head to tie it back. She shook it as Megan once did when her hair was long. He missed Megan. He missed someone to speak to.

37

Blair made his way back to Boz's mother's place. A warm glow suffused him. He was walking on air. He'd spoken to Sarah, and she'd smiled at him. They were almost friends. She wanted his number. My God. He opened the fridge and took out a Becks. He sat down and swigged. The cold liquid felt good in his throat. He switched on the T.V. Some woman was yelling at her husband and he was ignoring her. Then he walked towards her and slapped her hard. 'Yes!' From Blair. The front door moved. It was Boz's mother. She saw Blair but made no sign of recognition. He'd been here for several days and she'd only spoken to him once. Her coming felt like an open door on a freezing day—a chill draft that could only mean trouble. She wasn't bad-- looking Blair thought. In his heightened state of self-love, he thought he'd talk to her.

He knocked on her bedroom door then opened it. She was hanging up her coat by the wardrobe.

'Fancy a drink? Cup of tea, maybe? Raining, is it?' She turned to face him. A cold face.

'Blair, this is my bedroom. I don't want you in here.'

'I'm going as soon as I can find a place.'

'Where is Jack? I thought he was with you?'

'No idea.' She gestured him out with a sweep of her arm. He suddenly realised that she was afraid of him. He could almost smell it.

'You don't have to be afraid of me, Linda. I'm harmless.' He moved towards her. She stiffened. He was now a foot away. He noticed how her mascara was smudged by the rain. His finger moved to her eye. She drew back.

'No. Don't you dare!' But he had her now. A small forward movement and he enclosed her in his arms. Her perfume was strong. Lavender. He felt her knee rise then fall against his groin. A change of heart. She turned her head away and struggled.

'Stay still. Just a wee kiss Linda. You're an attractive lady and you know it...' He froze. The sound of the front door stopped him. Her face next to his now she whispered 'Fuck off!'

Blair pulled back, composed himself and went through to the lounge. Boz appeared in time to see Blair enter from his mother's bedroom.

'What the fuck is going on? Is mum there? What you doing in there?'

'Your mother wanted me to undo the zip on her coat. Fucking zips eh.' Boz was not fooled. Blair looked flushed. Boz went to his mother's room. Blair had a moment to decide; stay and explain or make a getaway. He would go.

'Boz returned a moment later, his mother pulling at his elbow. His face was contorted with rage. He picked up a book and threw it at Blair. It missed him and knocked over a vase.

'Boz. What the hell you doing…?

'Get out! Get out of my house, you bastard! The words floated in the air like burnt paper. Blair ran towards Boz and smashed a right into his face. Boz lurched then fell back. Blair struck again and felt the hardness of Boz's jaw. A sharp bang on his head and a momentary blackness that flashed bright, and Blair reeled. Boz's mother had hit him with something heavy. Blair rose, the mist clearing. He grabbed Linda's arm and twisted it till she screamed. She shrank back against the wall clasping her arm while
Blair gathered his few possessions and left, slamming the door. Homeless, homeless. Paul Simon's song played in his

head as he made the street. He touched his skull and realised he was bleeding.

Blair's diary:
Fuck me what a day. Losing my touch methinks. Wonder if Camus had this hassle. Homeless again. Maybe mother bird would shelter her wee chick...

38

Findon watched the street through a slit in the lace curtain. A patrol-van was there in full view. He knew what was coming. They were trying to flush him out. A hooter sounded from the quay nearby. He was down to his last cigarette. He'd been here for three days since one of his men had been taken off the street and interrogated. 'Loitering with intent.' Tomas said. Fuck off. He wasn't sure how Tomas would react. Now he knew. They were on to him. Out there waiting. He knew the score: the enforcer, then the splintering of the front door and the shouts as they swarmed the place. Maybe armed. He turned and glared at the four women on the settee. Squashed together, eyes wide with fear. What the fuck was he going to do? He'd mailed Paula two days ago but had had nothing back. They had her too, for sure.

'Don't go near that window. You hear? Go near that window and you're dead.'

The frightened women nodded vigorously. Two couldn't speak English but two could and they led. He went down the hall and down the stairs past the tiny rooms where the women worked. A window at the back looked out on a small drying green where some clothes hung on a line. The old brick toilet still stood, and its galvanised roof adjoined the neighbouring garden wall. This was his only chance. He knew the gate into the lane would be watched. They weren't stupid.

He went into the garden and up the slabbed path to the old toilet. Inside was an oil drum. He swivelled it out as quietly as he could and stood up on it exposing himself slowly. He couldn't see over the back wall so they couldn't see him either. The roof was waist high. He clambered onto it, piercing his thumb on a nail. On the roof he flattened himself and edged towards the neighbouring garden. As his head looked over, he saw the area was deserted. He would drop eight feet onto bare earth. Iraq came into his head. Only there he would've had an M9 submachine gun in his hands. He got into a sitting position and edged his way out. 'Timber!' He landed and felt an ankle give. FUCK! On his feet the pain found its root. He looked at the windows of the house and saw no movement. Then the back door swung open and two black figures ran towards him shouting 'Police! Get down! Now!' Findon froze. His game was up, and he knew it. They splayed his legs and cuffed him, then dragged him to his feet. They frog marched him through the house and into a squad car in the street. The hand holding his head down released early and his head struck the rim of the door. A thin trickle of blood made its way down his forehead to the amusement of the two policemen

39

The next morning. Wyllie's house in a quiet tree-lined street...

Digby parks. He looks up at the windows. No sign of life. He rings the bell. He hears it ring inside. He waits. Through the frosted glass of the door, he sees a figure approach then disappear. Strange, he thinks. He rings the bell again. No response.

He rings the bell a third time not releasing the pressure so the dring is continuous. He is angry now. He waits. A figure appears and the door opens. It's Wyllie. He's clutching a small white dog.

'Digby. You forgetting your manners? What kind of ringing is that?'

'Am I coming in?'

'Nope. Got company. Sorry Digs but it's just not convenient.' Digby pushes his way in and walks through the lobby.

'What the fuck are you on Digby! I said I'm busy. Get out of my house!'

' There were footsteps on the stairs. Annabell appeared, wiping her hands. Digby's breath failed him for a few seconds as he took in the scene. Annabell in Wyllie's house. Annabell wiping her hands free of paint because she fucking lives here. Annabell sat down opposite Digby.

'I told you not to come down,' said Wyllie.

'We need to settle this, Bill,' said Annabell. 'How are you, Digby?'

'Oh, I'm just great. He owes me money. And he's screwing my wife. Yeah, I'm just on top of the bloody world. Thanks for asking.' Digby rose and walked towards Wyllie. He was taller than Wyllie and he tilted his head to meet Wyllie's eyes. Digby made a sudden movement with his right arm and Wyllie jumped back. Digby smiled.

'I used to like you. Used to watch you playing cricket all those years ago. Whacking that ball for six. You were a kind of hero to me then. Did you know that?

I even liked you a few weeks ago in that tatty club of yours. But now… now I see what you really are. You're a liar and a cheat. You pretended to be my friend while you ran off with my wife.' He turned and addressed Annabell who had stood up as Digby approached Wyllie. 'And you, Annabell, chose him over me. We weren't great, but Christ Almighty, is this better?' He stood a moment, waiting for a response from Wyllie, but none came. He turned and strode out to the street, leaving the door open as if the house needed cleansing air.

In his car what had been rage turned to sorrow. Knuckles white on the wheel, he began to cry. His life seemed to spool in front of him: a terrifying rewinding film of his doomed days flickering in his skull; the face of Annabell, smiling as they walked in the woods at Eastlea; of days in the garden, the sun glinting on the glasshouse; of Robin in his cradle; of Blair, that beautiful face that turned ugly and smirking; the peeling, peeling everywhere as the house decaying around him…

'Sad bastard, eh?' said Wyllie in Annabell's direction. He released the dog and went out to the garden. He lit a cigarillo, his back to the house. Annabell made her way back up the stairs. She was calm but inside she knew something was broken. Something had been lost and she wondered if it would ever be found again. There had been a look in her husband's eyes that had shocked her. It was the face of hopelessness.

40

Blair looked at the knuckles of his right hand. The skin had ripped to white rags on the first and last knuckles and pale smears of blood had dried to stains. Boz's blood and his. Blood brothers. The pain was intense. A burning that wouldn't let up. The first knuckle seemed to have moved a bit and when he touched it, he winced. No-one had noticed. He was sitting in a dimly lit bar with only three others. Late afternoon, the dead time. He'd downed two pints and was on his third. He took out the thin roll of notes and his fingers played with them. He still had the other comfort of a tray wrapped in a tea-towel in his bag. His mind began racing. Boz's mother's face, the sound of the door and then all hell. He remembered little of hitting Boz, but his fists told another story. He remembered Tim though, now that day became clear. A smile on his face. Fuck it. Who cares? Boz is a fucking idiot and his mother had hair on her upper lip. Shit. New chapter about to begin.

It was then that he thought of his mother. Better looking than Boz's old woman. My old mater. He had her number on his phone. Should he? Where is she? Would she answer? Maybe if he crawled, she'd put him up. He felt sad, as if his brain had suddenly slumped. He needed a bed, a place to lay his weary. He pulled up Contacts. *"Mum."* Must have been entered when he liked her. Million years ago. He'd had the phone for donkeys. He pressed. It rang.

'Hi, it's Blair, your son. Remember me?' As he said it, he cursed himself for his tone. Contrite. That was what he needed. A bit of contrition. There was no answer.

'Look mum, I've been in with a bad crowd, and they've stolen all my stuff. I haven't a penny or even a change of clothes. I'm desperate.' He waited. He was shaking.

'Desperate.' Her voice. 'When have you been anything other than desperate? Where are you?'

'I'm in Edinburgh.'

'I know. Sheila told me you'd gone home and then come back. Where are you exactly?' There was a hiatus.

'It's nearly five. I need a bed tonight. Can you put me up?'

'Oh. A bit sudden. We'll see. I'll have to speak to someone. I'll phone back.'

'Ok. Speak then.'

Blair was cheered. He knew whatever lay between him and his mother she wouldn't allow it to eat him up. She'd give him money at least.

Annabell felt the day becoming one to remember. Digby and Wyllie, now Blair. What the hell was it with men? She had a fair amount in her bank account, but she was determined not to become an easy touch for Blair. Would this kid ever come good?

She'd speak to Bill.

41

Leckie slept late. He finally fell asleep about four then woke at seven when the radio burst into life. He fell asleep again and now it was nine-thirty. His phone woke him. It was McBryde.

'Morning. McBryde of The Force here. No thanks to you we have our man. We've also lifted his IT pal from the office for a few questions. We need to talk. Voluntary Interview. You won't need a legal chappie. I can send a van, or you can come and speak to me at ten. Your choice.'

Leckie had little choice. He dressed and shaved quickly. He ate a slice of bread with some marmalade and heated up a coffee. He realised he was now out of a job, but he was surprised about Simon who seemed a decent guy.

McBryde's office was stuffy with bodies and a strong sun shot speckled shafts of gold on to the desk through the high windows. The questions went on for an hour and a quarter. Leckie was tired and experienced feelings of disorientation. Here he was in the nick being questioned in the middle of a serious case. Not the first time, but he swore it would be the last. Too often the law and he had sparred, knights jousting. He was tired. He realised how easily he could have become an unwitting player in Findon's operations. Had that happened, he'd be wearing a set of cufflinks you wouldn't buy in any jewellers. He left with a handshake that was polite but not cordial. Outside the air was warm. A boy passed licking a huge ice cream cone. He phoned Megan who had left a message on his phone.

'Hi, How are you honey? Long time no speak.'

'Dad. I want to come back home for a spell. Is that OK?

'Of course. Something wrong? You sound a bit funny.'

'It's over. Sausage thief has been two-timing me. I'll explain later.'

Leckie felt a knife gutting him. He could feel Megan's hurt. Tricky Ricky, eh? He needed a drink. He walked to The Royal and ordered a Guinness and a double Macallan. Another message on his phone. Sarah.

'What's happening Donald? You said you'd get back to me.'

'We need to wire you. Get evidence. Without evidence the police can't do anything. I know it sounds a bit weird, but I've done this recently. It'll be OK. We just get him to talk.' As he said this, he realized how stupid such a plan would be. Stupid and dangerous. He'd scrub it when he saw her.

42

Blair unpacked his bag. He looked round the room. It was small, but the grey walls had been newly painted: pictures of stags, a salmon and a crest of some sort. The double bed had a tartan duvet; there was a beige bedside table with a beige lamp and a beige chest of drawers. Was this nicked from a Travelodge? He sat on the bed and rolled a spliff. A knock and his mother entered.

'Uh, uh. No smoking. Bill doesn't like it in the house. And especially that. We're in the garden. Get settled, then come and meet Bill.'

Bill was not a happy man. The episode with Digby had soured him of warm feelings for the Lithgows. Annabell was one thing, but her son was another. He had no children of his own and never felt the need for one. Now he had a young man under his roof that he hadn't seen for years, if ever. Annabell had sprung this on him, and he was resentful.

Blair appeared a few minutes later, tall, blond, smiling. Time to be nice.

'Bill. Good of you to have me.' This kid didn't lack confidence. Hands were offered and accepted. Blair winced. Bill's grasp surprised him with its strength.

'Bashed it on a wall. It's a bit sore,' said Blair.

'Your mum says you're homeless. That so?'

'Just temporary. I've something in the pipeline.'

'Sleeping in a pipeline. Not a good idea. Be bloody freezing.' A weak smile creased Blair's mouth. It was one his mother recognised. He thought it was all he could do. Keep on the right side of this guy.

'Well make yourself at home. But not for ever. Ok?'

'Thanks. Appreciate it.'

Wyllie left to play golf, leaving Blair with his mother. She told him he must respect the fact that this wasn't her house. She began to quiz him about the college but little by little she realised that Blair hadn't changed. His answers were guarded if not downright lies. He drank two beers before she made an excuse to return to her studio.

'Don't clear out the fridge. And no more beers. You should phone your father and make peace. He just wants you to settle down to something. Robin's in a new flat I hear. You could have all that, Blair, if you just tried.'

'Yes mummy.' Upstairs he jumped on the bed and stretched out, his hands behind his head.
That look on her face said 'same old.'

BLAIR
This is c-omf—y._ Old Bill seems a boring cunt. Mummy what've you done. Can't see this lasting long. At least I'll get fed. Fridge is bursting with goodies.

43

Leckie had had a change of heart. Maybe it would work. She could pull it off. She could pull anything off. He poured Sarah a glass of the only white he had. She was too nervous to tell him how awful it was. She sipped while he spoke.

'Right. We'll take this slowly. We get him to my office. Findon's gone but I've got a key. You tell him this is a friend's office. He's away in Spain on a business trip. He's an exporter. He won't quibble about this. He'll be only too happy to be alone with you.'

'And I'll be so happy to be alone with him.'

'Yes, yes, I know it's not easy. If you can get him relaxed and talking… We need to get him to convict himself.' She stood up and moved to the window, her back to him as she spoke.

'Peter won't let me do this. And he's right. This boy's a psychopath or a sociopath or whatever. What he did to Michael was way beyond normal behaviour. He enjoys violence, Donald. Let's not fool around here. He's too much for us to handle. We have to get the police involved. This isn't about me. Michael can identify him.' Leckie scratched his head then threw back his whisky.

'Michael may identify him but that won't convict him of anything. There's no evidence Sarah. I keep telling you this. We don't have DNA or anything.' She turned to him; her face changed.

'Then that's it. I'm done. I haven't seen him at the house for ages anyway.

Leckie sighed. He feared for this woman's safety, but he also feared that she was right. His plan could seriously backfire. If something went wrong, if Blair began to suspect something, he could explode. A part of him wanted done with all of this but he had feelings for this woman. He wanted her to be safe, to live her life without being threatened by this nutter.

'Do you like Chopin?'

'What?'

'Do you like Chopin?'

'Yes, I do. Why?'

'I'm going to play you some Chopin. How about a Nocturne? I've got the music here.' She looked up at him and smiled. She shook her head.

'You're something else. One minute we're trapping a psychopath and the next you're serenading me with Chopin.'

'"Serenading." Do you think I'm trying to seduce you or something?'

'Of course not. Just a word. Go on. Play me some Chopin and I'll sit here and try to calm myself.' Leckie pulled a book from a pile by the piano, settled himself, scanned the music for a moment.

'Nocturne in E flat Major. One of my favourites.'

He was nervous but found his touch quickly and soon lost himself in the piece. He struck the last chords and let his arms fall. Silence. He turned and saw that she was weeping. His instinct was to move to comfort her, but he turned on the stool and stared at her. She dabbed her eyes with a tissue and apologised.

'I know I'm not exactly Steven Osborne, but it's not that bad.'

She raised her head and smiled through her tears. It was a sun-shower.

'That was wonderful. My God, I didn't know you could play like that.'

'Started lessons last week. Teacher said I was making good progress.'

'Oh, stop it. You'll make me cry again.' Leckie laughed. He made her a coffee, and they chatted about music. She promised to bring her violin some evening and they could play together. The subject of Blair was lost in their delight at being in each other's company and was only alluded to briefly before she left. Leckie would deal with him. She should forget the whole thing. He wouldn't bother her again, he promised. She kissed his cheek and left, warmed by the man. But halfway down the stairs as she replayed his final words about Blair, she stopped. The scars caused by the hurts Blair had perpetrated on her new family seemed to vivify in her head. She wasn't a woman to leave her life in the hands of another. Leckie had tried but really nothing had changed.

All she wanted was to hurt this man. It wasn't a feeling that she relished but it was one that wouldn't leave her. Night and day it plagued her. She had to get him herself, not leave it to Leckie. Leckie hadn't been hurt, he was merely trying to help her. Leckie wouldn't hurt Blair the way she would. He didn't have the hatred.

Later that evening she was speaking on the phone with a pianist who had a small studio in town —a room with a small kitchen and toilet where she often practised. She asked him if she could borrow the room for an afternoon. She was becoming oppressed by household duties and needed some space to play in peace. Of course. He'd leave the key at the shop below. He was going to be out of town for two weeks. There was a kettle and some teabags in the kitchen, but she'd need to buy milk. There was also a small, high-quality recorder which he used. If she could run that and get Blair to talk about what he did then there was the evidence she'd need for the police.

But how to find Blair…
Sarah phoned Wyllie and Annabell answered.

44

Megan returned the following day. Tearful and angry. Sausage man was just like every other man in the world—a total bastard. Leckie thanked her and she punched him. As he heard her in her room noisily settling herself back in, he felt happy. She belonged here, with him. Safe from harm. It was a feeling that had never left him, though he knew it was foolish. She was a grown woman with a life to lead. Why was it that life so often seemed hurtful?

There was another person that he wanted to shield from life though and he had to do something to help. He opened his notebook. Blair's number. With those magic buttons pressed he would hear that voice again. If Leckie came within a mile of him, he'd run. For the first time, Leckie asked himself why he was doing this. And more importantly what he hoped to do. The guy was dangerous, out of control. He took a pad and jotted down:

1) McBryde. Find if any DNA taken —Michael x2
2) If none. No evidence.
3) Where is he now?
4) Scare the fucker shitless.

45

Digby Lithgow went home to Eastlea after leaving Wyllie's house. His mind was in turmoil. He'd been betrayed by someone he thought was a friend and he'd lost his wife. As he parked on the driveway, he felt his life was in ruins. Even Sheila was going. The house was empty, the garden, in the last fling of summer growth looked more unkempt than ever. He had to do something, but clarity of thought was lost as the two bottles of Genfiddich he'd brought back clinked under his arm. Later that evening and three-quarters of a bottle down, a log rolled from the open fire and the rug caught. He rose unsteadily and thrashed it with the fire shuttle. The flame died and he sank back into his chair, the acrid stink of burned carpet in his nostrils.

The next morning Digby stood before the cabinet in the hall. Where the pieces of silver had been, the spaces remained. He knew Blair had taken them but somehow at the time he'd been too concerned with the Wyllie business to care much. That, and the belief deep down that he would never talk to his son again. Now, though, things were different. The little bastard might come back and help himself to more goodies. No, this couldn't be ignored. He had to contact Blair and find out what had happened to his silver. He went up to Blair's bedroom. The bed unmade, clothes on the floor— a shambles. On the dresser, a sheath knife, some playing cards and a jotter. Digby read Blair's English notes for a couple of lectures and noticed the name 'Sarah' at the top of several pages. On a blank page was a drawing of a woman with long hair coloured with a red biro. Digby stood transfixed by conflicting ideas and emotions. He only knew one woman with such red hair, and it struck him that Blair might know her also. It couldn't be, could it? Was that Sarah? Wyllie's wife? Why would Blair obsess about her? She was old enough to be his mother.

He thought about calling Wyllie. He'd maybe know her number.. No. Can't speak to that bastard. Forget it.

At two o'clock on a bright afternoon Sarah Wyllie was in her car heading to Wyllie's house where she now knew Blair was living. She'd phoned her ex-husband concerned about some clothing she'd left behind and was surprised to hear Annabell's voice answer the phone. Annabell was obviously embarrassed by the situation, but Sarah kept calm and reassured her that what Bill did with his life was his business. Sarah then asked if Blair was in Edinburgh as she thought she'd seen him. Annabell told her he'd left college and was looking for a job. Did she know where Blair was living? She did. He was living there. Oh, that was very handy. Blair was out, but Annabell said she would take a message. Sarah said she'd phone back.

Sarah parked her blue Fiesta fifty metres from the entrance to her old house. She knew the street like the back of her hand: every cat, every dog, every tree, every woman who lived there and every man. She felt confident also that if Blair Lithgow noticed her, he would stop and talk. She would ask if he would like to go for a drink. She would be in control. If he walked up the street and didn't see her, she would drive up and stop him on some pretext.

46

Blair Lithgow sat in The Meadows Bar. He was reading a paperback he'd picked up in a Chest Heart and Stroke shop. He sipped his beer slowly, distracted by the words. He was reading 'The Thief's Journal' by Jean Genet, attracted by the writer's bio which described him as a 'petty thief in his early years.' He stopped reading after a short time and closed the book. At the bar he ordered another cider and asked the barmaid where the local library was. It was a gambit that worked wonders depending on the perceived intelligence of the girl. They began to talk and exchanged names. Her eyes were bright—a sure sign of interest.

'You a student?' She asked.

'Yep. Going to be a DOCTORRRRR.' The last word drawn out as if it were an apology—a youth's self-conscious nod to joining life's treadmill. She was impressed. Of course she was. They always were.

'That's great.' She resumed her glass-cleaning.

'Got a boyfriend?'

'Yes. A big boyfriend.' A well-rehearsed response. You don't survive in bars looking like her without a defence mechanism.

'Right. Really big?'

'Oh, big. Twice your size. Easily.' Blair laughed. She was flirting but it was a parry not a come-on.

'That's good. Cheers.' She smiled. He took it as one of those, 'if only' smiles that he sometimes met. She fancies me but she's too fucking moral to cheat on her stupid boyfriend, he thought. His ego remained undented. He took his drink and sat down again. He took a slip of paper from his pocket. There were three addresses on it. Two scored out. The third was a house in the Merchiston district that he had sussed out. He had opened a Bank Account and had deposited £2,075.

He had pawned some jewellery from the Mitchener house and a laptop but was wary now of being identified should the items be traced. Just money from now on. He regretted that he'd returned to the Mitchener's house. Linking two crimes was a mistake and could lead to a build-up of evidence. But he was hooked on burglary. That frisson of fear and excitement in a strange house with strange odours. He had broken into someone else's life with that life's qualia: the scents, the furniture, the floors, the carpets, the ornaments and most of all the photographs of the occupants—it all added to the addiction. He saw himself clearly now as above conventional moral constraints. Reading 'The Thief's Journal' only convinced him that what he was doing was an extension of his personality. He was gifted beyond the norm. He didn't need people, he told himself. Boz, and the others he'd befriended were holding him back. His purpose wasn't yet clear, he felt, but it would become clear as he proceeded. What he needed now was a place of his own. He'd stay with his mother for a couple of weeks then rent somewhere, maybe out in the country.

His mind was turning like a casino wheel clattering to a halt then spinning again. Now it stopped at Sarah. Bet on red. Faites vos jeux he heard as her face floated into view. He was excited. He was close now. Just a phone call away and she'd be there. He gulped down more beer as a dog's head brushed his leg. A collie with trusting eyes looked up at him. 'Hi there.' He stroked it as its master tugged it away with a 'Sorry.'

'No problem. I like dogs.' The pair moved to the bar where the dog settled. Blair's mind whirled back to Eastlea and his father's yellow retriever called Max that had been his constant companion in summer holidays. Blair had thrown a stick far out over the river one day when the current was strong, and the dog had struggled to get back up the steep bank. He'd waded in to pull it to safety. He chortled quietly to himself. It was the last act of kindness he could remember but it gave him some satisfaction.

He left the pub and strolled across The Meadows. The sky was still blue but slate-grey gobs of cloud had brought a few drops of rain. Folk began to rise reluctantly and pack up their belongings to take shelter. He'd find shelter too

47

Round another corner and into Chapel Road Blair looked across and stopped dead. He saw the dark hair of a woman in the driver's seat of a car. She looked up. It was her. He looked over his shoulder then crossed the street. She smiled at him. Her window rolled down.

'Hello. I'm looking for a Mr Wyllie.

'Hi. Think I know you. I'm living across there with my mother and …your hus…'

'My "ex?" How do you know that? Oh. I see. You must be Blair. Is that right?' He smiled when he heard his name coming from her lips.

'Why are you here?' He asked, his hands in his pockets now.

'Just picking up a few things.' Blair shuffled uneasily.

'You look nice.' Out of the blue. She flashed a smile wider than she felt, touched her hair distractedly. Her whole being strove to contain the hammering in her chest. All she wanted to do was get out of the fucking car and kick this little bastard in the balls. She wanted to stand over him with her shoe on his face and drop his crimes on him like molten lead till he squealed. When he reached in and rested his fingers on the sill she lifted her hand.

'Are you nervous? You're shaking?'

'No. I've got pills I take for this.' Well done, she told herself. Quick thinking. Whether he would believe her was another story, but it would do. But now any plan she had was dead. She couldn't sit with him in the car. She just couldn't be near him any longer…

'Oh God, is that the time. I must get going. I'll pick things up tomorrow. Must get going. Bye.' She put up the window and he pulled his hand away. He knocked hard on it. She opened it an inch or two, her finger on the button.

'How about a drink or coffee or something?' She began to panic. She'd seen the fish, but if she didn't cast, he'd be lost. Decide. Decide. She nodded.

'I'll drive if you're not feeling too good,' he said smiling. The fish was wriggling but now she wondered who was hooking whom.

'Well, Ok. We mustn't go far. I've to be back by five. She got out and moved round to the passenger side while he slipped into the driver's seat. He was aware of the flowery orange dress draped over her knees. He crashed the gears and laughed, and she laughed. 'You can drive, I assume?' He smiled, shoved into first then they eased away.

'Look I've to pick up some music from a studio. Can you drive there please. I'll guide you.' Blair was smiling. He'd never driven in Edinburgh before, but it didn't phase him. Just having the scent of her in his nostrils was enough to banish any fear. He drove cautiously through traffic, almost breaking a red as she guided him to the West End of the city. They drew up outside a Chemist's shop. By now she had collected herself. A red rage galvanised her. She still shook but she clasped her hands together, dug her nails into her palm till it hurt and every time he looked at her she stared ahead, her face motionless. She had to do it now. The key from the shop, then up the stairs to the small room with a piano and an armchair where she'd practised so often.

A calm settled, born of a determination to end this. Somehow. Anyhow. She no longer feared for herself. It was Peter and Michael she was thinking of. She'd offer him tea, distract him somehow. She'd take the recorder into the kitchen. She'd make tea. She'd switch the recorder on. If he noticed she'd say she'd done it by mistake. They'd sit and drink and she'd ask him about himself. If the recorder failed at least she'd have his cup. DNA...

Sarah got out of the car. She looked at her watch. Six o'clock. Home in an hour and Peter wouldn't be worried. She thought of running but what was she running from? A boy who'd just driven her? It was madness. She had to relax him. Make him feel that she liked him. He followed her up the stairs, taking off his blouson jacket and carrying it with one hand over his shoulder. She opened the door and stepped inside. The room smelled of sweat as if David Hickey had been here for hours playing away at full pelt. Music. That was why they were here. Pick up some music. There was no music. She laid her handbag down on the piano and pretended to search in the kitchen while Blair sat in the chair his legs wide apart. He was happy.

There was no recorder. Shit. Only the kettle and on a tray two grubby mugs, a jar with some tea bags and a bag of sugar turning to cement.

'He's taken my music with him. Some tea? I need a cup of tea.'

'Yeah. Fine. You practice here?' There was an excitement in his voice that made her anxious. It sounded as if he felt he'd achieved something just by being with her.

She filled the kettle and plugged it in. Her only hope now was his prints on the cup. She wondered what would happen when she said she wanted to go home. Would he take her home? Would he take her to the house where Michael might answer the door? To the place where she'd noticed him so often? What was in his mind?

Blair Lithgow was happy. He sat listening to the wheeze of the kettle coming to the boil and the clatter of cups. She was behind the door. He hadn't investigated the kitchen, so he didn't know there was nothing there but the sink. Underneath it in a cupboard was a brush and pan and a few rags. The tap was still running. Perhaps she was washing her hands or the cups. He could smell her. That flowery aroma that he'd noticed that day on the street. He began to grow hard. He twisted, trying to hide it but the bulge was obvious in his tight jeans. He stood up moved to the shiny ebony piano and lifted the lid. 'Yamaha' it said. He sat down. He fingered a middle 'C.' Sounded a lot better than the old concert grand at Eastlea. Then he played a C chord. In the bass he played a simple four note boogie pattern—C-E-G-E and hit a chord in the treble. She stopped clattering the cups. Christ. He plays. Or does he? Will he go further? The answer was no. Blair Lithgow's time learning piano was brief. A music teacher at one of his schools taught a group of them a basic boogie bass. He'd loved it but the baby grand at Eastwood was so badly out of tune that he made no further experiments. He played several tunes on his guitar, but he'd left it at Eastlea.

'Tea. Don't have any milk. Do you take sugar?' She heard herself speaking and wondered if it were someone else, someone who was entertaining a friend, not someone who had tried to kill her stepson. She was an actor in a bizarre play.

'One spoon please. I suppose it's shit tea, is it? Not that I was expecting anything else.' Just an edge, she thought. It reminded her of what she was dealing with. If this character was a psychopath, then there would be swings of mood.

'No, nothing fancy.' She'd cleaned his cup as thoroughly as she could. Doing something helped. Roses on it. On hers, a girl in a Hearts top. She gave him the cup holding the tea-towel round it.

'Hot. No biscuits I'm afraid.' He took the cup and sniffed it. She sat in the other chair facing him.

'Typhoo or something is it? Do you play the piano too? I know you're a violinist.'

'Oh, who told you that? Yes. Comes with the territory. Music. You?'

'Not really. Got a guitar. Maybe we could play together sometime.' She shifted in her seat. Now it was coming.

'So, you're living with your mother.'

'Yep. Nowhere else to go. Poor little homeless boy, that's me.'

'Poor you.' She offered a smile. He stared at her. Pinning her.

'You know I like you, don't you.' The suddenness took her by surprise. She pretended to drink, the mug covering her mouth. She smiled. Respond. Respond.

'That's nice.'

'I know you're living with someone and all that. I just wanted you to know how much I like you. Your hair is great. You've got amazing eyes.' She rose. If there ever was a time it was now. She had no idea where her words would lead but she didn't care.

Words boiled in her and broke. 'And you've been stalking me, right?' He hesitated, leaned down and put his mug on the floor by his feet. His eyes met hers. 'Yeah. I followed you once or twice. It's not a crime. Just wanted to see where you lived. Why not?'

'And then you beat up my stepson.' She was rolling down the slope. ' Was that just to see how he would cope with your punches?' He stood up. He moved to the piano and with one finger repeatedly pressed a note. She was aware of the immensity of his body. An 'A' she instinctively knew, though what difference it made angered her. It was as if a part of her brain didn't realise what was happening here.

'Beat up your stepson? A A A A A What are you talking about? A A A A A A A Why would I do that? Yeah, I went to lessons once. I was quite good. A A A A A D D D D'

'Please stop that. Because you didn't know he was in the house.' She remained seated as he moved to her. She was shaking now. He was towering over her now as if she might be crushed if he toppled. Her eyes were on his hands waiting for something to happen.

'He took you by surprise. I understand in a way. You weren't to know he was there and you panicked.' Her eyes were still on his right hand.

'"Panicked." I don't panic. He panicked when he saw me, the stupid idiot. If he'd just been calm, it wouldn't have happened.' She had him. The confession. The cup. Now she had to get out of here...

'You knew all this, didn't you. You brought me here knowing all this. For some reason, eh? You're not the person I thought you were. You're trying to trap me. Fuck you. I trusted you.' His fingers formed a fist.

'You trusted me?' She looked up at him. 'You tried to destroy my family, you shit.' She stood up, brushing his chest, facing him now, her eyes ablaze.

'You tried to kill my stepson by pushing him into the rhino pen. What the hell are you, a maniac?' She pushed him away and grabbed the metronome from the top of the piano and threw it at him. It struck him on the temple. He reeled, saw the blood on his palm and threw his mug at her, striking her head. Then in a moment was over her, punching. She fell back half-on half-off the chair in a vortex of pain. She couldn't feel her legs. She slumped to the carpet.

Standing over her, something in him burned now with the rejection. That ending that always seemed to come to anything he did. And now it bit deep into him, the rage, the injustice that life did him and he picked up the metronome and threw it at the piano. She was bleeding now, a gash on her cheek that stung. Her head bleeding too. In his head a switch had gone off. Now he was free of guilt, shame, you name it—anything that might make him human…

Sarah lost consciousness, lay like a mutilated rag doll. He bent and raised her dress. White pants. The bulge of her mons. A stain. She'd pissed herself. For a moment he wondered about taking them off, exposing her for all she was. No. His hurt was engulfing him. An anger that swelled. He rummaged in her handbag and took her diary. He'd snatch a look at a part of her life no-one would see. He picked up her phone but decided she'd need it later or she might die alone here—not compassion, but an effort to prevent his being a murderer. He looked at her again, lying there. She didn't seem too bad. She'd recover. 'You're a fucking tart. That's all you are. All fucking hair and eyes and all that shit. I've a good mind to fuck you right here. You know something, I can't be arsed. You ugly bitch. Old ugly bitch.' He spat and watched the saliva land on her stomach and bubble.

He went to the sink and washed the blood from his shirt and hands. He strode to the door and was gone, clattering down the stairs.

Some moments later she opened her eyes. She could still hear his words from somewhere as if they were still in the air. She looked down and saw how exposed she was. Her head turned in shame. She pulled her dress down and lay gasping for air for a few seconds, found her breath again—a rhythm, each beat of which brought pain. Instinctively she tried to lift her hand to her face, but her arm wouldn't lift. A shaft of pain shot through her shoulder and made her gasp. She could feel the warmth of blood on her cheek and on her forehead. Her finger tried her cheek and recoiled from the horror of split flesh. With her other arm she pulled herself to her knees and crawled to the chair as the tears came. The room spun. She sobbed, her whole body shaking. In and out the dark and the light. 'Oh my God!' she cried, to no-one. The room faded…

Blair kicked her passenger car door and caught a bus back to town. A small boy saw him and tried to tell his mother, but she just told him to get a move on.

BLAIR

Fuck. Fuck. Fuck. What the fuck was she doing! Stupid bitch.
That's me in trouble. But it's her word against mine. No problem. Deny everything. Daddy and mummy will vouch for me.

48

Leckie was quiet as Megan prepared their meal. Frying onions. He was distracted but would say nothing to Megan which might elicit a barrage of questions. He switched on the TV. It was 6.45. He'd had no call from Sarah. A magazine programme in which the two grinning presenters a man and a woman took turns delivering their mindless scripts. Photos from viewers of their unusual pets: a pot-bellied pig, a python, a furry thing with a huge tail. This was what kept millions of people amused every fucking night while the country burned. He switched it off and played Classic FM. Mozart as usual. 'Relaxing' music as usual. Christ, did old Mozart sit down every day and say to himself 'Now what relaxing music can I pen today Constanze?' Angry. Always angry these days. It's lonely being different. He stood by the window and examined the street below. He phoned Sarah's mobile. Nothing. Shops closing. Bolts being slid and padlocks clicked. Above the roofs the sky was a bluey grey. The rain had eased. In the glass he saw the slim form of Megan crossing the room.

'Won't be long dad. French fries in the oven.' He phoned again. Nothing.

'Smells good,' he said. Sarah again in his head. They ate their sausages and onions, Leckie toying with his so Megan asked what was wrong. Nothing, he said, just not as hungry as I thought I was. She was disappointed he could see, so he told her she'd become a good cook and now that the thief had gone, they could eat sausages again. She smiled.

By eight-thirty there was nothing from Sarah. He'd tried to watch a film on Netflix, but his mind was restless. The stomach pain had come back. It was as if someone was turning a knife in there. He said he was going to the pub, and she said she'd go. No, she should stay there as he was expecting a call and he might have to go somewhere. Just business honey. No sweat. She shook her head and settled back to the film. He tried Sarah again. Nothing...Then the phone rang. Peter Wells. Sarah hadn't appeared or called. He was worried.

Peter Wells tried to read, but his brain was elsewhere. Michael had gone away with a friend. He was alone, tortured by his imaginings. Was it that boy again? He phoned Leckie. He'd be over. Just hang on. She'd be fine.

Outside Sarah's house Leckie saw that there was no car in the drive. There was a light on in one of the upstairs rooms. Was Peter stalking the floor, wondering where she was? Leckie walked away and sat on a bench opposite. Then he remembered her plan to take Blair somewhere and how that had been ditched. He couldn't help her, for Lithgow had seen him. She'd be in danger if he sensed it was a trap. He got up and crossed the road. He pushed the bell. In a few seconds an out of breath Peter was at the door. His face fell.

'Leckie. My God where is she?'

'Sorry about the timing Peter. May I?'

'Is it Sarah? Something happened? It's getting late and she hasn't called.'

They moved to the lounge and Wells gestured Leckie to sit.

'Where the hell is she? Do you know? She hasn't phoned. Just nothing. It's not like her, Donald. She wouldn't put me through this.' said Peter. 'She's in trouble, I know she is.'

'No. Look, I want you to be calm, Peter. 'I know this sounds stupid. Peter, I want you to think. Do you know anywhere she might take him? Some place they'd be alone? I need to know all the possibilities. She wants to finish this.'

'We need the police. What's the point of imagining we can do anything?'

'Tell me where she might take him. Please. If they're not there then yes, we'll contact the police.' Wells stopped pacing and sat down, his head in his hands.

'There's a studio she sometimes uses. That's all I can think of. In the West End. Above a shop. But why would she take him there?' Leckie put his hand on Well's shoulder.

'I'm going there now. Give me an hour. If you don't hear from me then I'll contact the police. Is that fair?' Wells took his hands away. His face was white, and he was trembling. Leckie looked at him and knew this was a man so far removed from the things he understood that he was lost. Wells nodded.

'An hour. No longer. I love her, Donald. I can't lose her to this maniac.'

Leckie left and drove to the address Wells had given him. By now, the rage in him had swelled so much, he was contemplating violence.

49

Blair left the bus and walked to the nearest pub and downed a whisky. He was shocked by what had happened. The switch on again. He had lost control when it was least expected. Oh, there'd been other beatings, but he'd always known the consequences. Everything he'd ever done had been done with the knowledge that certain consequences would ensue, but he had brought on these consequences. Beating up Pringle had relieved him of the tedium of Birchbrae School. He had dumped his stupid friend, and he'd rid himself of his brother's narking. He had stalked the bitch and now got shot of her.

He felt free again. A man in control of his own destiny. He needed his mother for the moment but not for much longer. In his head he planned to find a woman with money and live on easy street. He was young, handsome, clever and talented. What was the problem? He could do as he wanted, and he would. He realised that Sarah knew where he was living but what could she do? Come charging in and say that he'd hit her? Who'd believe her? What proof did she have? And why would she ever be alone in a room with him? Nah. He'd forget her. He'd get out of Edinburgh though. Safest to get back to Eastlea. Fuck. She knew where Eastlea was. Then he remembered the diary. He flicked through hairdressers and doctors and dentists. A Sandy who did acupuncture. Then by chance he saw it— *'Findon Investigations' 0130688759. The next day 'Spoke with Donald. He can find who it is. Pray God!'* Donald. He looked up the firm and found Leckie's name. That must be the guy at Eastlea. Stupid fucker. How much was she paying that wanker to find him?

That evening Wyllie, Annabell and Blair sat at their meal. The gash on his temple he'd explained away as a boy in the park who'd thrown a stone at him.

'Did you steal his ball? asked Wyllie. Blair didn't laugh. 'So, how is the job search going young fella?' Annabell paused, her fork halfway to her mouth.

'Give him a chance, Bill. He's only got here. He'll get something.'

'But you don't want any old job, eh?'

'Nope. Not any old job. I'm going back home I've decided. Tonight.'

Wyllie's bushy eyebrows lifted. Inside he rejoiced. From the moment Blair had set foot in the house Wyllie had felt uneasy. There was something about this character that disturbed him and he couldn't put it into words. He was a beautiful house full of shit.

'Tonight?' said Annabell. 'Why so sudden?'

'I need a bit of country peace and quiet. Go for walks. Look at birds. That sort of thing...'

'Oh, Birds. I see,' said Wyllie, winking. 'Wondered about that. Have you got a special bird then? One that you're missing?'

'Yeah. She's got black wings with a white throat. She's a fucking penguin.'

Wyllie stared. Shook his head and ate in silence. Annabell apologised to Wyllie about Blair's language and chuntered on about a painting she was doing knowing that no-one was really listening. At nine-twenty Blair left with his rucksack to catch the ten-twenty train to Dundee. He declined his mother's offer of a lift. He had withdrawn into a shell that felt safe from anyone.

Four miles away, Sarah Wyllie woke, bloodied and bruised on the floor, the smell of old carpet and something else in her nostrils. She felt underneath her skirt with the fingers of her left arm. Her knickers were sodden. It felt as if her whole body was broken. Her head throbbed. She looked at her watch. It was dark outside now, only a light from outside hitting a small mirror on the wall. Nine-twenty. She'd been in this room for hours. She'd been unconscious for ages. The front of her orange dress had darkened and grown stiff with blood. Her right arm hung lifeless. When she tried to move it she gasped with the pain. Her bag with her phone was on the floor by the door but it might have been miles away. Every time she tried to move a leg or an arm the pain shot through her. She was cold now, chilled from inaction. There was dim light in the room, and she could hear birdcall. She had to move. She had to. Her coat hung on the door. And Peter… Peter would be climbing the walls wondering where she was…

Then she heard footsteps on the stairs. She cowered, imagining he'd come back to hit her again. She closed her eyes and froze. Nothing. Please God…She opened them to see Leckie filling the doorway. He was breathing heavily and red in the face. An angel.

'Good God Sarah. My God.'

'Leckie. Oh, Leckie…' She burst into tears and her whole body shook as he bent and clasped her. She smelled the faint musk of his cheek, the ridged weave of his coat's collar.

'My phone. Must phone Peter…' He helped her onto the chair supporting her arm.

Leckie called an ambulance. He could see that her arm was broken by the swelling and there were at least three deep gashes on her head. Strands of her long hair had tarred with it. She was ashen, trembling. He'd seen this before, this trauma after physical violence. Calm. Calm needed. He held her tight and detected the scent of urine.

'I peed myself. I peed myself, Donald. Sorry.'

'Pissed off, were you?'

'Oh fuck. I must look like shit.'

'Yes, you do.' He looked into her eyes. 'Why did you go with him Sarah? Where's he gone? Where would he go?'

She was too tired to think, to speak. She told him to get Wyllie's number from her phone.

Leckie tried to dab some of the blood from her face. The gashes were deep. He phoned the police and ambulance. How long? He couldn't stay with her and face the police. He kissed her forehead and said he'd wait outside. She'd fainted again. He sat in the Saab and in fifteen minutes two medics appeared with two police officers close behind. Leckie drove off. He prayed that she'd be OK... He couldn't get involved. He was in too deep as it was.

He phoned Peter, said he'd found her. She'd be OK. She'd phone him soon...

What if. What if she wasn't OK? The thought plagued him. He'd left her. Left a badly beaten woman lying there because he couldn't get involved...Shit.

Leckie only wanted Lithgow now. He phoned Wyllie. 'Good evening. I wonder if I could speak to Blair please. I'm calling from the College.'

'I'm afraid Blair isn't here. He's gone back home. Who's speaking? Would you like to speak to his mother?' Leckie switched off. Too late for niceties. Now there was only one thing on his mind and that was to get his hands on Blair Lithgow...

Leckie used his Trackplus app. He put in Blair's number. The position showed The Waverly Station. He was going home to Eastlea.

50

As Blair sat in the bar at the station, the thought of Donald Leckie plagued him. It was his appearance at Eastlea that bothered Blair most. He'd been that close. They'd spoken. And this guy was going to get him one way or another just for following her. *Well, not just that, a voice in his head told him. You did beat up her son and try to kill him. Maybe she thought that was serious!* He laughed. A man at the next table looked up from his paper. It was the old, seeing things more deeply than everyone else, syndrome, he told himself. Now the voices woke, and their clamour was outrageous.

In his head past events swirled and eddied and crashed against banks of reason and were rebuffed with laughter or anguish. Now these came more often, and the pills didn't help. This afternoon with that bitch had made them worse. And this fucker with the red cheeks was out to get him. This fucker who said his fucking car had broken down! What the fuck was he trying to do? Get into Eastlea? Go into my bedroom and look through my stuff? Get to the bottom of Blair? How much does he know about me? He caught his breath and heard the hubbub of the station: the disembodied voice of the announcer echoing through the steel cavern; the hiss of released brakes; the clunk of engaged carriages moving; the pluff of the coffee machine and the slurp of pouring coffee; the shout of a man whose wife was going to miss their train…

Blair was not going home. Blair was going to find Donald Leckie. Blair was going to teach Leckie a lesson.

He went into a hotel and asked for a phone book. Pray he lived in Edinburgh. The girl at reception was hesitant and asked if he was a guest. No, but he would be if he could just phone a number. Oh, I see. She gave him a phone book for the Edinburgh area. He sat in the foyer and searched for Leckies. Only three *D. Leckie*s. One in Blackhall, one in Liberton and one in the town Centre, on Hanover Street.

'Oh hello. I wondered if I could speak to Donald, please.'

'Sorry, there's no one of that name here. This is Dorothy…'

Then, two calls later. A young woman's voice: 'Who shall I say is calling?'

'Blair. Blair Lithgow. You Mrs. Leckie? Remember that name. Tell him my car's broken down.' He rang off.

BLAIR
I am a bad man. I am a bad bad man, mummy…

51

Leckie was on his way in the Saab when his phone went. He pulled into a lay-by off the M90, anxious about Sarah. It was Megan.

'Dad? Just had a call from someone called Blair Lithgow. I wondered if it was urgent…'

'Blair Lithgow? What did he say?'

'He said his car's broken down.' There was a moment of silence, then Leckie spoke. Shit. The bastard. 'Right. I'm coming back. Nothing to worry about, but don't answer the door till I get back. Do you understand? Do not answer the door.' There was a sigh on the other end. A deep sigh.

'Ok. Dad, tell me this isn't more trouble. I don't think I could take all that again.'

'Honey it's fine. Just the old cop stuff kicking in. I'll be home in forty minutes. OK?'

'Ok. Be careful.' It was twenty-five past ten.

"Be careful." she said. As if he was in control. As if he had a choice. He put the phone back in his pocket and sat thinking for a moment. *He knows where I live. Like he knew where Sarah lived. And we know what happened to her family…*

He drove to the next roundabout and made for home. It could be that Lithgow was going home. He could be on a train somewhere or a bus heading to Eastlea. Just wants to put the frighteners on me. Or he could be standing in the street looking up at my window watching the shadow of Megan crossing the room…

By eleven-thirty he was parking in the lane. A thin drizzle had started to fall, and the street began to shine. There was no-one about. Opposite he saw the blue flicker of a huge TV screen. He ran up the steps and used his key.

Megan was nervous. She wanted to know who Lithgow was and he had to tell her. No option. She sat on the blue sofa and stared at him as if he'd done something wrong.

'You've been helping this Sarah woman—trying to protect her from this man? Why didn't you call the police? Dad, you're not a policeman anymore. I thought you chased debt-dodgers and adulterers, but no, you're involved in serious crime. He's a maniac, isn't he? He stalks this woman and tries to kill her son. My God, Dad, how could you do this?'

He poured a whisky and sat staring at the blank TV screen. Words had deserted him. Nothing came to him that would allay her fears. Once before he'd got her into a hell that was none of her making and now he faced a possible re-run. What the hell was wrong with him, to involve her in all this?

Deep down he knew that when you engage with damaged people you risk the damage coming home. The Lithgows of this world use any means to gain revenge when they perceive they've been challenged. You dip your head in their murky lives and you stink of shit.

'What now?' she said. 'Another drink? Is that it? Let's have another drink and all this will just go away?'

'That's not fair, Megan. I didn't bring this home.'

'Phone the police. Tell them to catch this bampot before he does more harm.'

'They know. They came to help Sarah. By now they'll have questioned her and be on his tail.'

'A bit late. Why not before?'

'She didn't want the police involved. Her own reasons. I was trying to stop him without more police intervention, that's all. We needed evidence.'

There was no more to be said, he decided. He put his hands up and refused any further questions from her. In the morning he'd phone McBride and get it all off his chest. He wasn't looking forward to the reaction he'd get, but too bad. He wouldn't rest now till Lithgow was put where he belonged—Carstairs probably.

That night Leckie couldn't sleep. One twenty-five. He stood in his dressing gown. The curtains closed for once by Megan as if to shut out any possible danger, he opened a crack and peered out. No-one in the street. His leg was hurting. That searing pain down the shin that he hadn't felt for ages. Stress. He laughed. Fucking leg knows more than I do when there's danger. He poured a whisky, swilled it down then made a pot of tea before shuffling back to bed.

'You Ok dad.' Megan was awake. Outside his door.

'Go to sleep, honey. You need all the beauty sleep you can get.'

'Very funny. Night.'

Leckie fell asleep and woke as his radio kicked into life at seven. Megan was up clattering about in the kitchen. Too early for her. She must be worried. He showered and dressed and joined her at the kitchen table. A cup of tea. He wasn't hungry.

52

Sarah Wyllie lay in the whiteness of her hospital room watching a pigeon puffing itself on the sill. It seemed as if the pigeon came and went. It was odd. Her head was heavily bandaged, and her shoulder ached. They'd done tests but twice she'd vomited a grey bile, and this had made the doctor nervous. This was her second day here. Earlier when the nurse had been in, she'd fainted. Now her head ached fit to burst. A consultant had spoken to her and said they'd need to do more tests. He'd held her hand and asked what she felt. She said her hand seemed a bit numb. 'And this hand?' he asked taking the other one.

'Oh, I feel that OK.'

By her bed, Peter and Michael. Peter had been contacted by the police the evening before and had made his way to the hospital. He had been home and come again. It was ten thirty-five. Michael sat by a bunch of red lilies which cast a rosy glow on his face.

'You've gone pink.' said Sarah. Michael smiled. Sarah saw in his eyes a deep sadness that hurt her. She blamed herself for so much of what had struck this family. As if her coming had brought nothing but trouble.

'He's writing a novel,' said Peter, as if he too, perceived the way Sarah was thinking.

'It's not set in a zoo I hope,' said Sarah. She moved to face Michael and winced. That pain again.

'No. I'm over zoos. It's set in Majorca. Lots of sun, sea and sex.' Peter grunted.

'Good. You keep at it. Your dad will keep you right. He wrote a novel too.'

'Well. Kind of. A child stillborn. Wasn't much good.' Peter took Sarah's hand. 'They think you might get home tomorrow. Isn't that great.' Sarah smiled. The morphine was kicking in now and though she tried to speak, her tongue had forgotten how to voice words and the room faded mistily into a silent dark.

'We'd better leave her to sleep Mike. She'll be fine. I need to talk to the Consultant for a few minutes and then the police. I said I'd be there by eleven. You go home and do some writing.'

He left and drove downtown to be interviewed by two DC's. The whole story piece by piece as close as they could remember to dates and times. It emerged that Lithgow was one of several suspects for burglaries in the Marchmont area. A visit to the college had resulted in an interview with Boz, but he claimed to have no knowledge of Blair's activities outside college. With little to go on and a murder case on the Pentland Hills, only a set of imperfect fingerprints resulted from the crime scene search. If it had been him, he was too clever to leave any clues.

When Sarah was taken to hospital, the police had phoned her husband as well as Peter. Wyllie was watching TV with Annabell when the call came. Someone had attacked Sarah at her studio. She wasn't in danger but had been badly beaten. Wyllie's immediate impulse was to go to the hospital, but he decided to let Peter go first. He would arrange to visit her later. Annabell was shocked. Who would do a thing like that to Sarah? She thought Digby should know. He liked Sarah.

He'd be shocked too. She phoned Digby on the landline at Eastlea.

'Digby?'

'Yes.'

'It's Annabell.'

'Yes. Think I know the voice by now.'

'Now, now. I've got bad news. Sarah Wyllie's been attacked.'

'Attacked? What do you mean?'

'She was beaten in her studio yesterday afternoon.' Digby put down his whisky glass on the occasional table. Blair's notebook...

'Where's Blair, Annabell?'

'Blair?'

'He was with us, but he left last night to go home. Isn't he with you?'

'No. He's not here. You know he's got a thing about Sarah, don't you?'

'A thing? Sarah? Are you serious Digby?'

'Look I could be wrong about this, but I saw one of his college notebooks. Where was he yesterday? Was he with you when she was attacked?'

'I don't know. He was away in the afternoon. He came back in the evening.'

'And how did he seem? Was he normal?'

'Normal? Yes, I suppose as normal as he ever is. He had a gash on his head. Some kid had thrown a stone at him.' Digby stood, thoughts swirling in his head. A gash. Christ is this really happening. He told Annabell to give Sarah his regards and thanked her for letting him know. He'd send her some flowers.

Annabell was in her studio, a glass of wine in her hand staring at a canvas on the easel. She'd drawn the blinds and the room was dark.

'Why the dark?'

'I feel dark.'

'I've just been talking to Digby.'

'It was Blair, wasn't it? she said. 'It was Blair who hurt Sarah.' Wyllie sat opposite her. She had been crying by the tremor in her voice. A surge of pity welled in him as he realised the burden her son was to her.

'I think so. I'm sorry.'

She finished the wine in her glass and stared at the blinds.

'It gets worse and worse. It's as if we stand and watch our son sinking down to hell. The quicksand of hell. Down and down, he sinks…' Wyllie leaned forward and took her hand.

'We need to pull him out. Maybe the police will do that. Frighten him. Maybe gaol will scare him.'

'Bill. I need to go home now. I'm tired. I mean Eastlea, not Digby. I'm sorry.'

Wyllie left her. He poured a stiff one in the lounge and sat down. Suddenly everything had turned. Annabell that he had imagined would be a part of his life was going. Sarah's leaving that he'd begun to come to terms with now hurt him anew. He pictured her lying in that studio covered in blood. Maybe she called his name. Maybe. Maybe. Blair was Annabell's son, but the boy was nuts. He might've killed Sarah. Shit,

He had to be stopped somehow. Annabell would never know he had been involved…

53

Bill Wyllie had connections. In two of his pubs in the less salubrious parts of town he had employed two ex-boxers as doormen—Tony Caldwell and Joe Henderson, both trustworthy with a fierce loyalty to him won through special 'gifts' he bestowed after strenuous evenings. Caldwell had injured one of the punters who drew a knife on him but had been exonerated on the grounds of self-defence attested to by witnesses. Henderson was now unemployed and living in Sighthill with his mother.
Wyllie met with them in the rear room of The Saltire and told Sarah's story.

'Gentlemen, this is my lady we're talking about here. Lovely woman. Beaten up by this arsehole. Now don't get me wrong. I'm not asking for his liquidation, but I want you to make it clear to him in any way you like that what he did was wrong. Get me? And Joe, if this goes to plan there might be a job for you. I want a video of this character after the deed. Got it? I want him to squeal for mercy. Right?'

The pair eyed one another. They'd never done this kind of thing before, but they liked Wyllie and Tony had met her once. She was a honey. Besides the money was good.

'I'll set up a meeting with him. I leave, you follow. No weapons.'

The next morning Annabell left. Wyllie told her he wanted to help Blair find work. He needed to be trusted, wanted. That might just be what would do the trick. She smiled, kissed him on the lips and stroked his hair. 'Too late,' she said.

'If you see him tell him to phone me. Please.'

She slipped as she walked down the path to the taxi and he steadied her. No harm done. Inside, he went to her studio to see if she'd left anything. On the easel under a rag was a black painted canvas. To the right of centre, a roughly scratched head and a hand emerged. The pit.

'I'll find him a job alright. A job stitching his face back together.'

Downstairs on the kitchen counter he found Annabell's phone. She was always leaving it lying somewhere or other. He'd post it to her at Eastlea.

He knew her code.

'contacts'

Blair. He tried twice before lunch. Didn't leave a message. Late in the afternoon Blair answered.

54

Blair lay in the bland room of a budget hotel not far from Leckie's flat. The walls were bare but for a print of a beach with palm trees. Cramond obviously. He'd phoned Leckie's number and spoken to a woman. He'd get the message about the car. He switched his phone off. Now he knew Blair knew where he lived. Put the wind up the bastard he thought. He christened the bathroom floor which always brought him a perverse delight. Make the mugs earn their pittance. He switched on the TV on the wall opposite the bed and watched the Scottish news. It was 6.35. That slim black-haired presenter that he fancied. Two refugees had gone berserk in Glasgow and murdered an old woman. A series of murders in Edinburgh had been the revenge of a man who'd been abused by priests at a Home. A cold sweat came over him and he switched off the TV.

More and more now moments from his childhood came back to him. His dreams, once of school and shooting, had turned inwards. He was often in bed, and his father was near, whispering, whispering…The room was hot.

He opened a window behind the net curtain and let the swish of traffic in. Opposite his room he looked into an office full of computers. Some folk were still working but most desks were empty. The wage slaves. He couldn't imagine a life like that—sitting there at a fucking computer all day under those glaring lights. Mugs. He poured another Becks from the four he had bought and drank. He had four-hundred odd quid left in his rucksack. He ate a Twix.

Though the room was a good size, his head was crushed by thoughts that raced. Sarah Wyllie lying there bloodied and helpless; the look on Boz's mother's face when he tried it on; the stairway that Boz toppled down; that guy on the doorstep that he clobbered; the fucking rhino. Fuck man. What a character I am!

It was as if each memory fed the next, sucked the goodness from it and caused it to grow. Wankers. They're all fucking wankers. Was there no-one like him? Was there no-one out there that he could relate to? Just share the same thoughts. He'd tried with Boz and some others at college but in the end they were wankers too. What plagued him now was Leckie. Was it Leckie that had phoned him in Robin's flat? Has this guy been on my tail forever? Fucking bastard. I'm so fucking close to him now. What will he do now he knows I'm on him? Is he police? Is he a private investgator? Who cares. I need to get him out of my system…

Blair's mobile went. Annabell.

'Hi, It's Bill Wyllie. How are things Blair?'

'Good. This my mum's phone?'

'Yep. Can't find mine. You know I said I'd try and help you get sorted. Well, something's come up and I wondered if you'd be interested. Good money. Just need a bright lad. That's all.'

'Sounds a bit vague. What would I do exactly?'

'Night watchman. Read your books and put your feet up. It's a cinch.'

'Night watchman where?'

'I've just bought this warehouse. Out Sighthill way. Just let me show it to you. You'd like it. New place. You at home? Oh, that's handy. I know it. Thought you were going back up North. Right. If you're up for it, my man will pick you up outside at nine- thirty. Black Range Rover. Big guy with a bunnet. Names Tony.'

Blair was running out of money. He didn't particularly like Wyllie, but hey, he was practically in the family. The thought of being paid for doing nothing was appealing.

He agreed to meet this Tony guy. They'd drive out to the warehouse. What's to lose?

Blair felt a surge of enthusiasm. Life always comes up with something. A bit like Sheila when you're ill. Ah, Sheila. A missed chance. He should've taken her when he had the chance. Never mind. He saw himself in a room with a heater and a kettle, his feet up on a chair earning good money. How often are warehouses burgled? And if the unlikely happened it would be a good gig. He was afraid of nothing.

He washed his face and hands and shaved. His hair was getting long now and he liked it that way. Curling over the collar. He'd go out and spend a few quid on a good nosh then go to a club. Maybe he could sneak some chick up the stairs later…

Wyllie switched off the phone. He smiled to himself. There was no warehouse. What he knew there was in Sighthill was a deserted store within a car park. Caldwell would drive. Henderson would be waiting behind the store. It would be dark when they got there. He knew kids played there from time to time but it was unlikely there'd be any there at that time.

Blair waited in the cramped foyer till he saw a big man with a bunnet mounting the steps outside.

'You Tony?' said Blair.

'Yup. Blair, is it?'

Tony had parked along the street. Blair got in and belted up. He glanced at the big man next to him who smelled faintly of aftershave and tobacco. They drove off, Tony picking up speed as they left the city for the suburbs. The big fat hands rested lightly on the wheel the way they do with a confident driver. Blair was excited. This was new. Big car like his old man's but somehow this was a trip unlike any other. He looked out at the traffic which had thinned, the big red buses with the names of outlying schemes on the front— a promise of somewhere exotic. Not.

'Where are we going exactly, Tony?'

'Sighthill.' Tony's eyes never left the road. There was an ease about him which suggested he didn't want to talk. Blair felt a challenge.

'You work for Mr Wyllie then?'

'On and off.'

'You drive him places?'

'Yup.' Blair settled for silence. One-way conversations weren't his bag. He was used to more enthusiasm, particularly from women. After twenty minutes or so they turned into a tar-mac forecourt. It was getting dark and the lights of the car died. Tony turned to Blair. 'You Ok?'

'Yeah. I'm not afraid of the dark anymore.' Tony laughed. He opened his door and stepped out.

'That's us.' Blair looked at his watch. Ten o'clock precisely.

55

The place wasn't what Blair had expected. Didn't look like a warehouse. On one level, no doors wide enough to load and unload goods. He stood looking around while Caldwell slammed his door and moved towards a set of steps. There was something about Caldwell's manner—the way he kept looking back that made Blair uneasy. He'd hardly spoken and yet he was so keen that Blair should enter that dark building…

'We're up here mate.' Blair stood for a moment. Every one of his senses flashed red. He couldn't say why, but there was something odd about this. No lights on in the building or in the yard: not even a light over the double doors. How did he know what to expect? How did he know that Wyllie would be there at the door with a friendly greeting? Doing him a big favour because he liked him so much. No. He didn't like you, Blair. And maybe he's heard about his ex-wife. Maybe he's going to fuck you up Blair: here in the middle of nowhere with his friend Tony whose hands are the size of turnips…

'Come on. Boss will be waiting…'

Blair turned and ran, his trainers pounding a *slap slap* on the pavement. The road was well lit though there were no houses opposite. He knew as he ran where he'd go though. Out the gate and right towards the houses further down the road. He ran, his trainers shiny in the light from the orange of the streetlamps. Run. Run you fucker! Behind him he could hear Tony shouting something, but the words seemed far away. Run. Run.

As Blair disappeared down the street, Tony opened the door and shouted to Henderson. 'Joe! He's done a runner the wee bastard.! Fucking hell!'

Blair ran for what seemed minutes, his breath coming in gasps now. He couldn't hear anyone behind him, so he slowed a bit and stopped, bending over for air, his heart racing, the sweat on him cold now. He reached a bus shelter where two men stood in their parkas the hoods up. *'Keep going'* a voice told him. *'Don't assume they've given up.'* While another voice, the voice he'd always listened to intervened to say, *'You stupid fool—you've just lost a good job by being a bloody idiot!'* He knew if Wyllie didn't phone the next day, he'd done the right thing. If he did phone, it would be interesting to hear what he said.

He came to the next bus stop and luckily a bus appeared in less than a minute. A quick look inside. Three folk. Upstairs was empty apart from a young girl sitting at the front with a toddler beside her. The bus was stale with the stink of the day's passengers, the windows grimed and cloudy with condensation. He cleared a half-moon, wiped his moist fist, stared out as it moved away. His heart was still pumping. He was on his way back into town. He rubbed his legs and fingered his hair. Problem.

That guy knew where he was staying. Fuck. He could be waiting for him when he got back. It was a risk, but his things were still in that room.

He took a hundred out of a machine and booked into another budget hotel at the top of Leith Walk. He'd have no fucking clothes—no fucking anything, but he'd have his skin. Tomorrow he'd go back and get his

56

Leckie needed to trace Blair. He got Wyllie's number from Sarah in the hospital. He didn't go himself. He was ashamed to have left her in the room, but she thanked him for helping her and gave an update on her condition. He said he would find Blair if it was the last thing he would ever do. She laughed. 'It may be, Donald. Go home and cuddle your daughter.'
He would be at Wyllie's place.

'Hello, Is that the Wyllie's residence? I wonder if I could speak to Blair Lithgow.'
'Blair isn't here. Why are you phoning?'
'Ah. Well, I'm phoning from the College. Student Welfare. We'd really like to speak to Blair about his course.' Wyllie laughed.
'As far as I know he's chucked it.'
'We haven't given up on him. He's a clever lad. You wouldn't know how we could get in touch with him.'
'No. Good night.' The phone went dead. Fuck it, thought Leckie.
be in there for hours. OK. You're a resourceful bastard so think of something…

Wyllie's men were seated on a sofa, heads bowed, while he ranted on about how he ever imagined a pair of fuckwits like them could pull off something like this. 'All I asked you to do was get him into the fucking building and you couldn't even do that. Now he's scared and he'll suspect me of being after him. Christ knows how I'll get him now. Any ideas?'

Tony Caldwell looked up. 'If you've got his number, you could track him, find out where he is. He's probably back at that hotel.'

'Can we do that? Fuck me. OK Tony, get your shit together with this numpty and we'll give it a go.' He got Annabell's phone. 'Here's his number.'

'Needs you to put in your email and card number. Costs a pound. I did it to find out where Gary was one night. My boy. Christ did he get a shock when I turned up at the party.'

Wyllie grabbed the phone and watched as the map shrank and shrank from the globe to Britain to Edinburgh, from street to street, till it settled on Broughton Street, number 233. 'Bingo! We've got the bastard! Let's go.'

Leckie walked down Hanover Street, his thoughts on Megan when it hit him. A searing pain in his stomach that made him gasp. Again. He leaned against the wall and tried to remain calm. The leg was a constant visitor with its pain but this was new. Stress. It was stress. Chasing that monkey was taking its toll of an old man. Gradually the pain eased and he brushed his forehead. It was damp. He thought of Megan. Saw his own funeral with Megan in tears. Megan in black. Stupid man. A bit of pain in the tummy doesn't mean you're going to die for God's sake. Get a grip man. He looked up at the house, in darkness now, and his determination to break in evaporated. Fuck it, he wasn't going to die chasing this little fucker. He needed to go home and get some whisky in that stomach…

The pain was back the next day.

57

Blair knew his whereabouts could be tracked by his phone number. He switched it off. Then he wondered if that was enough. He poured water in the sink and watched his phone zig-zag down. If they tracked him now, he'd be under water somewhere. 'The body of Perthshire man Blair Lithgow was found today floating head down in a sink…'

He sat in a green bucket chair by his window. A light breeze nudged the curtain. On the TV a group of five politicians held a lying contest. One after another in their nice suits saying what they would do if elected. He switched to a commercial for a dishwasher. A chubby little child doll wearing a nappy was giving advice about cleaning pans. He necked another swig of lager and rubbed his fist which still stung. Eastlea. He had to get to Eastlea. Didn't matter if the bastard showed up. Make some peace with daddy. Get daddy onside and spin a story about being stalked by this geezer who wanted sex. Might work. Daddy has a twelve gauge. Fuck, yes.

It was half an hour later that Blair heard a commotion downstairs. Men's raised voices in reception. Then it struck him. The phone. They'd traced him.

Grabbing his rucksack, he made for the corridor. Left? Right? Left, the fire exit. He pulled the bar and headed down the stairs. Hoping to Christ it didn't take him to the lobby. No. Another door and through to the street. That black car that had taken him to Sighthill, parked half-on the pavement. The sounds in reception had died. They must be in his room now, the bastards. Run. Run anywhere.

He stopped by a brightly lit café to catch his breath. He looked in his rucksack and fished out a wad of notes. A hundred would get him a nice bed for the night. No phone, no tracking. Then tomorrow he'd go back to Eastlea.   Only one thing missing- his epi-pen. Oh fuck it, he hadn't needed it in ages.

58

The next day Blair pushed the bell at Eastlea. He was surprised when his mother answered.

'Blair. I thought Bill was giving you a job?'

'Is it possible for me to step over the threshold or is that too much to ask?'

'No, sorry. Come in.'

She was dressed as he'd often seen her and even the forced smile struck him as beautiful. Her hair was tied back in a blue flowery scrunchy.

'Have you eaten? I had something half an hour ago. Help yourself to the fridge.' She seemed very relaxed somehow. Perhaps it was a contrast to his own ill-ease. What did she know about Sarah? Something must have got back to her through Wyllie...

'Sheila around?'

'Sheila's gone. She chucked us. Can't blame the poor girl with all the comings and goings. Anyway I'm off upstairs. Are you staying or just passing through? Bill was keen to get you fixed up with a job.'

'Nope. Didn't meet my needs, as they say. Pity. Is pater here?'

'I wish you wouldn't refer to him like that. He's your father. You're not at Birchbrae now. Gone out for a drink with a friend. He'll be back later.'

She sighed and left, and he wandered into the kitchen for something to eat. It felt strange to be in the house with his mother and father again. He wondered why his mother was here. Had she split with Wyllie or was she intending to go back to Edinburgh?

59

Sarah was discharged from hospital and returned home to Peter and Michael. Much fussing and pampering of the recovering invalid. As she settled in again, she noticed little was said of the incident. It was as if she'd taken a fall in the street rather than having been assaulted by a maniac. It was obviously an agreement between the two, not to revisit the pain she'd gone through, but for Sarah swerving round the reality was not what she needed.

She'd spoken to Digby and to Annabell about Blair. Nothing about the assault, but how directionless he seemed: lost, in a way. How she'd wanted to help him, knew he was a bit troubled. How a psychiatrist friend had offered to help him if they thought that would be useful. Digby was adamant he didn't need a psychiatrist, but Annabell thought he did. And bit by bit his life in Edinburgh formed a picture—Robin's trashed flat, the College's report, the stolen silver. She'd contacted the college and had spoken to Boz. Another avenue walked down...

Leckie was coming. As sunlight filtered through the curtain of Peter's study, she picked up her violin and drew the bow over the 'E' string. She repeated the action and let her arm drop. She couldn't play. The usual excitement whenever she began to tune, wasn't there. Her arm still ached from the fall and her face stung from the scar on her cheek. That morning she'd carefully removed the bandage. The scar was livid as she'd been warned but reassured that it would fade in time.

She didn't want this cossetted treatment but neither did she want some sort of showdown with Peter and Michael.

She went downstairs and couldn't help glancing out of the landing window through which she'd first noticed him. No-one in the park. Leckie was coming to see her, and she liked the man. He was safe and kind if a little too stubborn at times to accept what she wanted rather than what he was determined to do.

Twenty minutes later He was sitting opposite her in the lounge with a glass of sparkling water in a glass.

'Hope you're impressed,' he said, 'I'm driving and dying, so drink is a no-no.'

'Oh, sorry to hear you're dying. Would that be dying for a drink maybe?'

'No. I'm not too good. Ulcer I think. Fucking painful too. Doc says I'm stressed. Did a couple of tests. Waiting now for the results. Well, who isn't stressed? This is a stressed society we're living in. Cost of Living, cost of drink, bars closing, restaurants closing, everything's closing. You ok?'

Sarah crossed to him and squatted.

'How do you like my scar? I think it gives me the air of a woman of the world, don't you?'

'Aye, maybe the underworld…'

He leaned towards her and gently traced his finger over the scar. He smiled.

'Don't take this the wrong way, but you were beautiful before the scar and you're beautiful after it. Ok? Believe me. No difference.'

'Ah, but there is, Mr Leckie. Before I got this, my life was good. There was no badness in my life. Even Bill Wyllie wasn't bad, just a bit limited as a human being. But now, when I lie awake at night I see that horror show again in vivid detail. I play it out in my head too, wondering if I could have

made better choices. What if I hadn't started to expose him the way I did? What if I'd just played along and let him happen rather than making it happen for him. What if nothing bad had happened and we'd both had a cup of tea? Or what if I'd managed to switch on that recorder and we'd have his voice…
Do you know where he is now? Where he is as we speak?'

Leckie wasn't expecting this autopsy. She was back in her chair and now she sat back waiting for him to say something.

'I don't know Sarah.' She leaned forward, her eyes drilling into his.
'I want to know. I need to know. Do you know why? Because he will harm another woman. He may kill another woman for all I know. And I'm going to do my damndest to see that doesn't happen.'

Leckie sat back in his chair. He'd come here to close this whole affair and now this. She wasn't letting go.
'Sarah, you've got to let this go. For your sake. Listen to me. You'll only bring more grief on yourself if you don't call this a day. I understand your concern. Yes, he's damaged. He's fucking dangerous. But not to you. Not now. If we'd got the police involved long ago, we could have had him behind bars or in a padded cell in Carstairs by now, but you didn't want that. God knows why they haven't caught up with him anyway, but that's by the by. No. Let this go now. Please.'
'Do you like me, Donald?'
'Do I what?'
'Do you like me. I mean do you want to kiss me.'
'Sarah…'

'You do. You want to kiss me, just like he did.'

Leckie stood up and placed his tumbler on the occasional table by his chair. He shook his head and smiled. This was a strange creature he was dealing with now. So direct. So in-your-face, that he imagined he was talking to someone new. His first instinct was to head for the exit, but something kept him standing there looking down at her…

'Oh sit down you daft man. I'm only pulling your leg. I wouldn't kiss you if you were the last policeman on earth. But…'

'But what?'

'But I will let you kiss my cheek if you hand him over to the police with no mention of his assault on me.'

'Then there'd be no evidence of wrongdoing and no case to answer.'

'Yes, there would. I've been digging. You forget I know the family. They're a bit dysfunctional themselves. Annabell left and Digby…well Digby's always been a bit weird. A guy who collects cricket bats! He's going to kill someone Donald.'

'Have you considered speaking to them? Telling them what he did. How he's out of control?'

'No… well… yes, I have. I phoned. Couldn't face them in the flesh. I mentioned a psychiatrist but as I said it, I thought how crazy that must sound to them.'

'And how do you imagine I'm going to hand him over, Sarah? Just tap him on the shoulder and say, "Come with me young man, we're going to the police so that you can be put away?"'

'I don't know, Donald. I'm just so tired of all this. I want a bit of peace. I can't play the bloody violin these days, my head's so full of shit.'

Leckie put his hand on her shoulder and blew her a kiss. In her eyes he saw a far-away look as if fear had driven her away from herself. She wasn't the woman he'd spoken to in the gallery now, she was someone whose world had turned bad, and he had seen this before in the eyes of victims, shocked, when violence came knocking at a peaceful door. He left her sitting there and strode down the street. What Sarah didn't know was that his own future was looking bleak. The pains he'd been suffering had been diagnosed as stage three stomach cancer. The prognosis wasn't good. Just less than half died within a year…

60

Blair went to his room and lay on the bed. That familiar smell, part-damp, part- age, part-sweat. He drifted off into a troubled sleep as the demons returned. He was a kid. His hands were tiny and he clutched the bear whose tatty fur gave him such comfort. A door opened and he turned to see a huge man, big, so big. And he smiled. He sits on the bed and strokes the boy's forehead. So gentle, that the boy sinks into a comfort that feels safe, soft…Blair woke suddenly. For the first time, that comfort that he had remembered so often turned in a moment as his father's hand moved under the covers to stroke and stroke. The boy didn't know what was happening. Only that his little penis was rising and that it felt good. The voice was whispering now. "There's a good boy. Feels nice doesn't it? And his father fumbled with his pyjamas and the bed began to shake. This is what we do…"

He woke. Why? Always the same dream. Such memories don't come from nothing. His father. His fucking father. Was it just because I hate him? That loathing wrought into a story. He was sweating. He didn't remember the whispers, but he remembered the secret. There was a secret shared between him and his father for months, till he was sent off to Penhouse.

He lay as if paralysed. He was exhausted. Running, always running. And now the thought came to him that this was his father's doing. Did his father make him like this? Bad. He was bad. He did bad things to people. He saw that. All that stuff about the poor was just shit speaking. What the fuck did he care about the poor. What the fuck did he care about anything. Was there really touching and stroking? Was all this his father's doing? The thought chilled him. He couldn't go on like this. There had to be a better way…

There was a light knock on his door and his mother's voice. 'You ok? I heard you shouting.'

'Yeah, I'm fine. Just a dream.'

'Your dad's back. Come down and we'll have lunch.'

Two days later Blair was walking in the woods. He took one of his father's canes with him. A silver goose head the weight of which was enough to decapitate shrubs and the occasional flower. He was about to turn back for home when there was a rustle in the scrub and a dog appeared. A collie. It came slowly towards him, and he could see that its fur was matted. Pieces of grass and twigs stuck to its shaggy coat. He squatted and waited to see if the dog would come closer. Sure enough, bit by bit it approached still he was able to stroke it. One of its eyes was milky. Was it blind? Had some bastard turned this dog out into the world because it was nearly blind? The good eye shifted here and there in fear of this stranger but the need for contact was greater. He knew dogs. He understood the need for calmness in his movements.

'Hi boy.' The sex was a mystery but 'boy' would do.

'You lost? Where've you come from?' He stood up slowly and looked around. The path behind after twenty yards or so was obscured by bracken. He strolled back a bit, and the dog stood still. There was no-one around.

'Dog here!' he shouted. Then louder. There was no response. The state of the dog suggested that it had been outside living rough, but he knew working collies can often get very grubby. He walked back down the path, and the dog began to follow him. He stopped and the dog stopped. He walked on and the dog followed him again. He stopped a third time and crouched, his hand out, and the dog came close. He'd made a friend.

When he returned to the house the dog came with him into the little washroom by the back entrance. He spoke gently to the creature, and it settled to allow him to remove some sticky twigs and grass. He poured a bowl of water, and the dog lapped it. A slice of chicken from the fridge disappeared in a moment. It was like old times when as a child he'd had Teddy, who followed him everywhere and slept on his bed. He'd keep this one. A real pal that wouldn't ask questions, that wouldn't hate him…

61

Leckie drank another tumbler and felt the liquid ease his pain. He was alone in the flat with the curtains half-drawn, a bit like his life, he mused. His life's curtains were closing and there would be darkness. He smiled. You couldn't make this up, he thought: a sick old man with no-one to love but Megan. Liz gone, Sarah wondering if he wanted to kiss her. Christ. Boy, did he want to kiss her! What if he'd said 'Yes,' what if he'd kissed her, maybe just lightly on the lips. That evening they spent together when he played for her, he'd gone to bed with thoughts of her swirling in his head. You know when you've made a mark. You know when a woman likes you, but she's not yours: she loves that mealy-mouthed professor. Now there's nothing ahead but a dark fucking road that leads nowhere. Am I on the right road? Well that depends where you want to go…

A year or less. It would be less. And the pains were getting worse. What could he do to make his miserable life worthwhile? Then he thought of Sarah again and he thought of Blair and he wanted peace for Sarah…

62

When Digby realised Blair was home, the lift to his mood that two doubles had given, quickly abated. He now had to face the problem of his demented son. The weeks of stewing at Eastlea and the moments when determination to deal with him took hold now seemed a chimera. In truth, he was afraid of Blair. He was afraid that that grim monster that had lain hidden in the shadows of the past might re-emerge. While Blair had been physically absent, at school and in Edinburgh, that monster had faded from Digby's thoughts. Now it was back, and it just might be more real than ever. Blair had never alluded to those bedroom visits in all those years but as time wore on and his life became chaotic, it struck Digby that in Blair's muddled head some clarity may have come, some questioning of why he was as he was. Didn't we all at some stage in our lives look back, to try to understand ourselves: our inclinations, our motivations?

It was now October and Autumn had established itself. The grass round the house wouldn't grow any more, but it needed cut. The beds were shrinking and folding as plants died off and this morning he'd plucked the damp netting from the fruit cages. Everything he touched seemed to scream decay, the year's dog-end.

Annabell was in her studio working with a fresh determination it seemed, from their brief conversations. She made his breakfast with a politeness that only pointed out the chasm that now existed between them. Their eyes rarely met. They talked about the house and what should be done and somehow a plan emerged. An aunt that Digby could scarcely remember had died and left him some money that would enable them to carry out repairs to the roof. A gardener would tidy the place up. A local girl could come in three days a week for cleaning. He would speak to the family solicitor in the village and discuss the future of Eastlea. He'd agreed with Annabell that shares would need to be sold. McGregor was a family friend and an easy man to talk to. He'd be able to give advice about what was best. Perhaps the sale of the house was inevitable, though it still held a pull for Digby that he didn't detect in Annabell.

Digby had driven back, whisky or no, with four bags of groceries from a list drawn up by Annabell. She had taken to drinking Kefir and wasn't eating meat now. A new Coffee machine was fuelling their days, and Digby had promised to drink less and tidy up his office.

He realised quickly that little promises made by him were bit by bit breaking the ice between them, though as he watched her sipping her morning coffee he couldn't get the face of Bob Wyllie out of his head. Nothing was ever said about the reason for her return. It was her house as much as his, and she was entitled to be here.

In the late afternoon, Blair returned. Digby could hear a commotion in the washroom at the back and wondered what was going on. Was Annabell scrubbing something?

Blair was bent over a dog that cowered from the jet of water that now drenched it.

'Blair. You're back then.'

'Found him in the woods. He needs a good scrub.'

Digby scrutinised the animal and shook his head.

'He must belong to somebody.' Blair turned.

'Everybody belongs to somebody, yeah? But some folk don't look after their pets. Some folk want rid of them.'

Digby couldn't but agree. As he watched the calm intensity of Blair's washing, he was struck by how seldom he'd witnessed his son caring for another creature.

'Are you keeping it, then?'

'Yep. Need a pal. He likes me.'

'Well Teddy liked you too, I remember. Poor Teddy.'

Digby turned on his heel and left Blair to it. Every time he saw his son now it was as if an old wound had opened and oozed a poison. How much of the Blair he knew now; the stealing, the lack of direction, the disrespect, was down to him, to those moments so long ago?

As he mounted the stairs Annabell came out of her studio.

'Did you get everything?'

'Yes. Didn't have any health drinks though. Too far out in the sticks for healthy people, I suppose.' She stopped and smiled.

'You need a haircut.'

'Yes. Probably. Sheila was cutting it for me.'

'Ah. Of course, Sheila. What will we do without Sheila.'

'We get another Sheila. I've got a girl who's agreed to come three days a week. McGregor mentioned her and I phoned. Seems a nice girl so I'll speak to her here tomorrow. Painting coming along?'

Annabell passed him and he caught the pleasant smell of oil paint. She waved her arm in answer but said nothing as she disappeared down the stairs.

'Oh, by the way, Blair's found a friend.' Annabell stopped and turned. 'He said he found a dog in the woods. He's cleaning it up. Looked a bit rough, I must say, but he's at it anyway.'

'A dog? My God, I thought you meant a human being for a moment. Now that would be something. Chicken casserole do for supper? Tesco's finest I'm afraid. Hey ho.'

'Lovely. Seven?'

'Seven.'

Annabell went into the washroom where Blair was towelling the dog.

'What do you think? It's a she. Prickless.'

'Lucky her. She's a good-looking beast. You going to keep her? I can't believe she hasn't got an owner.'

'Well I called and called but there was no-one about. What was I to do, just leave her?'

'No, you did right. If she does belong to someone, I'm sure we'll know soon enough.'

'I'm calling her Tess.'

'A hardy beast, eh?'

'Ooh, clever. That's it. It's a good name, I think.'

If there was one part of Blair's life which had always provided a connection for Annabell, it was her son's love of books. She was sometimes astonished at the extent of his reading and his ability to remember details of what he'd read. Her own love of books had dwindled as the years pressed on her, but she knew how bright he was and it pained her to see him waste his brain in the way he did. Now he was back home, showing interest in this animal, she was oddly touched. Pray God, she thought, he may become normal at last. Pray God. Whoever she is.

Blair spread a couple of blankets on the floor by his bed that evening and the dog lay down. As he lay, his bedside light low, he looked at the animal's slow breathing and felt a warmth spread through him. 'Tess,' he whispered. 'Tess,' and the dog raised its head as if it knew its name.

The next morning a light rain fell as Blair took his stick and went into the woods followed by Tess. He was happy. He picked up a fallen apple as red as blood, but unmarked and began to eat it. Along the path he'd gone the day before he walked, his stick over his shoulder, the dog trotting at his heels, when he heard a voice coming from in front of the house.

'Izzy!' Again, louder, 'Izzy! Come on. Come on!'

Blair knew someone was calling a dog. Dogs often ran off into the woods chasing rabbits or sometimes roe deer. The calling continued and became hoarser. 'Izzy! Come on.' Tess's ears pricked up and she ran off towards the voice. Then through the trees he saw a hooded figure appearing, Tess in tow. It was a girl.

His heart sank. Tess was her dog. She wouldn't have bounded off like that towards a stranger. Shit. Shit. He walked towards her.

'Hi, you know each other then.'

'Oh, hi. Yes. Oh my God, I thought I'd lost her.'

She dropped her hood. She was beautiful. Blonde hair tied back. Bluish eyes, a pert little nose.

'Did you find her?' she asked.

'Yeah. Found her yesterday. She's mine now. Finders keepers.'

The smile left her face, and a puzzled expression took its place.

'Just joking. I can see she's your dog. She slept on my floor last night. Farts a bit, doesn't she?' The girl laughed.

'Yeah, she does a bit. She's ten now. They do as they get older.'

The girl stood up and slipped a lead round the dog.

'She didn't have a collar,' said Blair, otherwise I'd have phoned you.'

'No. She slipped it somehow. She's been wandering about here for two days, the silly mutt. You live here?'

Blair pointed to Eastlea which was partly visible in the drizzle.

'She was in a bit of a state. I cleaned her up. You want to come in for a cup of tea or something. You look drenched.'

Her gaze held a moment, then she smiled. 'That would be nice. I'm Molly, by the way. You got a name?'

'Blair. Ok. Come on Tess, we're going home. I called her Tess after Tess of the thingies.'

'Oh I read that at school. It's a nice name, isn't it Izzy.'

63

A night's sleep had given Leckie a clear head and a chance to think. The empty bottle sat there, a reminder of his foolishness. He made coffee and buttered a slice of toast. His phone sang. It was McBride.

'Morning squire. You up already- it's only ten thirty.'

'Would fuck off, feel appropriate to you?'

'Ah, what a way with words you have, Leckie. Look, we didn't quite hit it off last time, but this time it'll be different. I've a fish on my line and I need him netted.'

'Never fished in my life. So why me?'

'Seems you've been busy lately working for Sarah Wyllie.'

A chill shot through Leckie. How the hell had McBride learned about Sarah? This would need all the brain cells he could muster…

'Who?'

'"Who?" Oh come on, Leckie. We've spoken to her. Give me a bit of credit. You know who. Very nice-looking woman who plays the fiddle and who was beaten up recently. Beating people up is against the law. And if you know who beat her up and are concealing this crime then you are complicit. Now get that fucking chip off your shoulder and stop being an arse. This is the second time that you've been close to a crime. You Macavity the Mystery Cat or something?'

'What the hell are you talking about?'

'Ah, sorry, literary reference. Forgot you were illiterate. Anyway, to the point. I need a witness statement from you regarding Mrs Wyllie's alleged assault at 47 Shandhouse Road, on the…' Leckie knew the game was up. Sarah's hope not to get the police involved was a dead duck. But how had this happened? Had she changed her mind? Had someone else spilled the beans? Leckie knew he was in no danger of arrest, but now McBride had something on him that he couldn't wriggle free from.

'Look. I'll come and we'll talk.'

'Good. I'm not fucking happy chasing you, Donald. You need to remember which side of the law you're on, old buddy. Word has it our little friend has gone home to mummy and daddy. Three o'clock. You know where. Ciao.'

Leckie sat down. He felt his heart slamming against his ribs. His breathing became difficult. A wheeze like an accordion. 'Calm' he told himself. 'Just calm down, man.' In a few moments he felt better. Then the reality of the situation came to him. He had concealed a crime by buggering off before the medics arrived. She was ok, but she knew he'd come and seen her. Has she really gone to the police and reported the whole incident, including his appearance? Shit. And could he blame her? Wanting that character locked up? No. McBride would be smiling like his fucking cat this afternoon now that he had something on him,

64

    I'm desperate for a glass of something but that will only set him off. Get the fucking brush moving. Fat with cerulean blue, I'm doing a sky that takes me back to a sunny day on Cramond beach. I feel my shoulders burning but I'm a kid so who cares when you're a kid, you get digging or whatever. She was behind me reading a book if I remember, rarely engaging with me in my efforts, when I turned and saw the gull land on our rug and snatch a sandwich. The bright beak grasping the white bread and that twist of the head before it was off, the wings flapping triumphantly. I remember that moment as if it were a photograph. That was our lives: a mother lost in herself while a child is left to escape her world to attend to reality.

    It was one of those moments that never leave you: I was like that bird- invisible as long as she was in her own world. And I became more invisible as I grew. She knew nothing nor seemed to care as the hormones kicked in. Oh hell, was I different? Who knows, we only attend to our own world don't we. That evening she put calamine lotion on my back and shoulders. The strange feeling a mixture of searing pain and the cool of the lotion. Don't remember what was said but my father was angry that she'd let me burn. Have another drink pet, she'd say any time he was angry, and he would. We lived in a house of drink. Whisky, port and lemon, gin, the drinks table a clutter of bottles with big labels like shields. 'Inchview' was the name of our house—a big house with a big garden overlooking The Forth. That was when I started painting. Never really got over the beauty of the flowers in *our garden. Crayons at first then for Christmas when I was ten a set of Windsor watercolours. From Inchview to Art school in Edinburgh and then Will, handsome Will whose family owned a big house in Peebles.*

Will wasn't my first man—plenty of Art College boys, but when we made love, I knew something was different. I adored that man so much it hurt. A doctor he was. I remember the first time I met him he was draped in a multi-coloured faculty scarf unlike my rather dull one, and there was a mystique about medics. It was snowing outside, big fat flakes outside the Cafe window. And I recognised the faculty. Clever then. And useful. Never mind the floppy brown hair, the nose that had been broken playing rugby. I remember his first words to me: 'I'm a doctor you can trust me.' and he laughed. Then you fast -forward eight years...

Christ. How do you shatter a world? I know. You send a male and female in black uniforms and they deliver a rehearsed few lines. Do you mind if we come in. The faces are serious. You fill with fear. Something is wrong. The rest is history as they say. A car crash on a wet road. He hit a tree. That was it. My life smashed. Then Digby. I was drifting. Trying to get into galleries that frowned on flower pictures. He was smooth-talking with his public-school confidence. At first, I wasn't interested but he persevered and gradually we came together. He lived in this house with his parents then, Wilma and Peter. I liked them, friendly and welcoming. Made me feel a part of the family from the off. But as time moved on Wilma's brain went and she was put in a home in Edinburgh and Peter bought a flat there to be closer to her. That was it: Digby and Annabell and three children now filling Eastlea. I loved the garden and the older man who helped, Willie. But as the kids grew, the school fees kicked in. Digby wouldn't consider anything but public schools for them, so for much of the time they were away and the two of us lived here with empty rooms and a roof that was ageing. Digby liked to drink and that became his crutch as the business began to fail. He'd pour over accounts with his accountant, nodding, his face serious and his fists clenched as the reality of our finances became desperate. Robin was taken from school and sent to another in Edinburgh whose fees were a lot less. A day school. He stayed with his grandfather for a couple of years till Peter died suddenly of a heart attack. He was seventy-seven. I moved down to look after Robin till he went to university, leaving a shaky marriage behind and met a few people including the Wyllie's. All this while Blair was moving from school to school taking his problems with him. Looking back I wish we'd seen him more clearly as a boy with issues, as they say, these days, but we were always reacting to things happening and were never pro-active with him. A psychiatrist maybe, but that seems harsh. When he came back from Birchbrae I was back here. It was the final straw for me with my own son. It seemed there was something of the devil in him. That incident with Sheila brought it home suddenly. We couldn't live with him here. And now he's back. Older, a bit slimmer than he was, but still with that brittle temper.

Bill phoned to ask how I was. Told him Blair was back and that was affecting how I was. Poor old Bill, still in love with Sarah. Bill will always be in love with Sarah. He asked if he could try again to help Blair. I said we'd think of something, and he rang off.

Spoke to Digby last evening about the silver Blair took. He was oddly calm about it, as if that was all he expected really. Don't know how I feel. Just seen him with that dog and a young girl in the kitchen. Molly. You know there will come a time when I no longer care about him or what he does, but

*that time has come often. The trouble is it won't stay. Fuck it, he's my son after all and I just live in hope that he'll change. He seemed to like her. Pretty
little thing...*

65

Dinner. 8pm. Digby at head of table. Annabell on his left. Blair on his right. They are eating a Tesco chicken casserole with a Muscadet. Blair is drinking a Becks lager.

Annabell: *She seems nice.*

Digby: *This the new girlfriend?*

Blair: *Not girlfriend. (he eats, drinks)*

Digby: *She's a girl and she's a friend. That's a girlfriend isn't it?*

You don't have to be coy about it. What's her name?

Blair: *I've forgotten. I'm not being coy.*

Annabell: *Digby, if he doesn't want to talk about it, let's leave it.*

Blair: *What's there to talk about for fucks sake.*

Annabell: *I'm on your side. Let's just eat and talk about something else, shall we. We're going to get a girl in to help.*

Digby: *Someone should be happy. Get some order around here.*

Blair: Who should be happy?

Digby: Well, you, for a start. Get your room sorted out.

Blair: Nothing wrong with my room.

Annabell: Sheila used to tidy your room. That's what we paid her for.

Blair: I don't want anyone in my room, if that's ok with you.

Digby: The ceiling needs doing at some stage. Better start clearing it up before we get someone in.

Annabell: There's plenty of time for that. (she sighs)

Digby: What's that about?

Annabell: What's what about?

Digby: The sigh. You bored or something?

Blair: Her mind's elsewhere.

Digby: You tired?

Annabell: A little.

Blair: Holding a brush must be exhausting. (he drinks)

(Annabell stares at Blair. He winks behind his bottle.)

Annabell: Well tiredness isn't something you'll ever suffer from.

Digby: Let's not...

Blair: Oh mummy, don't hold back, just let wee Blair have it.
He's such a lazy boy.

Digby: Right, this is going the way it always does. Can't we just sit and eat without the warfare?

Annabell: He thrives on warfare, don't you darling. Love a bit of biffing. More fun that being normal. I suppose.

(Blair attempts to speak but is interrupted by Digby...)

Digby: Where's the silver you took?

Blair: What silver?

Annabell: The silver from the cabinet in the hall. You took it.

Blair: Is there silver in that cabinet? News to me. This is quite tasty isn't it. I mean for a Tesco meal...

Annabell: 'Is there silver in that cabinet?" Do you take us for morons? How long have you lived in this house and you never noticed the very shiny silver collection in the cabinet. A collection *which by the way you would have a share of one day...*

Blair: OK. I took a couple of things. I was skint. It was coming to me anyway, you just said it. So I took it early.

Annabell: No, you didn't take it--- you stole it.

Blair: Define 'stole' please? Genet would have got it.

Digby: Genet? Is he a friend of yours?

Blair: Never mind.

Digby: But I do mind. I mind very much that my son is a bloody thief. *(Blair smiles, gulps down the last of his beer. Annabell folds her napkin and crosses her arms. It is Annabell's assertive pose. Battle lines arranged, she is settled for battle...)*

Annabell: Digby, we've been to this movie before, as they say. And do you know something? I've run out of patience with re-runs.

Blair: Right. I wish you both a very good evening. I'm off to see my girlfriend.

(Blair leaves the dining room dropping his napkin on the floor. Annabell is a seated statue. She has not moved. Digby carefully lays down his knife and fork and pours another glass of wine. He sighs.

Annabell: I'd like to kill him. I would. I'd really like to kill him.
I can't forget Sarah's call. My God Digby, he assaulted her.

Digby: I know, What can we do? If we call the police, he'll go to prison. Our name will be dragged through the shit. Let me know when you're ready. I'll join you. But seriously, we've got to get him out of this house. I just don't trust him not to steal more stuff. He doesn't seem to have a bloody conscience about anything he's done. He does need help. A psychiatrist or psychologist or one of those fellas.
Can you see him agreeing to that? Me neither..

66

Leckie woke from a nap. He looked at the clock. Ten-past six. Only ten minutes or so then. Lately, when he tried to read a book or a newspaper, the mist would roll in and he'd begin to nod. Two pages in and that was it. Now the pains in his stomach had become more tolerable with the pills he'd been given. But every waking moment he imagined a green fungus growing inside him eating away at his stomach. Why green? Who knows. Red maybe but chewing away as if he could hear it.

Megan was in her room studying. And it came to him quietly, slowly, the thought that he was dying and that that was a kind of giving up. He wasn't a man to give up, even with this. There were things to do. There were still people to be made to smile and others to be made to suffer. He knew which. Fuck it, he knew clearly which. McBride's lot can't finish this. Lithgow would be a first offender. Posh boy from a good home: Public school, and all that. Maybe probation or Community Service Strutting the streets with a brush and a smirk while Sarah and Michael's lives have changed…

He went to his room and packed a bag. Two nights. Just two nights would be enough. He knew where he was going. Knew what he had to do. He'd crossed the line. Posh boy was going to squeal. He'd take his phone out and video it. 'Say you're sorry. Say it!' And he'd beat it out of him. The policeman was going to break the law big time, but it was a good thing he was going to do. He imagined Sarah's face when she found out. She'd be shocked. Leckie did it? Leckie? No. Yes, it was Leckie. And maybe that's what killed the old man…

No goodbyes to Megan. He knew his eyes would fill if he looked at her. Might be the last time. Close the door quietly. Slip away.

It was still light, but the roads were quieter now that offices were closed, and most workers had driven home. In an hour and a bit he was there, over the bridge into the sleepy little town.

He took a room in the Station Hotel. Mr Lewis. There was the smell of a deep-fat fryer somewhere. Patterned carpet, a stag with attitude on the wall. A chair by the window with scuffed arms. Welcome to Scotland's country hotels, folks. On Groupy and on the skids.

The bar was empty. A young girl with a pony-tail served him a double Bowmore and he took a seat by a radiator. He took out his phone, scrolled through his mail. Two Arts events, three mails from Megan, green cord trousers going cheap from a Highland Country Clothing firm, some stuff from The Guardian about donation to Child Aid…

The pain was sudden and made him gasp. He swallowed his drink and ordered another. She smiled weakly but didn't engage. From somewhere he recognised Oasis singing 'Don't Look Back in Anger' Megan a big Oasis fan and a song she played over and over.

'Oasis eh?' She looked up and the smile widened into a real smile.

'Yeh, Great, aren't they?' He lifted his glass and drank at the bar.

'One of my favourites. I'll have another.'

By ten o'clock, the bar had begun to fill up. Some older women in puffer coats, two tattooed men in t-shirts, bellies bulging. A couple of young women with nails that could scrape clean a rusty ship…

Back in his room Leckie undressed. He stood in front of the mirror in the corner and two massive hairy shoulders stared back at him. He flexed his arms. Impressive bulges still. His head dropped. But the belly let it all down. Once it was flat. Once Liz remarked on how she could see where his six-pack had been. 'Had been?' he'd joked. 'Well you're not twenty anymore.' Now the memory of a six-pack had faded and standing in the shower he could no longer see his penis. A fat man. For 'six-pack' read 'barrel.' That's what he saw in the mirror. A fat man who used to be strong. And could this fat man take on a twenty-year-old? Could a dying fat man do this? Early in his police days he's been trained in restraint. How to pin a struggling suspect down. No tasers then, no sprays, just words and if they failed then the truncheon or a wrestle. Now? It was nearly midnight. He pulled back the curtains and looked out on an empty street. A cat strolled by close to the wall. A Landrover passed, its engine loud in the still air. He undressed and took a book from his bag. He switched on the bedside lamp, but it didn't work. The central light was glaring. Just sleep then.

The mattress was too soft, the duvet too thick. He lay, his feet out of the duvet as still as death. Then his phone played its tune. Megan. Yes, of course. She didn't know where he was…

'Hi, it's me. I'm ok. Just had to take a trip up North.'

'Dad, what were you thinking. I was so worried. Why didn't you tell me where you were going?'

'I know. I didn't want a conversation about it. Look, I'll be back tomorrow or the day after.'

'Where are you?'

'A wee town in Perthshire. Came to see a friend.'
'You don't have any friends.'
'Maybe I do. Look honey, I'm tired, I need to sleep. Speak soon.'
Shit. He hadn't even given Megan a thought since he'd left. It was what was happening to his brain lately. Couldn't keep two thoughts in his head at once.

67

Blair's diary:

Last night was so fucking predictable. All that stuff had to come out sooner or later. The fucking silver. Thought I handled it pretty well though. See his face when I asked, 'what silver.' He's such a prick. She had to chip in and help, didn't she. Poor mama being married to him. And poor me for being the result of his sperm. Jesus what a thought—him lying on her pumping away to produce me.
Molly. M..o…ll,…y. I like it. Kind of old-fashioned. That look when I called the dog Tess. As if I'd stolen something from her. Great. She's OK. Nice eyes. She lives over by Butterhill near the loch. That's why I've never seen her before. Said her dad's a butcher in town. Might get myself some nice steaks if I stick in there. 'Hi mister Molly's dad, I'd like two fillet steaks please and make that half-price and I won't screw your daughter…' Ha. Now there's a thought. She said she'd be in town tomorrow in Fraser's Café meeting a friend. Well I might just mosey on to town and pop in. Fuck it, I like her. I really like her…

DIGBY

Bill Wyllie wanting to come and see me. Finished screwing my wife so he thinks the old-pals act can resume. Bloody fool. How many times is he going to cheat me? Come within a mile of Eastlea and I'll blow your brains out with my trusty twelve-gauge.

Annabell did well with Blair. Got to hand it to that girl—she has a tongue on her that's useful sometimes. Glad she's here really. Can't imagine handling all this stuff without her. Getting old, old boy. Just getting old.

68

Bill Wyllie was missing Annabell, but thoughts of Sarah wouldn't leave him. He imagined her in that room being beaten and the thought sickened him. He wasn't a man to forgive. His credo in life had always been that those who treated him badly had to pay for it. And harming Sarah was treating him badly. Now he was driving North with Tony Caldwell beside him. Always useful to have a bit of unprincipled muscle beside you when violence was in the air. The only thought in Bill Wyllie's head was to make Blair Lithgow wish he'd never been born. The details would come with the deed.

'You want some music, Tony?'
'Yeah. Got any Oasis like?'
'Oasis? Nope. How about Franz Ferdinand?'
'Don't' know him.'
'Them.'
'What?'
'He's a *them*. Name of the band.'
'Oh, Aye, right-o.'
Franz Ferdinand play 'Take me out.' Caldwell doesn't like it.
'Fuck me. That's shit Bill. Anything else but that.'
'OK U2? You'll like this. "Sunday Bloody Sunday." They got that right, eh?' Caldwell goes silent. He's settling rather than pushing it. They drive on through the clamour.
'Where we going exactly Bill?'

'Eastlea. Big house. Where the cunt lives. We wait for him and then get the bastard…'

69

Blair woke to the patter of rain on his window. Leckie was in a café with a coffee and a bacon roll.

Wyllie's wipers performed their languid sweep as Caldwell dozed beside him. Ten minutes later they were parked opposite the gate pillars leading to Eastlea House. It was close to where Leckie had once parked a while previously.

Blair made his way to the kitchen and scrambled two eggs. He toasted two slices of white bread and made a coffee. He was sitting eating when Digby came in.

'Morning.' said Digby.

'Yup.'

'Any plans today?'

'Going to town for a mosey.'

'Any chance of some help in the garden? No, I suppose not.'

'Oh, I'd love to, but I promised my girlfriend I'd see her.'

'She's not your girlfriend. Remember?' He opened the fridge to discover there were no eggs.

'I thought we had eggs.'

'We did. Somebody ate them. Maybe mummy.' Digby peers over Blair's shoulder.

'Maybe you.'

'Maybe me. A growing lad needs an egg in the morning.' Digby makes himself toast and takes it through to his study.

'Poor daddy, no eggies for breaky.' Blair finishes, puts his plate in the sink, grabs his coat and goes out.

Outside his vehicle and up the drive a hundred yards or so, Wyllie takes out his binoculars. The house is two hundred yards ahead.

Nothing doing. Caldwell has been sent into the woods adjacent to the house to keep a look out for anyone going in or out. He rushes up to Wyllie with the news.

'It's him Bill. He came out about five minutes ago. Almost saw me, but I ducked behind a tree. He's off somewhere.'

The pair make tracks to follow Blair and soon spot him sauntering along the path towards the town. He is whistling some tune they don't recognise, obviously pleased with himself. Wyllie puts a hand on Caldwell's shoulder.

'Get ahead of him and start talking to him. I'll come up behind him.'

Blair was a contented boy that morning. He was going to see Molly in the café and invite her back to the house. He had hopes of some intimacy after their chat the previous day. She'd laughed as he told her stories about Boz and how he'd taken some silver from the cabinet. Molly thought he was a card. Always a bit of a rebel, she was entranced by this good-looking boy and his exploits. He mimicked his mother and father, and she laughed some more telling him that her father was too boring to even talk about.

A crow screeched and Blair looked up. Somewhere in his head he was back in these woods as a kid, running wild in the trees, when he saw a figure approaching. A man he'd never seen before. In a moment his mood changed. Who was this coming towards the house. Heavy with guilt the appearance of a stranger could only mean some kind of threat. As the man drew closer, he recognised Caldwell. Flight or fight? Don't run. Play it cool. Be prepared. He's on his own. You're strong. If it comes to it, you can beat this guy…

'Mornin.' The face was florid, smiling, but not a good smile.

'Morning.' Pretend you don't know him. 'Out for a stroll?'

'Don't I know you from somewhere' said Caldwell. He saw Wyllie forty yards away approaching.

'Don't think so. Anyway I'll be on my way…' Blair never finished the sentence. A. strong arm throttled him and pulled him backwards while a punch from Calwell caught him in the midriff. The air left him. Blair tumbled to the ground and felt Caldwell's fifteen stone's worth of shoe press his cheek. He couldn't move.

'How you doing my man? Not whistling any more. Shame.'

The shoe pressed harder, and Blair couldn't feel his mouth. A kick in his groin caused Blair to retch a colourless bile. He tried to kick Caldwell, but his legs only met air. He lay still. What next he wondered…

'Get him up,' said Wyllie. Caldwell removed his foot and yanked Blair to his feet. He was winded and had no energy to resist.

Caldwell held him while Wyllie delivered blow after blow to his face and stomach. Between blows he called Sarah's name. 'Think you can beat up my wife you fucking little cunt. I'll teach you, you little fucker…'

Blair sank to his knees and lay lifeless. He was no longer a body but a lump of pain. Wyllie's fists were throbbing by the time he stopped. Caldwell's face took on a look of concern.

'Bill, that's enough. He's fucked. Anymore and we'll kill him'

It seemed that Wyllie didn't care what he did to Blair. A rage had taken him and stopping was difficult. Caldwell pulled him away and shouted, 'No more Bill!' There was no one around. The trees saw it all and said nothing. The birds were quiet. Only a black slug moved near Blair's head. The pair turned and made their way back to the car in silence. Caldwell was concerned. Blair hadn't moved since the beating stopped. Was he dead? This had turned out badly. He was angry with Wyllie, feeling he'd been duped into something he'd never imagined…

70

Leckie was nervous. He'd taken two pills but as he walked the pain came back. His leg ached, his stomach ached. He kept going, his mind slowing and churning as if he were sleep-walking. Down a path that led to the river then to the right towards the trees. He stumbled but righted himself. He could hear ducks slapping the water. An engine revved. A crow in a juniper squawked and squawked to add to the chorus of sounds that seemed to bait him.

The clear-thinking of the day before had clouded now and he felt as if he'd abandoned his body to some intent far beyond him. He saw himself from above: an old man walking unsteadily along a path, the pale morning settling on his grey head as he walked. His fists were clenched. He unclenched them. Calm. Calm.

It was all coming back to him in a rush: Sarah's face, the boy's fair hair, that smirk at the door…and here he was heading towards what? Heading along a strange path from a small town, intending to settle something. Did he even know what it would take to settle this, this catalogue of misdeeds? The callous cruelty of this kid. Walk. Just walk Leckie, for while you walk there is intent. When the intent goes you are nothing…

And then it happened. Rounding a bend, there on the path was a man lying still. Leckie's brain woke with a start. The fog cleared and the old instinct kicked in. He began to jog towards the body.

And then he saw the hair, the shoulders. A young man. He stood over the body and saw the defeated face, dark with blood, the hands limp, the legs curled as if in a desperate effort to protect himself. He put a hand under the head and an eyelid fluttered. He wasn't dead. A sound like the sound of a baby came from the burst lips.

Leckie dialled 999 and asked for an ambulance. He knew he couldn't support this guy. He told them about Eastlea and that the victim was on the path towards the town. He'd stay with him, keep him warm.

Then it dawned. In the panic of discovery, somehow, he'd overlooked the obvious. This was Blair. Someone had assaulted Blair. Now, what? Should he wait for the medics and give his name?

Should he walk away now knowing that help would come? The boy was alive, but how damaged was he? Leaving him now to shiver in his pain might be the end of him. His folks were ten minutes away

finishing breakfast. If he went to Eastlea to tell them, what would they think? Good Samaritan or assailant? How could they know that

he had nothing to do with this. Then who did it, if not him? The odds seemed stacked against him. He fingered the phone in his pocket. Should he? Proof for Sarah. He promised some resolution. No. He couldn't do it. Not now.

As he pondered outcomes, it was as if his feet had already decided. He was moving away after covering the boy with his Barbour.

He didn't see the dog coming but heard a female voice shouting 'Izzy! Izzy! Come on!' before a young girl appeared. She saw Leckie and the body and froze.

'I found him,' shouted Leckie. 'Someone's beaten him.'

If the girl panicked and ran, she would go to town believing Leckie had done it. If she came closer at least he'd be able to talk to her and explain.

She walked slowly towards Leckie and as she came closer to the body she screamed. She'd recognised Blair.

'I don't know who he is,' said Leckie. 'Do you know him?'

She bent down and stroked his hair.

'It's Blair. Oh God, Blair, what's happened?'

'He's alive,' said Leckie. 'I've phoned for an ambulance. They shouldn't be too long. Eastlea House is that right? Just along the path?'

'Yes. He lives there.' She held him, tried to straighten his legs. She whispered to him that it would be OK. Leckie saw his chance.

'Look, you stay with him, and I'll go to the house and get someone to come who knows him.' This was easier now. The girl seemed to believe he hadn't done this. As he strode away, he feared for the boy's life: he'd taken a massive beating, but at least he'd moved.

He rang the bell. Waited a moment or two before Digby opened the door.

'Your son's had an accident. Just along the path there. Can you come with me. I've phoned for an ambulance and the police.' Digby's face froze in horror. He turned, went back into the house and shouted 'Annabell! Come here! Blair's had an accident! He grabbed a coat , thanked Leckie and followed him along the path…

71

Six months later...

Blair Lithgow suffered a broken cheek bone, a broken nose, damage to his right eye, a broken ankle and three broken ribs. Suspected injury to his spleen had healed well. He remained in Perth Royal Infirmary for two weeks before returning home. He was in a wheelchair for two months during which time Molly came to see him every day, his mother fussed over him in a new way and his father faded into a reclusive state seemingly unable to come to terms with what had occurred. Repeated attempts to identify the attacker or attackers by the police and Blair, failed.

As the weeks passed, it seemed that Blair Lithgow had changed. The irascible nature had settled to a new calm. Molly came every day and read to him. He had accepted the vulnerability that his condition had conferred on him and his mother rejoiced in her new-born son. 'Molly has changed him,' she told Sarah, 'Molly and the accident.' No-one was charged. Blair remembered nothing, he said, and Leckie was thanked for his help. A physical examination of Leckie proved that he was innocent of the assault. McBride phoned him and asked how it was going. 'Macavity strikes again, old son. One of these days…'

Blair returned to Edinburgh in the Autumn and resumed his studies at college, living in Robin's old flat while Robin had gone to London. Molly didn't join Blair, something had happened between them to end their relationship.

72

Donald Leckie was horrified by the state Blair was in when he found him. He helped carry him into Eastlea and gave his number to Digby who although puzzled by this man's part in the affair, could do nothing. The police were contacted and Leckie's description and number was given to two police officers who visited Eastlea a day later. Leckie was questioned in Edinburgh and exonerated from any part in the affair.
The same evening Megan served Leckie his supper. She was quiet, he thought and asked why.

'That boy you were chasing was almost killed in a brutal attack, and you seem quite happy about it.'

'Happy? Who says I'm happy. You should've seen the state of him. Of course I'm not happy, honey. But I had nothing to do with it. I found him, that's all. And if I hadn't found him, God knows what might've happened. I'll pay them a visit. I owe them that. The old man was a bit suspicious, I could see that, but he'll know now that it wasn't my doing. His mother was beside herself rushing about with cloths and dabbing him all over. You know the odd thing? He was quite quiet. Didn't say a word or even moan. Just lay there. Couldn't say he was smiling through those burst lips, but…

The next evening Leckie was in The Royal when the news came through that Findon had been sentenced to a minimum of ten years for people trafficking. Findon Investigations was no more, and Donald Leckie was an investigator no more. He smiled and ordered another dram. He turned to look at the door, but it remained closed. He was half-expecting to see McBride walking in with a big grin but there was no McBride as was. He'd retired at last to his cabbages and the wind.

Sarah Wyllie played in a private 'do' two days after Blair's assault. Bill Wyllie sat in the audience two rows from the front on a chesterfield settee. At the interval with a plate in one hand and a glass of red in the other he approached Sarah.

'Sorry to hear about that boy. Terrible thing to happen, that. What sort of animal would do a thing like that to an innocent kid, eh? But at least he won't be bothering you from now on.'

Sarah smiled. 'Yes. Horrible news that. They thought Donald had done it, you know, but I knew he'd never do a thing like that to anyone, however hard he tried to stop that kid from harming us.

'How are you? I hear Annabell is back with Digby. Sorry about that. Perhaps she should never have left. Some folk don't know when they're well off. And I wouldn't eat that trifle if I were you. Putting on a bit of beef there are we? Tut tut.' He laughed, and she excused herself and made for a group by the window among whom were Peter and Michael. Wyllie patted his stomach and reflected on her comment. Maybe she was right: who would want a fat man?

73

Annabell was in her studio when Digby came in. It was late morning, and he had just answered the landline phone.

'Annabell, just heard the news. It's bad. That was Sarah. It's Bill. There was a fire. He didn't get out…I'm sorry. Such a shock.'

end